LIKE ASIF

PHILIP SAGAR

APEX PUBLISHING LTD

First published in 2005 by
Apex Publishing Ltd
PO Box 7086, Clacton on Sea, Essex, CO15 5WN, England

www.apexpublishing.co.uk

Copyright © 2005 by Philip Sagar
The author has asserted his moral rights

British Library Cataloguing-in-Publication Data
A catalogue record for this book
is available from the British Library

ISBN 1-904444-51-2

All rights reserved. This book is sold subject to the condition, that no part of this book is to be reproduced, in any shape or form. Or by way of trade, stored in a retrieval system or transmitted in any form or by any means, electronic, mechanical, photocopying, recording, be lent, re-sold, hired out or otherwise circulated in any form of binding or cover other than that in which it is published and without a similar condition, including this condition being imposed on the subsequent purchaser, without prior permission of the copyright holder.

Typeset in 10.5pt Baskerville

Production Manager: Chris Cowlin

Cover Design: Andrew Macey

Printed and bound in Great Britain

AUTHOR'S NOTE

For reasons of security, and after discussions with the publishers, it was agreed that the details contained in the passage describing the construction of letter bombs should be deleted. These deletions occur on pages 80 and 81 of this book.

Thank you for your understanding.

CHAPTER ONE

It was TV time for Alan Corbett. Outside, the evening air of early winter was already chilly. He settled into his well-upholstered armchair, picked up the mug sitting on the table to his left, sipped his tea, glanced at the log fire which was burning to his satisfaction and shifted his feet against the weight of the black labrador who had found a space between the newspapers on the carpet. It was a scene of contentment which might have been duplicated in many British households on that winter afternoon; but there were some differences between Alan Corbett and the average British household. The average British household did not have five television sets in the same room. Alan Corbett did. The average British household had perhaps current or recent copies of the *Daily Telegraph* or *The Times* or the *Daily Mail* or *The Guardian* or *The Sun* or *The Mirror*, with possibly a regional paper, lying around the place. Alan Corbett had them all and more; and not just current or recent copies but several weeks' worth of them, piled in neat stacks through which he and the dog would wend their way for TV time.

The battery of TV sets and the piles of newspapers were evidence of Corbett's mission; his life's mission; the mission he had set himself after Annie's death.

Annie Corbett had died just over a year ago, written off by a hit-and-run driver, eighteen years old and high on drugs and alcohol. The Corbetts had been married for thirty years. The driver got a five-year jail sentence and a three-year driving ban. How convenient, Corbett had thought; as soon as he gets out of prison, probably after around three years with good behaviour, he'll be able to go and do the same thing again.

Corbett didn't think about that now. The shock that he had experienced on that dreadful day was followed by such feelings of desolation, misery, despair and dreadful loneliness that he knew that he had to do something brutal if he was to carry on living. So he had forced himself to close the window. He had put aside any question of loyalty or disloyalty to Annie's memory. What was done was done. Annie was gone. No point in looking back. Nothing to be gained by pining over her. It had taken him a month or so to stop thinking or talking in terms of "we" and to replace it with "I". He had forced himself to put aside all emotion when he poured only one glass of whisky instead of two, took out only one set of cutlery with which to lay the table, hung only one bath towel in the bathroom. The window was closed. In closing it he had drawn on inner reserves of strength which he did not know he possessed.

Occasionally he regretted having sold the business some months before Annie's death. He had sold it well. Given the shortage of housing in Britain, there were plenty of buyers for a well-established brownfield site demolition, conversion and reconstruction company. The intention had been to cash in his chips fairly early so that Annie and he could live comfortably without financial worries and enjoy a decent quality of life together, with some good foreign holidays to exotic destinations thrown in before it was too late; travelling first class, of course. Now, the trouble was that Annie wasn't there any more. He didn't really fancy exotic holidays by himself. There had been no children of the marriage. Without the business he had time on his hands.

Corbett was by no means a recluse. He had chums from his earlier Territorial Army days, business acquaintances whom he saw periodically and a sister who had already invited him to spend Christmas with her and the family. He played golf reasonably respectably and he enjoyed the occasional day of rough shooting, and these activities, plus walking the dog and doing a bit of gardening, provided him with the amount of exercise that he and his doctor considered appropriate for his time of life. Fortunately the heavy garden work was done by Fred Downing, and, even more fortunately, Fred's wife came in twice a week to do the housework and the all-important washing and ironing.

So, one way or another, Corbett was pretty well placed; but at the same time he had reached a point of crisis, hastened by Annie's death. Like so many others in their early sixties, he was standing on the top of the slope that leads from being middle-aged to being old. He stood there and asked himself the age-old questions: what was life all about? What was he doing here? What had he contributed to the world? What was the reason for his existence? Earlier in his life he had been too busy and too confident to bother with such questions. Too busy growing up, enjoying himself, falling in love (more than once), marrying Annie, setting up the business, working hard to ensure their future. Well, the future was here now; and with it had come the questions.

A few months earlier Corbett thought that he had found the answer and now, after some weeks of research, he knew that he had found it. This would be his mission, his purpose in life, his contribution to the world. This was what his life was all about.

He had thought about what was wrong with the world or, if not the world, with Britain, and how he could help to change things for the better. God knows, there were plenty of things to choose from, even though he was broadminded enough to differentiate between those that genuinely needed changing and those that might be regarded as representing the prejudices of a grumpy old man who yearned for "the good old days".

He had plenty of pet hates of the grumpy old man variety. Politics and all politicians for a start. Couldn't trust any of them. Most of them were incompetent anyway. No point in trusting someone who was incompetent. No future in relying on someone who, though competent, couldn't be trusted. Going into politics was not the answer. Even if he were ever elected, which was unlikely, there was precious little hope of changing politics or politicians for the better.

He deplored all forms of political correctness too and everything that went with it. It all seemed so forced. It went against all reason. It led to the formation of countless quangos and the introduction of new rules and regulations and targets and red tape which, in his view, made it more difficult, rather than easier, for people to get on with their jobs – doctors, nurses, police, the armed forces, teachers and – well, just about everybody. Worse, it made a mockery of common sense. In the same day's letters column of *The Times* he had read separate letters from the heads of the Equal Opportunities Commission and the Commission for Racial Equality, both signing themselves as "Chair". What was wrong with "Chairman" for the man and "Chairwoman" for the woman? Might as well sign off as "Table". The following day there had been a letter from someone describing himself as "Chair-person". Not much courage of his convictions there. "Chair-person", "spokes-person", it was all so laughable; but it niggled. God, how it niggled! Worse, it was growing like a cancer.

Alongside political correctness - almost part of it - was the growth of the

'Nanny State'. Children were not allowed to 'fail' now. Mustn't let the poor things be upset by 'failing' their exams or, come to that, 'losing' in a sporting contest. Chestnut trees were being cut down in case anyone was injured by falling conkers. Snowballing was out in case anyone got hurt. Anything adventurous which might involve the slightest degree of risk was discouraged. Window boxes hanging over pavements were banned for fear of accident or injury. The whole population, of whatever age, was gradually being forced to live inside a giant cocoon of 'health and safety' regulations; like a huge spider's web from which, once you were entangled, there was no escape.

Another thing that got up Corbett's nose was spin. Not just political spin but all spin, which, so far as he could see, was either downright lies or change for the sake of change, coming from a newly created head of a newly created PR or marketing department who had just finished this or that course in this or that business school and thought that he or she knew better. There was nothing particularly new in this. It was nothing more than hype and gimmickry, directed at the presumed to be gullible consumer. He remembered years ago, when the railways were still nationalised, that someone had decided to paint arrows on the sides of the trains; but the arrows did not make the trains go any faster or any more punctually. Now it was getting worse. In the year 2000, a recorded announcement had welcomed him to "Paddington Station, centre of the Millennium Capital of the World"! What a load of rubbish! More recently, on the Gatwick Express a recorded voice had informed him that he could buy a ticket from "a member of the On-Train Team". The mind boggled. He had conjured up images of a bunch of track-suited people running up and down the corridors shouting, "Rah! Rah! Rah!" What was wrong with good old "ticket inspector"? Only the other day, driving home, he had come across a sign saying, "Workforce on Road". What was wrong with "Roadworks"? Either way, there was no sign of anyone actually doing any work; just the usual cones and temporary traffic lights, with their accompanying traffic jam.

All these things niggled Corbett. They might, in some cases, be minor, but they still niggled. Coupled with binge-drinking, hooliganism, the issue of condoms to under-age teenagers, the over-payment of footballers, the development of the "celebrity" culture and countless other trends, they were all ongoing proof that the country was going to the dogs. Sadly, though, Corbett realised that such a condemnation on his part would put him firmly in the camp of the Colonel Blimps, the "disgusted of Tunbridge Wells" and the old fogeys. Any opinions or even actions from someone in that camp would be ignored or dismissed as outdated and old-fashioned. The expression of such opinions would at best be mocked and would achieve nothing. He already had proof of this. He had frequently written to the media about a number of his pet hates. Not a single letter had been published. He had telephoned the BBC and ITV. His comments or complaints had sometimes been politely acknowledged but nothing else had happened. He had even written directly to some of the miscreants themselves, including the "Chairs" of the Equal Opportunities Commission and the Commission for Racial Equality. Neither of them had even deigned to reply. Writing achieved nothing. Telephoning achieved nothing. Direct action was what was needed. Some kind of direct action, aimed at one or more specific targets.

Not a deep thinker as such, he turned his mind to the problem and its solution as best he could. He concluded that civilisations and all that they stood for, such as the Egyptians, the Greeks or the Romans, had frequently been attacked from the outside and had, more often than not, been successful in defending themselves. So long as the civilisation was healthy, a threat from outside could be withstood; but if the threat came from the inside it was only a matter of time before the civilisation became sufficiently weakened for the predators on the outside to pierce the defences and eventually destroy their prey. Vulnerability came from within. As the core became more rotten, so the process of decay would accelerate until the inevitable collapse ensued. Whichever past civilisation you examined, the process was the same: the decline in standards of behaviour and morals; the replacement of responsibilities to others by the "rights" of the individual; the dwindling of a sense of duty to others or to the state; the perception that it was the state's job to look after the people rather than for people to look after themselves; the growing culture of greed and selfishness and "me too". The symptoms were visible time and time again and they were only too visible today; and in Corbett's view, so far as Britain was concerned, one of the elements central to the problem was the decline of the English language.

Paradoxically, in an age when the use of English was growing faster than ever before through the development of computers and the Internet and through the globalisation of commerce, the standards of spoken and written English were falling equally fast. Perhaps this was only to be expected when you thought of the increasing numbers of people who spoke it or what now passed for it, either as a first or as a second language. But most of them had an excuse. They were foreigners. The British, on the other hand, had no such excuse. If the British didn't know how to speak or write English properly, albeit with various regional accents, who did?

The decline of the English language, Corbett felt, was due largely to a "couldn't care less" attitude which was becoming more and more prevalent. There were, to be sure, people who spoke or wrote English badly because they didn't know any better. Inadequate education, class and lifestyle combined to contribute to this. But there were others who did know better and yet they too, rather than providing an example to the others, spoke and often wrote just as sloppily and lazily as everybody else. He remembered a teacher who, when interviewed about the way children at her school would say or write "would of" or "I done it", or, even worse, "I dunnit"; merely said that "That's the way children speak nowadays". Of course it was if she made no attempt to correct them. She just couldn't care less.

Corbett thought that she should care. If she didn't, she should either be persuaded to or she should be sacked. This is where he, Alan Corbett, came in. He couldn't do the sacking, so he would do the persuading. He had decided that his mission, his role in life, would be to save the English language.

Saving the English language would be no mean task. Corbett realised that. But he had time on his hands. The first thing to do was to narrow down the countless potential targets and then to decide how they should be approached. He picked up the five remote control handsets and switched on the five television sets. The dog wagged his tail, settled his nose on his front paws and closed his eyes in contentment. He knew the routine. He knew that he would be able to lie idly in the warmth of the fire for an hour or two. Then it would be time for his evening walk. Then supper. Then back to the warmth of the fire.

Corbett had four TV sets tuned to BBC1, BBC2, ITV and Channel 4 respectively. With the fifth he would roam randomly through various digital and satellite channels. He had all the sets on simultaneously at low volume. When one showed a picture that merited particular attention he would turn up the volume on that set. Until a few weeks ago he had had a sixth set, but that was now in the barn with a smashed screen. One evening he had been so incensed at the utter banality of a so-called celebrity reality series that he had thrown a glass of whisky at it and had scored a bull's-eye. It was an expensive gesture but it made him feel better, though he regretted the Waterford glass.

Corbett's TV research occupied the afternoon and evening. He had reserved the mornings for his newspaper research, accompanied by the radio in the background. It was hard work, which required concentration and dedication. By his side, next door to the mug of tea, he had his notebooks – one for each TV set. Periodically he would scribble a few notes in one or other. He had a similar set of notebooks for each pile of newspapers.

The notebooks were already well-thumbed and, in some cases, nearly full up. They represented the four months during which he had been following this routine. They represented his compilations of the many examples of the slow destruction of the English language. Deliberate or unwitting? He couldn't be sure, but either way the result was the same.

Initially, surrounded by an *embarras de richesses* from which to choose, Corbett had tried to note every single example of malpractice. The words or phrases in all their horror, the grating pronunciation, the grammatical errors, the malapropisms, the non sequiturs, the dumbing-downs and the inanities. But he soon found that the sheer volume of them was too much to handle. It was also too much for his blood pressure. The "thank yeeou". Where had the "ees" come from? The "naow". Whither how now brown cow? Farewell old bovine friend! The split infinitives. The "obviously" when it wasn't necessarily obvious to him. The irritating American habit of turning nouns into verbs. American spelling, which was becoming alarmingly common usage in Britain. He soon realised that his constant explosions of anger or disbelief might actually pose a threat to his health. He decided that he would have to be selective.

So far as monitoring television was concerned, he had decided to eliminate plays and, with some relief, soap operas and sitcoms. After all, whatever the actors were saying had been written by a scriptwriter. The words they spoke were not their own, so the actors could not be regarded as prime targets. Perhaps he should, one day, act against scriptwriters but for the time being he had enough on his plate. He would cross that bridge when he came to it. Documentaries depended on whether they were live or not. Where they included "live" comments or interviews they would be fair game. So would chat shows. (He hoped that Parky wouldn't let him down.) The news slots would certainly need to be watched. Whatever the news contained carried authority. News bulletins had the endorsement of the BBC or ITN or whichever entity was delivering them. Moreover, they had a large audience. The news and the newsreader were certainly prime targets. TV presenters, sports commentators, quiz show hosts and their participants and weather presenters would all need to be observed closely. So too would political broadcasts and *Today in Parliament*. Those who were supposed to lead us should have a particularly strong duty towards the English language.

Corbett's policy of being selective would need to go further than just deciding which TV programmes to monitor. It was no good generally lamenting the fall in the standards of English. He would get nowhere criticising the way English was spoken, no matter how painful the virtual disappearance of the letter 't' - not just from the Essex or Estuary vocabulary but, alarmingly, across the whole of Britain - might be to him. Spelling mistakes and grammatical errors were two a penny, but he was aware that these too would be defended by the liberals and modernists who disdained tradition, claiming that it wasn't important, or who would, time and again, use as an excuse the claim that English was a living language and that over time living languages needed to change. Change would enhance and embellish a language. Without change a language would atrophy and eventually die. Corbett did not dispute this for one moment. Of course change was healthy. It could even be fun. He loved the expression, "to total a car". It was a natural extension of "write off", or even of "pranging", and certainly a lot more descriptive than "crash". But the claim of the modernists did not apply to slipshod English, where sloppiness, laziness or just plain ignorance were allowed to pass unchecked. It did not apply to "would of" or "dunnit". Both were just plain wrong. He looked back to his schooldays when, at the age of eight, he had written "I could of" in an essay. He hadn't known any better. People spoke the phrase as "could've" and so did he. He assumed that "could of" was the way to write it. The English master, good old Gaffer Hill, had gently corrected him and had explained how it all worked. Corbett had never forgotten that moment - the flash of light, the feeling of ... knowledge! It was wonderful! Why couldn't that bloody "couldn't care less" teacher do the same for her schoolchildren?

Narrowing things down even further, Corbett concluded that of all the mistakes or examples of sloppy, ignorant usage of English, the one that got up his nose most was the use of the word "like". Funnily enough it was not the use of "like" to replace "said" or "felt", as in "he was like - 'that's fantastic'", or "I felt like 'OK, let's do it'", that irritated him. It was, he hoped, a passing phase through which all teenagers, starting with the Americans, had to go. It grated, but it didn't send him up the wall, unless of course it was used by a mature, well-educated adult, who should know better. What got up his nose was the use of "like" when the correct phrase was "as if" or "as though". Weather forecaster - "It looks like the South East could be having a wet day tomorrow". Sports commentator - "He must feel like that punch went right through his ribs". Chat show guest (usually some kind of "celebrity") - "I felt like all my Christmases had come at once". Corbett would go bananas when he heard it and when he read it. It was an error, a knife in the back of the English language, which occurred not only in the spoken but also in the written word - even in *The Times*! Worse still, it was used, with increasing frequency, by people who should know better.

He had to start somewhere, so the use of "like" instead of "as if" would be his prime target. That and the people who used it and who should know better. During the past few weeks he had concentrated purely on this phrase and its perpetrators. It had not been easy with all the other ghastlinesses that he had to read or listen to; but he had disciplined himself to close his ears to them and concentrate on "like".

He had gradually compiled a list of the worst offenders. A weathergirl named Mandy Drake; blonde, big boobs, low neckline, short skirts and an even shorter knowledge of meteorology. She had used "like" incorrectly ten times over the past three weeks. A weatherman named Justin Harper, who looked like Frank Bruno and spoke like him too, had used "like" eight times over the same period. Were they in cahoots, these weather people? A woman presenter of the National Lottery named Tracey Carroll had used it three times in each programme for the past month. A woman – an actress/celebrity of whom he had never heard – named Fortunata (she didn't appear to have a surname) had used it four times in the space of ten minutes on the Parkinson show.

The other targets on his list comprised a sports commentator, a quiz show host, a tennis player, a number of columnists in five national newspapers (three tabloids and, beyond belief, two broadsheets), two TV foreign correspondents, a TV newsreader, a radio show compère, a business pundit, two corporate executives quoted in the *Financial Times*, and a Labour politician. The list numbered twenty people, all well known for one reason or another and all of whom had no excuse for mangling the English language. He was ready for action.

As Corbett rose to his feet he paused to add another tick opposite Mandy Drake's name, when she committed her eleventh offence. Then he went over to the coffee table on which he had earlier placed twenty sheets of white A4 paper, twenty envelopes, a pair of kitchen scissors, a pair of surgical gloves and a roll of sellotape.

He pulled on the gloves, picked up the scissors and approached the piles of newspapers, which represented three months of patient reading. After a moment's reflection he decided on *The Times*. Nothing but the best for the recipients of his first message.

Carefully he cut out twenty capital A's from the newsprint and repeated the process with S's, I's and F's. Not all were the same size. That didn't matter. One by one he laid the twenty sheets of paper on the carpet and patiently arranged the letters ASIF neatly on each. Then, painstakingly, he cut twenty lengths of sellotape and affixed the letters to the A4 sheets. When he had completed the task he gathered up the three copies of *The Times* which had served his purpose and placed them, page by page, on the log fire, waiting until each had flared up and burned before putting on the next one.

Having decided on his twenty initial targets, he had already addressed twenty envelopes using labels printed on his computer. The research required to find their addresses had taken time and patience but, on the whole, it had been easier than he had thought. Copies of the members lists of the National Union of Journalists and the Royal Institute of Journalists had provided the necessary information covering over half his targets.

Electoral rolls and local telephone books had filled most of the other gaps. A visit to France and some calls to France Télécom's international directory enquiries service, which was more free with information than its UK counterparts, had completed the remainder. Only two of the initial targets were ex-directory or too elusive to find. He had replaced them in the list, albeit with some regret.

Corbett folded the twenty A4 sheets and placed them in their envelopes, which were self-adhesive, as were the first-class stamps that he had neatly stuck on the top right-hand corner. No finger prints. No saliva. No DNA. He didn't really expect any comebacks from his first message but you couldn't be too careful and at all times he would follow the process of strict discipline that he had imposed upon himself.

Corbett stacked the envelopes, which he would post the following morning. Tomorrow would be a long day, but by the end of it the first shots would have been fired.

He checked his watch and saw that he had enough time to take the dog out before the 6 o'clock news. Just because he was going to fire the first shot tomorrow, it didn't mean that he needn't continue with his TV monitoring vigilance. He put a log on the fire, placed the guard in front of it and picked up his empty mug to take to the kitchen. The dog looked up and gave a slow wag of his tail. "Come on, Carstairs," said Corbett. "Pee time."

CHAPTER TWO

Corbett posted the twenty envelopes the following day. Before leaving the house at 9 a.m. he put an envelope containing Mrs Downing's weekly money on the kitchen table, with a note explaining that he would be away for most of the day and would she please let Carstairs out during the afternoon.

Picking up *The Times* which had been delivered earlier that morning, he went to the car, put the twenty envelopes on the passenger seat in a plain carrier bag, slipped on a pair of light driving gloves and set off down the lane to the village. From Rudgwick he drove through Billingshurst and Pulborough to Chichester, where, still wearing the gloves, he posted three envelopes. These would carry a Portsmouth postmark. From Chichester he retraced his route to Rudgwick and on to Guildford, where he posted three more envelopes, which would carry the Guildford postmark. From there he carried on to Dorking, parked the car in one of the few spaces outside the station, posted three more envelopes, which would carry the Redhill postmark, and returned to the station where he bought a cheap day-return ticket to London Victoria. The train was only delayed ten minutes and the journey passed quickly enough as he perused the newspaper. By the time he reached his destination he had not come across any more examples of "like"; but the offending columnist did not appear in that day's paper.

At Victoria he posted all but two of the remaining envelopes. Then he walked to the Underground and took the Victoria Line to Warren Street, where he changed onto the Northern Line. A train arrived after only a short wait and ten minutes later he got out at Hampstead.

Turning right out of the station into Heath Street he realised that he was hungry and, glancing at his watch, saw that it was already 1.30. He dropped into a Pizza Express, ordered a calzone with a half carafe of red house wine. He enjoyed his lunch, paid the bill and carried on up the hill for a couple of hundred metres, then turned into New End. He passed the New End

Theatre, where many years ago the body of Karl Marx had been laid out on a cold marble slab when the building had been the local mortuary, and, a few metres further on, came to the address that belonged to Mandy Drake; she of the big boobs, low neckline and short skirts. He was indifferent to whether she was in or not. He slipped her envelope through the brass letter box of the red-painted front door.

The last address was in Anderson Street, just off the King's Road in Chelsea. After changing trains at Camden Town, Warren Street and Victoria he got out at Sloane Square and walked the five hundred metres past Peter Jones to where the corporate executive lived. Corbett assumed that he would still be in his office in the City. He would presumably need to put in the odd appearance there to justify the £1 million bonus he had been paid by his company last year. Corbett put the final envelope through the letter box and returned to Sloane Square station.

He was back in Rudgwick to the usual boisterous welcome from Carstairs by 6 p.m. He was pleased that the first shots of his campaign had been fired, although he did not expect any results from them. They were merely warning shots across the bows. Just pieces of paper with four letters stuck on them with sellotape. But it had been a successful exercise. He had been pleased that at the two addresses where he had hand-delivered the envelopes he had felt perfectly calm. No trembling of the hand. No noticeable feeling in the pit of his stomach. No quickening of the heartbeat. Not that there would have been any need for nervousness. They were only pieces of paper after all. He had been doing nothing illegal; but it was good practice, nevertheless. Good practice for the next shots, which would not be aimed across the bows but at the waterline; and the next shots would not be legal.

After a short walk with Carstairs, Corbett brought in more logs from the woodshed, and relaid and lit the fire. He settled down in his armchair and turned on the five television sets. He would catch up with the other unread newspapers later. He wondered whether Mandy Drake would have received and opened her envelope before going to the studio in time to read the weather report. Not that it would make any difference – four letters on a sheet of paper. Sure enough, there she was, gesticulating towards the map where a cold front was moving in from the North Atlantic and where it looked like Scotland would be getting more snow showers before midnight. Later that night the presenter of Business News warned viewers that following the publication of new GNP figures it looked like equity markets might be due for a breather. This was repeated on the radio just before Corbett went to bed.

* * *

For the rest of the week Corbett's vigilant routine was unchanged, save for a trip to Tesco's, where he stocked up on food and drink supplies, and a chilly nine holes of golf at Slinfold, down the road. He had not expected any reaction from his opening salvo and he needn't have done. Mandy Drake opened her envelope the evening he delivered it, read the four letters on the sheet of paper, turned it over, looked into the envelope again to check whether she had missed anything, shrugged and threw envelope and paper into the bin in the kitchen. The corporate executive did the same. During the next two or three days the other recipients did likewise. The sports commentator asked his wife whether they knew anyone or anything called ASIF and, on receiving a negative response, screwed up the envelope and the paper into two small balls and attempted to drop kick them one by one into the waste-paper basket in the corner of the room. He missed both times. The tennis player was away playing a tournament in Eastern Europe and would not be back to pick up his post for another week. None of the recipients gave Corbett's message a second's thought. None of them recognised it as a warning shot.

* * *

On the Saturday night, Corbett went to the half-yearly get-together of the Royal Marines Reserve Old and Bold Club in Bermondsey. He enjoyed these occasions in the Sergeants' Mess, meeting chums of all ranks, talking about the good old days and generally drinking a lot more than one should. Grey hair, where there was any, and expanding waistlines were the order of the day, but they were a good bunch of people and an evening like this made a change from his self-imposed routine.

After dinner he manoeuvred himself into a group at the bar which included Colour Sergeant Jakey Dobbs. After the usual backslapping and another round of drinks, Corbett raised the subject he had planned.

"Jakey," he said, "my bloody moles have come back again. Buggering up the lawn all over the place."

"Tried broken egg shells?" asked Jakey.

"I've tried everything. Broken egg shells, broken glass, bottle tops which give a whistling noise when the wind blows, anti-mole pellets, stink bombs, smoke bombs, you name it."

Jakey nodded sympathetically. "Tried prickly rose branches? They're supposed to work."

"No good. I've even tried peeing down the bloody holes, but no joy. And when the holes are sometimes fifty metres apart you need to have a hell of a lot of beer on board to be able to get round them all. I thought it might be worth trying thunderflashes. If the blast doesn't kill 'em it should at least scare the bloody shit out of them". He laughed.

"Could work," said Jakey.

"Any chance of getting some?"

"Shouldn't be a problem". Jakey looked round the room and gave a shout. "Oi, Ginger! Over 'ere a jiffy."

Ginger Evans, the current Quarter Master in charge of the unit's stores, ambled over with a pint in his hand. "Jakey. Alan. How goes it?"

Corbett and Jakey returned his greetings and Jakey lowered his voice. "Ginger, Alan's got mole problems big time. Any chance of your 'losing' a few thunderflashes?"

Ginger smiled. "It'll cost you a pint, Alan."

"My pleasure," Corbett replied. "Plus a chaser?"

"Of course. How many d'you want? A box do you?"

Corbett concealed his delight. Thunderflashes came in boxes of fifty. "Lovely," he said. "Could you make them the Mark IVs? I need to get them in deep and then block the hole so that the blast goes as far as possible along the runs."

"Mark IV? Delayed action fuse? No problem." Ginger passed the empty glass towards Corbett. "I'll go and dig out a box right now before I forget. You can pick it up on your way home."

"Thanks mate," said Corbett, taking the glass and lining it up with his and Jakey's on the bar.

Two hours later Corbett lay in his bed at the In and Out Club in St

James's Square. Before turning out the bedside light he looked with pleasure at the box of fifty Thunderflashes Mark IV in the brown paper "plain wrapper" which Ginger Evans had so thoughtfully provided.

* * *

A week passed, during which Corbett maintained his TV and radio watch and his perusals of the press. He was not short of examples of more usage of "like" instead of "as if". He duly noted them and began to draw up a reserve list of offenders in case he might need to take any names off the No. 1 list.

He still found no evidence of any reaction to his opening salvo. Nor had there been any. No police station had received any complaint from anyone. The letters ASIF had not produced a single ripple of disquiet. Not yet.

* * *

At the end of that week, Corbett began preparations for salvo No. 2. He had given this a good deal of thought and had decided that he would build up the pressure on the offenders slowly. He wanted them to mend their ways, of course. The future of the English language depended on it. But he didn't expect them to do so immediately. He wasn't expecting his targets to see a flash of light on the road to Damascus. It would require gentle pressure which, over time, would bring them to ask themselves, "Why me?", "What's going on?", "What's going to happen next?", "How long is this going to go on for?" and finally, "What do I have to do to stop it?" He wanted them to progress from complete lack of awareness to full understanding, initially through curiosity, but eventually, if necessary, through fear.

Once more he laid out the twenty sheets of A4 paper and affixed the ASIF letters, again cut out of *The Times*. He ran off the twenty labels on the computer and stuck them on the envelopes. The envelopes were slightly larger this time, of the Mail Lite Gold pattern, manufactured by Sealed Air and lined with bubble paper. He had purchased them months ago from a stationers in Earls Court. In the kitchen he had stacked a pile of twenty Jiffy bags.

The Jiffy bags were designed to hold the dog turds. The turds would squidge a bit, of course, but they would remain safely sealed inside the bags. The bags were white, so that the contents would not be visible from the outside. Corbett wanted the offenders to open the bags in order to learn what they contained; and to smell his little gift.

Carstairs would provide the turds. This was going to be a team effort. The following morning, armed with a pooper-scooper, Corbett took Carstairs out for his morning constitutional. Carstairs didn't normally stray far off the beaten track unless there was a rabbit or squirrel to be pursued, usually unsuccessfully. Corbett was able to walk and observe without difficulty. After five minutes, three hundred metres and a few false alarms as he stopped and sniffed the grass, Carstairs squatted and did his stuff.

"For God's sake! What the hell are you doing?" Corbett's anguished cry made Carstairs look round in surprise. The dog's "stuff" was runny. There was no way of getting that into a Jiffy bag.

"Oh Carstairs!" said Corbett reproachfully. "Carstairs, you've let me down."

* * *

After a couple of days Corbett was relieved to see that Carstairs was back to normal. Helped by a few handfuls of rice which Corbett had added to the dog's diet the squitters crisis was over. During the following five days Corbett collected the required twenty turds and stored them in a biscuit tin which he placed in the barn in the same locked chest as the thunderflashes. He didn't want Fred Downing or his wife coming across either by accident, even though Fred knew that there were still a few demolition materials stored there, left over from the sale of the business. The turds were of different sizes, but all were respectable enough to be up to the job. Corbett chose a particularly turgid looking one for the corporate executive's Jiffy bag.

The delivery of the second salvo of Corbett's campaign to save the English language occupied the next three days. The three addresses in Sunderland, Chester and York, belonging respectively to the Labour politician, the quiz show host and the tennis player, were really too far for hand delivery. Corbett mailed these envelopes from Victoria, Sloane

Square and Warren Street. The remainder he delivered personally to addresses in London, the Home Counties and the South East. He would need to hand-deliver the thunderflashes in any case, so he wanted to spy out the land.

Two of the London addresses were in apartment blocks, one on the third floor and one on the fifth. They had their mailboxes in the ground-floor lobby, which was a pity because, although the dog turd envelopes would find their way to the recipients, it meant that the thunderflashes would explode in the mailboxes rather than in the front hall of their own apartments. That was a real shame but there was nothing to be done about it. At least the thunderflashes would make a fine mess of the mailboxes and anything else that was in them.

Corbett was disappointed to find that Fortunata lived in a new, modern secure complex of up market mansions near Sunningdale. The complex had an imposing set of ornate gates which opened and closed automatically, presumably operated from somewhere inside the complex or by remote control from the residents' cars. The whole place was surrounded by a high wall topped by electric wire and razor wire, which reminded him of the upmarket residential parts of Johannesburg. The mailboxes were alongside the main gate. Ah well! You can't win them all, he thought. An exploding letter box was better than nothing.

One of the newspaper columnists lived in a rather nice Queen Anne house near Guildford. The house was set about seventy metres from the road at the end of a well-tended drive. There was no gate or letter box at the start of the drive, so Corbett assumed, rightly as it turned out, that the letter box would be in the front door of the house. He brazened his way on foot up the drive ready to mutter something about "special delivery" if anyone appeared, but nobody did. So much for the turd. What about the thunderflash? The delayed action fuse would give him just thirty seconds to strike the thunderflash, put it through the letter box and get down the length of the drive to his car before the explosion. A bit dodgy, but probably do-able if he left the car with the engine running. He ruled out driving right up to the house. The risk of someone seeing his number plate was too high.

The remaining addresses presented no surprises or problems, and Corbett had no reason to believe that, save for the explosion, the delivery of a thunderflash would be any more difficult than the delivery of a dog turd. The seventeen destinations represented no more than a lot of driving in weather that was becoming increasingly inclement as the winter closed in. During the three days, Corbett had needed to exercise iron self-discipline in order not to exceed the many different speed limits through which the route took him. It would not do for his car to be stopped and possibly searched when carrying dog turds, let alone thunderflashes.

"Well done, Carstairs. We did it," he said when it was all over on the evening of the third day. He gave the dog a fine-looking marrowbone which he had bought at a butcher's in Alresford.

* * *

Although he had not yet delivered the thunderflashes, Corbett would not have been disappointed at the verbal explosions that occurred in various parts of the country as the contents of salvo No. 2 reached their recipients. Some explosions occurred not only in the houses or apartments where the salvo had landed but also in a number of local police stations where the recipients had gone to make their complaints.

Mandy Drake, who, despite her regular TV appearances, suffered from a mildly nervous disposition, burst into tears when she opened her Jiffy bag and was still sobbing at Hampstead police station when she arrived there ten minutes later, carrying the offending article held at arm's length in a pair of oven tongs. The duty sergeant was sympathetic and promised to look into it, though he explained that these kinds of unpleasantnesses happened from time to time. Kids' pranks, racial tension, gang rivalries, that kind of thing. Not nice but at least no violence or bodily harm were involved. Did she have any enemies? Was she aware of anyone who might have a grudge against her? She didn't think so. Mandy showed him the sheet of paper with ASIF on it and explained that this was the second time she had received it. Did it mean anything to her, asked the sergeant. No it didn't. It didn't mean anything to him either. He would ask around. If there was anything to report he would get in touch with her. In the meantime he was very sorry for the inconvenience she had suffered and would it be all right if he asked her for her autograph as he and his wife always enjoyed watching the weather when she was presenting it. Somewhat mollified by his request, Mandy gave him her autograph – "To Kevin and Tracey" – and returned home wondering why it was she who had been picked on.

Similar scenes took place in other police stations in London and the South East. Most people blamed racists or children. Fortunata blamed the Post Office or whatever it was called nowadays until the policeman reminded her that the envelope didn't have a stamp on it. One broadsheet columnist, questioned by the police, said that yes he did know someone who had a grudge against him; it was his editor who was a piece of shit himself; but he decided to decline the police's offer to bring in the editor concerned for questioning. A tabloid columnist said that he might bring the whole thing up in his column next week. Nobody knew what the country was coming to. Everyone agreed that the Government's war on crime should be stepped up. Several people said that they would complain to their MP.

The only MP who had actually personally received a dog turd was very angry indeed. He and his colleagues, in all parties, in the House of Commons sweated blood and guts for the people of this country and this was how he was repaid. But at least the turd had not come from anyone in his Sunderland East constituency. The envelope had a London postmark. Even so, this kind of behaviour could not be tolerated. Given the opportunity, he would raise the whole matter in the House of Commons. He didn't know anything about ASIF, but he had spoken up frequently for the Asian community in his constituency, so he knew where the letter had come from. The British National Party. They should be banned.

Only three people didn't complain to the police. A tabloid sports columnist, who had already received some mild hate mail from Australia following his criticism of the demeanour of the Australian Prime Minister while presenting the Rugby World Cup winner's medal to Jonny Wilkinson, and had recently commented unfavourably on the behaviour of an Australian tennis player after being knocked out in the first round of a grand slam tournament. He put the dog turd down to some Australian nutter and assumed that ASIF represented something to do with Australia, probably some epithet that could not be printed in a family newspaper. He threw the turd over his garden fence. The quiz show host shrugged in much the same way as he had when he received the first ASIF communication and took no further action. The tennis player complained to his coach,

20

who told him not to let such a minor incident put him off the main task of working to improve his backhand volley.

In all, seventeen complaints were made to seventeen different police stations spread across the country. No liaison took place between the police stations, who regarded minor incidents on their own patch as not meriting wider distribution or reporting on a national basis. Incidents regarding dog turds, though not that numerous, were not uncommon and were regarded as no big deal. The letters ASIF which were included in the envelopes were duly noted but, again, were not reported nationally. A couple of officers gave more than a moment's thought to what the letters might stand for but abandoned the question when other incidents took priority.

There it might have remained but for the sports columnist of *The Sun* giving the subject some space one Wednesday when he needed to fill six more inches in his regular column. This in due course led to two letters from *The Sun* readers; one came from Mandy, the other from someone who had not even been a victim of Corbett's salvo No. 2. Other readers also responded and they were accompanied by a comment in the leader column deploring the fact that more motorists were being arrested than burglars and that the putting of dog excreta through people's letter boxes was symptomatic of the inadequacy of government policies for tackling crime and nuisance; but after a few more days the story ran out of steam.

Then the Labour MP for Sunderland East got involved. He first wrote an open letter to the British National Party, which was published in the *Daily Mirror*. Then he gave an interview on the *Today* programme, which was followed by a photograph in several national newspapers of him standing outside his house captioned with his declaration that, "Now I know how the Asian community suffers". The next day he received another turd, this time courtesy of the British National Party.

The following week he put down a question for Prime Minister's question time in the House of Commons. When he rose to speak he was cheered by his party colleagues, while the opposition benches echoed with shouts of "Woof, woof!" and someone even gave a part rendering of, "How much is that doggie in the window?".

"Is the Prime Minister willing to recognise the fact that the behaviour of some political parties in this country makes a mockery of democracy and freedom of speech?" the Labour MP bellowed. "And is he prepared to instruct the Home Secretary to take stronger action against crime and the causes of crime, including the banning of political parties who behave in this despicable way?"

Corbett, who had been delighted at the results of his salvo No. 2 so far, was enjoying himself as he watched. Carstairs and he, albeit anonymously, had made it onto television. He wished he could somehow call them and tell them who should really be taking the credit.

The Prime Minister rose to reply. "I am aware that the honourable member for Sunderland East has been through some unpleasant experiences recently and he has my sympathy, as does anyone of any race or creed who has suffered in a similar way. I am assured by the Home Office that the police are doing everything in their power ... "

His voice was drowned by shouts of "Tough on crime and the causes of crime" from various parts of the chamber, including, he was alarmed to note, from some of his own backbenchers.

As the Speaker cried, "Order, order", the Prime Minister raised his own voice. " ... are doing everything in their power to pursue and bring to justice the people responsible for these regrettable incidents. But," he raised his voice even higher, "But let us try to keep things in perspective. These things are probably done by hooligans who are seeking publicity of some kind. They are not threats to democracy. It's not like we're dealing with terrorism here."

As the Prime Minister continued, Corbett's jaw sagged in shock and disbelief. "Bloody hell!" he said. "Did you hear that Carstairs? The Prime Minister. The bloody Prime Minister! It's not LIKE we're dealing with terrorism here. IT'S NOT LIKE WE'RE DEALING WITH TERRORISM HERE." He repeated the sentence twice more, shaking his head, almost in pain. The Prime Minister! In the House of Commons! AND on television to boot! It was unforgivable. Beyond the pale. The man should be impeached; and then hanged, drawn and quartered!

Corbett found himself shaking; partly with fury, but partly with excitement. This would raise the stakes all right. He grabbed a notebook and added the Prime Minister to the list of targets. Carstairs would get an extra large dinner tonight, with a good handful of rice thrown in. There was no chance of hand delivery. Not to 10 Downing Street. He would mail Carstairs' contribution tomorrow, with the ASIF letters as well. Corbett was under no illusions that the Prime Minister would open the envelope and Jiffy bag personally. He assumed that there was some kind of security set-up which would do that. A pity, but the shot would still be fired. It had to be fired, at this target above all. To protect the English language.

CHAPTER THREE

The wheels of bureaucracy tend to turn extremely slowly in all departments of the Home Office, even the Metropolitan Police. But when an incident involving 10 Downing Street occurs the wheels accelerate impressively. Corbett's salvo landed on a Wednesday morning and by Wednesday evening Chief Superintendent Michael Rayner was sitting in his office off Whitehall with instructions from the Home Secretary no less to get to the bottom of the problem and solve it. Given the contents of the envelope concerned, Rayner thought that the Home Secretary's instructions could have been worded differently.

Detective Sergeant Zoë Henderson was already establishing herself in the next-door room, which she knew Rayner would name the war room once the investigation got under way. The usual battery of desktop computers and laser printers was already in place, plus two high-speed photocopiers, telephones, radio sets, the whiteboard covering ten metres of one wall, and three flip charts, all virgin at the moment, but she knew they would gradually be covered with a growing list of data, names, places, theories and even hunches as information came in. At least, she hoped it would come in. There was little enough to go on so far.

"Okay Zoë, what have we got?" Rayner's voice summoned her into his adjoining office.

Zoë went in with a file containing what they had so far and a few notes that she had made. Facing her was the man she had got to know and come to like after working with him on a number of problem cases over the previous ten years: well built; not much flab or jowl for his fifty-three years; hair still intact – not much grey, cut short; green eyes with laugh lines round them, although she and others had known the full force of their angry stare if their owner had reason to believe that anyone was giving less than one hundred per cent to the job; clothes always conservative but well cut, be they formal suits or informal leisurewear, though she remembered that every now and then he would indulge in an outrageously loud tie when he was in a good mood and felt like bringing people, normally his superiors, down to earth – she had sometimes wondered how his wife let him get away with them; patient when dull, painstaking research had to be done, but impatient when anyone in his team was too slow to see something – an implication or question or conclusion – that he himself had seen or thought he might have seen.

Zoë sat down opposite Rayner and began to go through what they had so far. The Prime Minister's envelope had been opened by security at Number 10. The Prime Minister had not personally been involved but had been informed. The envelope, the Jiffy bag and its contents, and the sheet of A4 paper with the letters ASIF were with forensic now. They had contacted the Sunderland police station to which the Labour MP had taken his first complaint. The ASIF paper was on its way to London by dispatch rider. They thought that the Sunderland turds might have been ditched.

"Pity," said Rayner.

They were chasing up the various people who had written to the media after the sports writer's column in *The Sun*. The sports writer himself was out of the country following a UEFA cup football match but should be back tomorrow. That was about it for the time being.

"Right," said Rayner, and then remembered to add, "Well done" before continuing. "When can we expect something back from forensic?"

"It's been given priority, Sir. They should be able to give us something on the Number 10 ... sample later tonight, and the Sunderland bumph sometime tomorrow morning, with any luck, if they get it soon enough."

"The Labour MP?"

"Still at the House, Sir. I've left a message with one of the whip's secretaries and he'll be ready to see you at the House after 9 o'clock tonight. Is that all right?"

"It'll have to be," said Rayner.

"I'm sorry, Sir."

"Don't be. I have a gut feeling that a lot of people will be burning a lot of midnight oil, including you and me, before this is over. Right. Here's your midnight oil for starters. I want all county police forces contacted to see whether they've had complaints of similar incidents over the past, say, one month."

"All of them, Sir?"

"All of them. Plus all the stations in London."

"That's already in hand."

"Good. If they've still got any materials on file – turds, envelopes, paper, Jiffy bags, anything at all, I want them over at forensic soonest. Plus a list of every individual who's made a complaint. Okay? Have a nice evening."

As Zoë rose and turned to go, Rayner added, "A. S. I. F. Mean anything to you?"

"No, sir."

"Nor me. Not yet. Neither did Al Qaeda until 9/11."

* * *

The meeting with the Labour MP was unproductive. Rayner hadn't expected anything else. The MP didn't know anyone named Asif. Nor had he thought of any entity whose initials might be ASIF. Asian something or other, perhaps, but why would anyone in the Asian community want to put a turd through his letter box? He was on their side, remember. Anyway, it wasn't them. It was the BNP. They'd left a bloody compliments slip on the bloody doorstep.

"Maybe. The second one. Or from somebody purporting to be the BNP. To dent their image," Rayner said.

"Their image doesn't need any more denting, so far as I'm concerned. But are you saying that they didn't both come from the same source?"

"We don't know," replied Rayner. "We're investigating. It takes time, I'm afraid. Do you know whether the Sunderland police kept the stuff, the paper, the bag, the envelope?"

"No idea."

"Or the ... turds?" The dispatch rider hadn't arrived before had Rayner left his office.

"Why the hell keep the bloody turds?"

"The forensic boys might make something of them. What kind of dog, for example."

"Superintendent, I don't give a bugger what kind of effing dog they came from. German shepherd, labrador, greyhound, Jack Russell, chihuahua. It's all the same to me. All I know is that they came through my effing letter box. I don't want it happening again and it's your lot's job to make sure it doesn't."

"Sunderland have made arrangements to check your mail and watch your house, Sir."

"So I should hope." The Labour MP indicated that the meeting was over. "Anything else, you know where to find me."

"Thank you, Sir," said Rayner and made to leave.

As he did so the MP delivered a parting shot. "What makes you so sure it's dog shit? For all I know it could be human."

Rayner headed for his car. He hadn't thought of that one.

* * *

The following morning Rayner was up at 6 a.m., had taken his wife, Betty, a cup of tea in bed, wolfed down a bowl of cereal, a glass of orange juice and a slice of toast and Marmite, and was in his car by 7.30. In the car he tried not to feel too guilty about letting Betty down. The previous night she had again asked for his help, or at least his advice, in dealing with the Governor of Holloway prison. Surely, she had asked, the prison authorities could see the benefits in helping prisoners learn to read and write? According to the latest figures, more than twenty-five per cent of prisoners countrywide were illiterate. Would it not make sense to encourage them to pick up a book? If they could at least be taught the basic skills of reading and writing, surely they would be better placed to find employment when they completed their sentences, instead of going straight back on the streets again? She had tried to get her message across, but, more often than not, particularly in the case of the Holloway Governor, it was like talking to a brick wall. Rayner agreed with Betty and had said he would give some thought to the problem. Her ideas made sense to him; but not now. Betty's project, Step by Step Reading Plan or whatever it was called, would have to wait. He had other things on his mind for the moment.

After an uneventful drive up from Reigate he reached the office just before 8.30, where he found Zoë Henderson shuffling a pile of faxes and e-mail printouts at her desk. A coffee machine was percolating away, from which Rayner served them both, taking his mug through to his desk. Zoë knew better than to disturb him until he had finished his coffee and smoked a cigarette outside on the balcony.

At his desk Rayner opened the lower left-hand drawer and removed two packets of Benson & Hedges Silver. One was empty and bore, in large black letters on a white background, the message in French – *Fumer tue*. The other one was full and bore, in similar large black on white letters, the same message in English – Smoking kills. Carefully, Rayner transferred the cigarettes from the English packet to the French one. This was necessary because Betty thought that he smoked only ten cigarettes a day, whereas he actually smoked closer to twenty. A month ago they had come back from a day trip to Calais, bearing with them, amongst other things, 400 cigarettes, still a good deal cheaper in France than in England despite the recent French price increases. By now, at ten cigarettes a day, Rayner should still have nearly 100 of the Calais cigarettes left, in their French packets; but at eighteen cigarettes a day he had run out a week ago. He would have to maintain the subterfuge for a few more days in order to appear to be keeping his promise to Betty that he would cut his nicotine consumption. Had he but known it, Betty didn't really believe that he only smoked ten a day. His cough told her that. But she loved her husband and knew from experience that too much nagging would be counterproductive. So she turned a blind eye and pretended not to notice the subterfuge. Twenty a day, or whatever it was, was a lot better than the two packets he had smoked a year ago.

Rayner knew he was lucky to have a balcony on which to indulge his habit. Others in the building were not so lucky and had to make do with a smoke-filled Smokers' Room in the basement which stank so filthily that it was a deterrent to all but the most hardened nicotine addict. Soon that was going to be done away with and what few determined smokers were left would have to brave the street, where most of them would probably die of pneumonia long before lung cancer caught up with them.

He took a last drag, stubbed out the cigarette and placed the butt in the now empty English cigarette packet. Settling at his desk he started the working day.

"Morning, Zoë."

Zoë's "Morning, Sir" preceded her entrance into the room.

"Well?"

"Forensic report on the Prime Minister's turd ... "

"The Prime Minister's turd?"

"Sorry, Sir. It's ... Well, it's just the way I've taken to thinking about it."

"I see," Rayner chuckled. "Very descriptive I must say. I've no objection. More fun than just numbering them. But it doesn't go beyond this room. Okay?"

"Yes, Sir." Zoë had not been too worried about Rayner's reaction.

"Well, let's have it then."

"No prints on the envelope or the A4 paper or on the newsprint."

"I didn't think there would be," said Rayner. "But blast anyway!"

"We've checked with all the press and *The Times* say that the newsprint is theirs."

"So Asif reads *The Times*."

"The turd, Sir ... "

"The Prime Minister's turd."

Zoë smiled. " ... Could come from one of the larger breeds of dog. Forensic compared it with samples they got from the Battersea Dogs' Home. They've only got the Prime Minister's one so far, of course, and any others, if there still are any others, may be different."

"Of course."

"They would plump for a german shepherd, labrador, dalmatian or rottweiler for choice."

Rayner sighed. "So, so far we suspect someone who wears gloves, may read *The Times* and, unless he's just picked the stuff up in the park at random, may be the owner of a german shepherd, a labrador, a dalmatian or a rottweiler. Or," he added thoughtfully, "all four. Wait till I tell that to the Commissioner."

"The dog had eaten Pedigree Chum – the mixed variety – and there were also traces of long-grain Camargue rice ... "

"A Frenchman!"

"It's early days, Sir," said Zoë defensively.

"I know. I know."

"The stuff from Sunderland came too. Same story. No prints. And they hadn't kept the turd."

"Can't say I blame them. What about the county forces? Anything back from them?' Rayner's question didn't sound particularly hopeful.

"I was coming to that, Sir." Zoë sounded almost cheerful. "Chester and York have both confirmed identical incidents. Also Berkshire, Surrey,

West Sussex, Herts and Hampshire."

"Really?"

"Plus seven more in the Metropolitan area, not counting the Downing Street one. With Sunderland that brings the total to eighteen so far."

"You've been busy, Zoë, good work."

"Thank you, Sir. I asked for nil returns as well. Plenty of them. Only a few still to report back."

Rayner breathed deeply. "Eighteen. Well there's certainly plenty to get our teeth into. And they all contained the ASIF note?"

"Yes, Sir."

"Names of the recipients/complainants? Addresses? Telephone numbers? Occupation? Any other details?"

"Already requested, Sir. Some have come through already. We should have a full list pretty soon, provided the local stations can get hold of the people concerned."

"Right. Okay Zoë, start getting the stuff on the board."

"Will do, Sir." Zoë managed to conceal the excitement in her voice. The task of entering the first pieces of data onto the whiteboard in the war room made a case real, brought it to life. Over the next few days, if other cases were anything to go by, the presently empty thirty feet of wall would begin to bloom, sometimes slowly, sometimes with a great spurt of acceleration, as the laborious hours, days, even weeks of research produced first the skeleton and then the flesh to cover the bones. As she left the room, Rayner picked up the telephone and stabbed the numbers to put him through to the Yard's information technology centre.

Half an hour later, Rayner was sitting in the office of Mark Telford, head of IT.

"ASIF," said Telford after Rayner had filled him in with what little data they had so far. "Someone's name possibly? Christian name or rather ... "he corrected himself, "a first name. Someone with a name like that's hardly likely to be Christian is he? Muslim, more like. Hindu; Arab; Pakistani; African perhaps?"

"Could be," Rayner nodded. "Which raises terrorism with a capital T. Except that putting dog turds through people's letter boxes doesn't smack of the kind of terrorism we've been seeing over the past few years."

"True," Telford agreed. "And I don't know any Irish Asifs."

Rayner shook his head. "In any case," he said, "Muslims or Hindus or whoever, are usually the ones on the receiving end of things like dog turds. Normally delivered by skinheads or the BNP, as our MP for Sunderland East said. No, I don't think this is a racist thing."

"Pity," said Telford. "If we could limit disagreements to people chucking dog turds at each other the world would be a safer place and our job would be a lot easier."

"So," said Rayner, "if ASIF stands for something, what the hell does it stand for? That's where I hope you can help us, Mark. It's just a question of choosing a list of names, synonyms or whatever, and running a load of permutations through those computers of yours. With any luck they'll squirt out a few ideas that we could get to work on."

"In theory, yes," Telford replied. "In practice it's not as easy as that. Depending on how many names or words we choose, we could end up with millions of potential combinations of words beginning with those four letters."

"I'm not suggesting it'll be easy. But we've got to start somewhere."

"And, of course," Telford continued, "it's not just those four letters or the four words they signify. There could be others that aren't even included. Take RSPCA. That's five letters for five words. But the full title includes 'the', 'for', 'of' and 'to'. That makes nine. See what I mean. Those millions of combinations could turn out to be billions."

Rayner shrugged. "I know, Mark. I know. But as I said, we've got to start somewhere. Some inspired guesswork might narrow things down a bit instead of having to try every word in the whole bloody dictionary that starts with A, S, I or F. What about," he paused for a moment, "Afghan Socialists for International Freedom? That's not bad, off the top of my head." It wasn't actually off the top of his head. Rayner had been wracking his brains half the night.

"Never heard of them," said Telford.

"For God's sake," exploded Rayner. "Nor have I. They probably don't exist. But maybe, just maybe, they do exist. It's the kind of organisation that might spring up overnight; and if that happens, the sooner we get our tabs on them the better. Look at Al Qaeda."

"Okay, Mike, Okay. I get the message."

"Afghanistan, Albanian, Algerian, Argentinian, Aggression,

Abomination, Animal." Rayner reeled off the list, jabbing his fingers in the air as he did so.

Telford took over. "Alarm, Activist, Action, Abolition, Aberystwyth, Abagavenny, Aberdeen, Armagh, Antrim ... Bloody hell, Mike, we could be looking at Welsh Nationalists, Scottish Nationalists, Irish Nationalists, all on our own doorstep, without even going across the bloody Channel."

Rayner returned service with, "Anarchism, association, asylum seeker, assassin, assassination, army, Aldershot, Andover, Ascot. All right, try the S, sabotage, saboteurs, socialist, sedition, slaughter, Saudi Arabia, Spanish, Soviet, Swiss ..."

"Smite, secret, Satan, spearhead, strike, strategic." Telford began to sound as if he was enjoying himself. "International, imperial, immortal, invasion, inflammation, Ireland, Indonesia, Israeli, Islamic ..."

"Incendiary, immoral, incarcerate, indecent, India, Inverness, Inner Hebrides." Rayner gave the beginnings of a giggle, and soon both men were laughing out loud as they almost turned the problem into a contest.

"Fellowship," said Rayner.

"Federation," said Telford.

"Fatherland."

"Fight."

"Foundation."

"Faith."

"Flame."

"Force."

"Fundamentalism."

Gradually, with each new word, with each demonstration of the size of the task they were facing, their laughter died.

"France, Finland, Front." Rayner stopped. For a short while there was silence between the two men.

"Fear," said Telford.

"Fat farmer," said Rayner, but his ensuing smile was serious. "Well, Mark? Computers to the fore?"

"We'll give it a whirl," Telford replied. "And what then? Suppose we come up with a dozen, a hundred potential titles of organisations. What then?"

"Then we start our enquiries," said Rayner. "In London, across the country, abroad if necessary. In the hope that someone, somewhere, might come up with a lead."

"And if no one does?"

"Then we've drawn a blank," Rayner replied. "And I shall have wasted your time. For which I apologise in advance."

Telford thought for a moment. "If it is an organisation or group of some kind, won't they claim responsibility at some stage? They normally do. Think of the trouble that would save us."

"I wondered about that," said Rayner. "But claiming responsibility for a few dog turds? No, I don't think so. But bombs, even suicide bombers, and loss of human life. That's when these people start claiming responsibility or even credit according to their perverted way of thinking. And that's what we've got to try to forestall."

"Fair enough," Telford said.

On his way back to his office, Rayner hoped that it wouldn't come to him having to apologise. Part of him felt that all this was a pretty pointless and time-wasting exercise. All this for a few dog turds? What the hell? It happened all the time; and yet Rayner regarded every case as a challenge. He didn't like to be beaten, even if it was only dog turds; and he certainly wanted to prevent any escalation. At the office he nodded in approval as, thanks to Zoë's efforts, he saw that the war room was coming to life. But it was pretty sparse at the moment and he knew it. So, from the look on her face, did Zoë.

Rayner tried to cheer her up with an optimism he didn't feel. "All systems go at the IT centre," he said. "We're being given priority."

"That's something anyway," she said. "But it's a long shot, isn't it, Sir?"

"Anything's a long shot at this stage of an enquiry," he replied. "What about those interviews?"

"On your desk, Sir. Twelve arranged so far. I've tried to fix them as conveniently as possible but not everyone's available at the ideal time."

"Thanks, Zoë." Rayner left the war room and began to examine the names of the recipients of Corbett's second salvo with whom Zoë had managed to make appointments. Checking the different times and locations, he could see that he was going to have a busy couple of days. He noted that Zoë had already booked a reserve driver. The thought of driving round London and the Home Counties, to say nothing of up to Chester and York, didn't fill him with excitement, but it had to be done, and, as was his custom, he would be the one to do it. Surely one or more of these people would be able to give him a lead to what ASIF meant? With relief he saw that the reserve driver was PC Roberts, a smoker. That, at least, was something. Who the hell, or what the hell was ASIF?

* * *

A leak from someone or somewhere had ensured that news of the package sent to the Prime Minister reached the press. Led by *The Sun* and *Daily Mirror*, all of the national dailies gave it a mention. *The Sun* and *Daily Mirror* ran it on the front page as well as in their editorials. Not to be outdone, the *Daily Mail* decided to commission a readers' poll.

Corbett's delight was tempered by disappointment that none of them mentioned his accompanying ASIF note, but for the time being the publicity was most encouraging. He particularly enjoyed the results of the *Daily Mail* poll. Sixty-two per cent of respondents thought that the package and its contents represented what they thought about the Prime Minister and the Government. Twenty-five per cent thought the whole thing was shocking. Only thirteen per cent were "don't knows". The accompanying editorial commented that it was fortunate for the Government that Britain's democratic process was expressed through the ballot box rather than through the letter box. The following day the cartoon on the cover of *Private Eye* showed a sign stating, "Fouling Footpath – Fine £10" to which someone had affixed "Fouling 10 Downing Street – Reward £100".

As Corbett carried the box of thunderflashes Mark IV from the barn to the house, he hummed happily to himself.

CHAPTER FOUR

Corbett put the box of thunderflashes on the kitchen table. As he unwrapped Quartermaster Sergeant Major "Ginger" Evans's package, he told an optimistic-looking Carstairs that there was nothing here for him, then smiled at Ginger's message, "Death to Moles", accompanied by a rather well-executed cartoon sketch of an exploding molehill with its occupant blown high into the air. Corbett didn't know that Ginger was an artist.

He cut the seal on the box with a kitchen knife and raised the lid. There they were, the little lovelies, neatly laid in five rows of ten. Each thunderflash was shaped like a tube, four inches long and three-quarters of an inch wide. Down the side of each was a red tag in the form of a long strip. Tearing the tag sharply along the length of the tube would detach the cap at the top and ignite the fuse. On the Mark IV version the delayed action fuse would burn for thirty seconds before the thunderflash detonated.

Thunderflashes were made of heavy-duty cardboard and were not designed to be lethal. They were used on military exercises to add realism; they simulated hand grenades in house-clearing operations and shell or mortar fire during advance to contact or assaults on enemy-held positions. Sometimes they were distributed and used by infantry trainees in battle conditions, while frequently they were thrown gleefully into section or platoon positions by umpires who delighted in watching the reactions of the surprised and part-deafened infantrymen. They made a hell of a bang.

Only the Mark IV had a delayed action fuse. The other versions, though varying in size and noise of bang, all had the shorter four-second fuse, approximately the same as a hand grenade. As in the case of ordinary, standard fireworks, improper handling could lead to injury. You pulled the tag and threw. Holding on to the thunderflash for too long was not recommended. Corbett had seen one man hesitate too long while deciding where to throw it and the resulting mess to his hand made by the detonation was not pretty to see. The man had lost a finger. Corbett had heard of another occasion when an umpire had thrown a thunderflash into a slit trench, whose occupant was too slow to evacuate and who had failed to turn away from the blast quickly enough. The thing had gone off in his face, causing him to suffer not only painful burns but also the loss of an eye. Thunderflashes were not to be treated lightly.

  Corbett's first task was to test the weapon that would form salvo No. 3. Shutting Carstairs in the kitchen, just to be on the safe side, he walked into the garden, taking one thunderflash with him. There actually were a few molehills at the far end of the lawn, so, thinking that he might as well kill two birds with one stone, he picked up a spade en route. Pausing to gauge the probable direction of the mole run, he began to dig carefully so as not to destroy the run. The light December frost had not yet hardened the ground, and, about twelve inches down, between two groups of hills, he gave a grunt of satisfaction as he found the run. He checked to make sure that it was clear of cave-ins in both directions and then cut a solid piece of turf with which he would contain the explosion, ensuring that the detonation would spread along the run rather than being wasted by exploding upwards into the air. He tested the size of the turf over the hole, took the thunderflash from his pocket and tore off the tag, beginning to count as he did so. He placed the now fizzing tube into the hole and tamped down the turf over it. Ten seconds. He walked away for a few metres, still counting, and turned to observe. Twenty seconds. Continuing to count, he began to worry that his tamping down had been too efficient and that the lack of oxygen had extinguished the fizzing fuse, but as he reached the count of thirty there was a muffled but still satisfying explosion. The turf lifted slightly and gradually wisps of smoke rose from along the run. He nodded, pleased with the test. That would give them something to think about; and he didn't just mean the moles.

* * *

In the Commissioner's office Rayner shifted uncomfortably in his chair. He would never have admitted to squirming – he would never squirm for anyone – but it was a close-run thing. The Commissioner had listened to his report in silence. No questions, no comments, just silence. A silence that Rayner could only describe as icy. He didn't blame the Commissioner. He didn't blame anyone but himself. Before he had left the house that morning, aware of the interview that lay ahead, Betty had done her best to comfort him as she sipped her early morning tea.

"Nobody could have done any more than you, darling. The Commissioner can't expect miracles, you know. You're worrying too much."

"Three weeks," Rayner said. "Three weeks and we've got nothing. Nothing. A population of over sixty million in the country and he could be any one of them."

"That's an example of pessimistic exaggeration for a start." Betty tried to make light of it. "From what you've told me, he might be a she. So, either way, you're talking about one in thirty million, not sixty."

"That's very helpful of you, I must say," said Rayner morosely. "We don't even know what sex he, or she, is. The Commissioner'll have my guts for garters."

Then he remembered. "Sorry, darling. Here I am worrying about my case and forgetting about yours."

"Mine?"

"Your Step by Step Reading Plan for prisons."

"Oh that. I just persevere; but nobody seems interested. On the contrary. In some prisons they seem to be positively against the idea, particularly Holloway."

"Positively against?" Rayner sighed as he shared Betty's frustration.

"Oh they don't say that as such. They just bring up excuse after excuse. Lack of amenities or space. Disruption of prison routines. Staff shortages. Vetting books. Can't have prisoners reading porno literature, can we? And so it goes on."

"I've got to go." Rayner looked at his watch. "But I'll try to come up with something. As soon as this case is over."

* * *

When the Commissioner finally spoke, he didn't mention either guts or garters. "And that's all?"

"That's all, Sir."

"Not very much, Mike, after three weeks. God knows how much this enquiry has cost already, in allocated IT time, let alone the number of man hours in what appears to be every station in the country."

Rayner, who, with Zoë, had probably put in more man hours than all the rest of them put together including the Commissioner, tried to keep his temper. "We were clearly instructed to make this a priority enquiry, Sir."

"I know, I know," the Commissioner interrupted. "But we've got a budget to stick to. Targets to meet. You know that as well as I do."

"Next thing we know they'll be telling us to operate at a profit," Rayner retorted. "Treating us like some corporate entity listed on the Stock Exchange. Trying to value us in terms of share price, dividend yield and price earnings ratio. Well, as far as I'm concerned our shareholders are the general public, all of them, and the less we hear of them or from them the better we'll be doing our job. No reports and no complaints, mean no incidents and no crime. What better compliment could we, the police, seek than to be taken for granted? That's what I think we should be aiming for."

The Commissioner smiled thinly. "Not if we go over budget, Mike. Right. What's your next step?"

The question was the one that Rayner least wanted to hear. None of his painstaking interviews with the recipients of Corbett's second salvo had yielded anything whatsoever. The letters ASIF meant nothing to anyone. Mark Telford's IT team had come up with a large number of possibilities for the four letters, many of which were discarded at once as being too unlikely to be worth following up. Amongst those to fall by the wayside were the Aldershot Society for International Friendship, Alliance for the Secession and Independence of Felixstowe and Auxiliary State Information Foundation. A shortlist of the most promising permutations was being pursued, but there had been no comeback so far, and in his heart of hearts Rayner reckoned that they had drawn a blank, although he did still hold out some hope for Arabian Society for Islamic Freedom. Apart from that, he frankly hadn't a clue.

Rayner cleared his throat. "We wait, Sir."

"Wait? For what?"

"For any developments." Rayner spoke with a certainty that he didn't feel.

"Such as?"

"I've no idea."

"No idea?" Rayner thought that the Commissioner sounded as if he were playing Lady Bracknell in the handbag scene. "No idea? After three weeks?"

"Let's look at it this way, Sir. So far we've drawn a blank. Might as well face it. We don't know who or what ASIF is or what he, she or they want. Until now there've been some unpleasant incidents involving a number of people. Unpleasant, yes, but not dangerous or violent. No damage done. Now ... ," he paused to collect his thoughts, "... whoever it is may decide to escalate things ... "

"In what way?"

"We don't know yet. But that's been the pattern so far, what little pattern there is. First, just a sheet of paper with four letters on it. Then the dog turds, with the same sheet of paper and the same four letters. Next? Who can say? Maybe something completely different. Graffiti of ASIF all over the place? Letters to the press? Or perhaps something still aimed at the same people. More turds? Broken windows? Cars vandalised? Or worse. Personal violence? Letter bombs? You name it."

"You're guessing."

"Certainly I'm guessing, Sir." Rayner hoped he had managed to keep the exasperation out of his voice. "Whether it's inspired guesswork remains to be seen. Of course it's possible that we've seen the end of it. Some kind of nutter, who's protesting about something but we don't know what, but who's shot his bolt. In which case, we leave the file open but take no further action. No point in throwing good money after bad."

"So you're suggesting that we admit defeat. Then we tell the Home Secretary that, despite all the time and costs of this enquiry, we haven't got a clue and we hope it won't happen again."

"Certainly not, Sir," said Rayner. "I don't subscribe to the theory that it's all over. Personally, I think that we'll see some form of escalation. That's why my suggestion is to await developments. I'd like to put twenty-four-hour surveillance teams on all the people involved. Their houses, their movements, even their families. Number Ten's already taken care of, of course, and we also have the Labour MP's place in Sunderland under surveillance. I'd like to extend that to all of the others."

"Out of the question." The Commissioner shook his head. "The PM's covered, as you say, and so is the Sunderland fellow. But that's only for PR purposes. You know that, Mike, as well as I do. The cost of full surveillance of all the others ... plus the strain on resources ... no, I'm afraid it's not on."

"It's your decision, of course, Sir," Rayner replied. "But ... "

"No way. It's only a few dog turds, after all."

"I was aiming to protect people if the next stage turns out to be something worse than dog turds."

The Commissioner considered for a moment before continuing. "If there is a next stage. I think we should look on the bright side. Okay. Number Ten can look after itself. You can maintain the Sunderland surveillance for, say, another couple of weeks. That should be enough to keep him happy. But that's it."

Rayner shrugged. "Very good, Sir. And my team and me? Back to normal duties?"

"Who have you got with you?"

"Detective Sergeant Henderson, Sir."

"The little blonde one?"

"She's damned efficient. Oh, and PC Roberts as reserve driver."

"Okay. Tell you what. How long will it take to complete the follow-up of what came out of the IT effort?"

"A week or two, Sir. Not that I'm too hopeful."

"Right." The Commissioner reached his decision. "If you have something specific by then, fine. If not, then we close the enquiry down. Keep the file open, of course." He indicated that the interview was over.

Rayner broke the news to Zoë, who shared his disappointment but expressed no surprise. She shared Rayner's view that the bottom line should be the prevention or solving of crime, but she was realistic enough to realise that nowadays the bottom line meant money.

* * *

Corbett decided that his third salvo would be fired by night. The thunderflashes would obviously have to be hand-delivered and the cover of darkness would be helpful. His turd deliveries had served to provide the level of reconnaissance necessary to ensure that he should not meet any unexpected hitches during the process. Besides, he didn't want his targets to be out of their dwellings when the third salvo landed. He wanted them there, eating or reading or watching TV or sleeping, when the thunderflashes exploded. He wanted to scare the living daylights out of them. He didn't necessarily want to harm them. The total blast area of the explosion was only a metre at the most, if that; and he didn't imagine that anyone would be fool enough to actually pick up a thunderflash that was fizzing on their doormat. The danger of fire was also minimal. There would be a hell of a bang, a certain amount of smoke and that would be that. He would, of course, include the ASIF message with the salvo. This time he would put the A4 paper with its four letters into a fairly stout Manila envelope, just to make sure that it wouldn't be damaged or ignited by the blast. He didn't want his salvo to go unrecognised.

Corbett was sorry that Fortunata and the occupants of the apartment blocks would only suffer damaged mailboxes rather than a night to remember, but he hadn't been able to work out a way round that particular problem. So far as the Prime Minister was concerned, he had toyed with the idea of brazening it out, walking straight up to the door of Number Ten, waving a bundle of papers and stating that he was delivering a petition of some kind, bearing two hundred thousand signatures, in the hope that he might somehow manage to ignite and throw the thunderflash through the door or a window or something. But it was just wishful thinking. The windows were probably made of bulletproof glass, even if he could get close enough. Such an act would be suicidal, and he had no wish for his mission to save the English language to be mistaken for an attack by a Hezbollah suicide bomber. He would content himself with mailing a thunderflash to the Prime Minister, accompanied by the ASIF note, perhaps with an additional message regretting that as a result of the Number Ten security it was not possible to deliver the package personally.

During the previous week he had taken a further precautionary measure. Although he considered it unlikely, he thought it just possible that the residences of at least some of his targets, particularly those who had been the subject of press comment as a result of salvo No. 2, might be put under police surveillance of some kind. So, dull though the task had been, he had visited each of the locations to check for any indications of a police presence. Some he had checked from his car, stopping close to the address to show that he had nothing to hide and ostentatiously studying an A - Z map or talking into a mobile phone whilst scanning the surrounding area for suspicious signs. Others he had checked on foot, parking the car some way away. Carstairs had accompanied him on a lead to avert suspicion. On one occasion he had a huge fright when he thought that the dog was actually going to let go a poop right in the middle of a pavement, with a policeman approaching only thirty metres away. Luckily it turned out to be a false alarm and he had hurried Carstairs back to the car before any damage could be done. It would have been poetic justice if he and Carstairs had been nobbled for a footpath fouling offence after everything else they had already achieved. He noted the presence of the policeman, but was inclined to think that it was coincidental. The address in Sunderland was a different ball game, however. He had driven slowly along the Labour MP's street and had immediately noticed a white van, parked thirty metres short of the house. Driving straight past the van he saw two men in the front seats. With plenty of space available, he drove on for fifty metres before parking. He judged he would be too far away, at that distance, for the van's occupants to be able to read his number plate. After a few moments he got out, locked the door and walked slowly back towards the van, speaking into his mobile phone as he did so. He assumed an expression of frustration and spoke in what he hoped would be taken for a Thames estuary accent as he approached the van. "Can't find it. Dunno. No I 'aven't got a map. 'ang on, I'll ask someone."

He stopped by the van and was pleased to see that the passenger window was half open. With any luck they had heard his conversation. "'Scuse me. I'm lookin' for Waterfield Road."

There were no markings on the van. Both men were wearing ordinary-looking clothes, jeans, T-shirts and leather jackets. So far as he could see, there was nothing to indicate a short-wave radio or any other communications system. But they looked like the law. He could somehow sense it.

"Sorry, don't know it." The driver spoke and his companion shrugged his shoulders.

"Thanks," said Corbett and turned back to retrace his steps to his car, still speaking into the phone. Police. He was sure of it. They had seen his face, sure, but that didn't really worry him. He was doing nothing illegal. He was a law-abiding citizen, lost and asking for directions. He got into his car and drove away. So they were watching the MP's house. Round the clock? he wondered. He'd better be careful with this one, but he had the advantage now. Forewarned was forearmed.

* * *

At six o'clock that evening, Zoë received the routine report from that afternoon's Sunderland surveillance team. Nothing special except that a passing motorist had stopped to ask them for directions. No, he didn't look suspicious, but they would send a description, such as it was, by fax. No, they hadn't noted the car's number plate. He'd parked too far away for them to pick it up and it didn't seem worth leaving their post to get a reading. Zoë had asked what directions the motorist had been enquiring about. Waterfield Road, had been the reply; but so far as they knew there was no road of that name in Sunderland.

* * *

During his reconnaissance for signs of police activity in the region of his chosen targets, Corbett had also been making a time appreciation. From the evidence of a probable surveillance team outside the Labour MP's Sunderland house, he realised that so far luck - in the form of scarce police resources - was on his side. But time wouldn't be - not after a few thunderflash explosions had been reported to the police, who would probably put two and two together pretty quickly. He thought it almost certain that within twelve hours of the first couple of explosions, possibly a lot less than that, there would be police surveillance on all the target addresses. His window of opportunity for hand delivering salvo No. 3 to all his targets would be limited.

Although he had carried out his reconnaissance of the seventeen addresses in London and the Home Counties at different times of day, spread over four days, he had kept a close note of how long it had taken in total. He calculated that after deducting the double counts of the initial journey from Rudgwick, he had spent around eight hours on the reconnaissance task. This included stops of between two and five minutes for observation. The delivery of the thunderflashes would take much less than that. Furthermore, night-time traffic would be a good deal less heavy than that which he had experienced during the day. Taking these factors into account, he reckoned that, given no unexpected hitches, he could deliver salvo No. 3 throughout London and the Home Counties in six hours or less. He had factored in his prudent policy of observing speed limits in this estimate. If he started out from Rudgwick at, say, 7 p.m. he would hope to deliver the first thunderflash at a London address by 8.30 and the last one, at the newspaper columnist's house near Guildford, by 2.30 in the morning. It might be cutting things a bit fine, but Corbett was fairly confident that an explosion in, say, Anderson Street, London SW3 at 8.30 would be unlikely to lead to a police surveillance team being on the spot at a Guildford address by 2.30 a.m. He didn't think that the wheels of police force reaction would turn as fast as that.

This left the three northern addresses – the Labour MP in Sunderland, the tennis player in York and the quiz show host in Chester. What to do with these? He had thought of catching an early morning flight to an equidistant airport, perhaps Manchester, hiring a car and getting the thunderflashes delivered to their destinations, with luck, during the same morning. But by that time he might well encounter police surveillance problems in both Chester and York, as well as in Sunderland, where his gut feeling told him they were already in place. Besides, such a plan of action would mean a daytime delivery, during which it was probable that his targets would not be in residence. He didn't want that. So he rejected this course. It was a dilemma, and for a moment he regretted not having chosen targets to whom access would be less complicated. But then he remembered why they had come to be selected. He remembered how their names had been ticked again and again in his notebook as they murdered the English language.

Eventually Corbett concluded that the only solution was to put the three northern addresses on hold until the heat was off. After salvo No. 3 had been delivered in London and the Home Counties the heat would be on for how long? A week? Two weeks? Then, gradually, vigilance would be lifted. They couldn't keep it up for ever, could they? He was confident that, in time, the coast would be clear again. Then he would strike in the north. In the meantime, he would have to make do with sending them a repeat of the first ASIF salvo in the biggest capital letters he could find. To keep them on their toes.

Corbett decided that he would give the salvo No. 3 delivery day a code name. He named it 'T day', short for thunderflash. It was to be a Wednesday. There was no need to give it a code name, but he enjoyed it and noted T day in his diary and made sure that Carstairs was let in on the secret name. H hour would be 1900 on T day. The day before T day, he gave Carstairs a particularly long walk, which he repeated on T day at H minus ten hours. Carstairs would be spending a long time in the car later. After returning from the walk, Corbett loaded the thunderflashes into the car with the envelopes containing the ASIF message. He covered them with a rug. Onto the rear seats he also put a dark wool overcoat, a raincoat, a camouflage smock and two anoraks, one red, the other blue. He added a brown trilby, two different coloured ski hats and two different coloured baseball caps. For shoes he decided on the trainers that he used for playing squash. They would be silent and, if necessary, faster than ordinary shoes. They were also commonplace. He didn't speak or think of them as "trainers" but as "my squash shoes". A few years ago they would have been known as "gym shoes" or "plimsolls", but today people seemed to wear them for everyday use and called them "trainers". He sometimes wondered what they were "training" for. He judged that, worn in different combinations, the outfits would be sufficient to ensure that in the event of his being observed by people or by CCTV cameras during the deliveries there would not be too many consistent descriptions of him.

Before lunch, Corbett filled the car with petrol and windscreen washer fluid and put an eight-gallon petrol can in the boot. On the floor of the passenger seat he placed a cold bag containing two 1½ litre bottles of Evian water, two ham and two beef sandwiches, both with a liberal spreading of mustard, four bananas and two Mars bars. These should be sufficient to get him through what would be a long night. As an afterthought he added a box of Bonios and a water bowl for Carstairs.

At H minus six hours he ate a lunch of spaghetti bolognese, accompanied by two glasses of pastis, which he knew would lull him to sleep. At H minus five he set the alarm clock, stretched out on the sofa, covered himself with a light rug, closed his eyes and slept like a baby. On the floor by his side Carstairs slept like a baby too.

The alarm woke Corbett at H minus two hours. He made himself a cup of tea, gave Carstairs half a tin of Pedigree Chum and, when they had both finished, took the dog out for a fifteen-minute stroll so that he could do his stuff. Back in the house, Corbett shaved and showered, then dressed in dark corduroy trousers and a plain shirt, both as inconspicuous as he could find. By H minus thirty minutes he was ready to go. He felt rested, fit and calm. He had made all the preparations he could think of; he was not aware of any loose ends. He locked the house, loaded Carstairs into the car, got into the driving seat and started the engine. They were on their way.

CHAPTER FIVE

Corbett turned left off the King's Road and parked the car in a day and night underground car park in Sloane Avenue bang on time at H plus one hour and twenty minutes. He donned the blue anorak, put a grey baseball cap on his head and stuffed the two ski hats into the anorak pockets. He had decided to do the six local addresses, all in the SW region, on foot and by public transport. Then he would return to the car, guarded by Carstairs, and drive to the other London addresses before heading for those located in the countryside. He had wondered about taking Carstairs on the SW run to divert suspicion, but the route might involve some journeys by tube or bus where he thought the dog might slow him down. Neither could the possibility of urgent withdrawal or even, if it came to the worst, flight from pursuit be discounted and he couldn't see himself hauling Carstairs over a wall or fence in an emergency. Carstairs would be safe in the car as well as acting as a deterrent to would-be vandals or thieves who might come across the remaining thunderflashes.

Corbett took six thunderflashes and six envelopes from the car and distributed them in the remaining anorak pockets. He gave Carstairs a farewell pat and a Bonio, locked the car and headed for the car park exit.

Ten minutes later he stood at the door of the corporate executive's house in Anderson Street. Waiting until there were no pedestrians visible in the immediate vicinity he took out one envelope and one thunderflash, cast a last look around him and then, in one fluid movement, which he had practised several times at home, tore off the red tag, noted the fizz and thrust envelope and thunderflash through the letter box. Bombs away!

As he turned away he began counting and walked the thirty metres to the King's Road. He walked fast but did not run. Not only did he not wish to arouse suspicion but also he was automatically following the training he had received as Officer Commanding Support Weapons in the TA. On the ranges, when blowing up any unexploded mortar bombs, he had been taught to light the fuse of the detonation pack and walk away at a normal pace. To run might involve tripping and falling. Tonight the thirty-second fuse would give him ample time to distance himself from the resulting explosion without running any risk. By the time he had counted twenty-five he was round the corner and heading west along the King's Road, which was busy with the comings and goings of late-night shoppers and early diners. He did not hear the explosion. Nor did he expect to from his position, screened by thirty metres of buildings; but, sitting in his drawing room sipping a whisky with his wife, the corporate executive did.

Corbett's route took him a few hundred metres down the King's Road until he turned left into Oakley Street, where one of the TV channel's foreign correspondents lived. The foreign correspondent had figured frequently on TV during news bulletins on the Iraq war, looking macho in helmet and body armour and speaking dramatically about the latest insurgent attack on the occupying forces. Tonight, without helmet or body armour, he wasn't looking macho. Nor did he behave in a very macho way when the thunderflash exploded in his front hall.

By this time, with a change of headgear, Corbett was already striding out back across the King's Road, up Sydney Street and across the Fulham Road to Onslow Square. Here the majority of the elegant Victorian houses had been converted into flats, in one of which lived the sports commentator. His mailbox was the recipient of Corbett's attentions and Corbett thought he heard a satisfying thud as he turned out of Onslow Square towards South Kensington underground station. He glanced at his watch and was pleased to see that the delivery of the first three thunderflashes had taken only twenty minutes.

At South Kensington he changed hats again and caught a train the two stops to Earls Court, walked up Earls Court Road and delivered a fourth missile without mishap at another apartment block just before Kensington High Street. He was amused that this delivery was only a couple of hundred metres from the local police station.

A bus from Kensington High Street took him past the Albert Hall to Knightsbridge, where he made an uneventful delivery in Hyde Park Gate, from where he walked through Wilton Crescent and Belgrave Square to Eaton Mews North, where a columnist for a national daily broadsheet newspaper was putting the finishing touches to an anchovy sauce to go with his halibut. The explosion in his hall caused no direct damage, but led indirectly to a burned, glutinous mess of an anchovy sauce, which quite spoiled the columnist's dinner.

Within just over an hour and a quarter since leaving it, Corbett was back at the car. He gave Carstairs a pat and ate a ham sandwich. Bombing people had given him an appetite. He replaced the blue anorak with the red one and put on the blue baseball cap. All in all he was delighted at how easy the first six deliveries had been. He wondered what was going on now in the respective households. Presumably they had contacted the nearest police stations. Perhaps in some of the earlier cases the police were already there, collecting pieces of charred cardboard as evidence, asking questions, taking statements, and so on. Quite possibly, with their minds on terrorists and Weapons of Mass Destruction, they were cordoning off some areas. He wished he could be there to observe their activities, but he had things to do. He hoped they were all too busy running around like headless chickens to start taking coordinating action with any central command organisation which might lead to surveillance teams being sent out too soon.

He drove round Hyde Park and up the Finchley Road, through St John's Wood and Swiss Cottage towards Hampstead and Mandy Drake. After delivering Mandy's thunderflash he heard a dog bark. He had only counted up to twenty-five and was passing the pub next to the New End Theatre when he heard the explosion of the thunderflash. The fuse must have been faulty. He had to admit that it was a pretty good bang, even when muffled by Mandy's front door. He was well ahead of schedule and he needed a pee, so he walked up the steps of the pub's forecourt. From the pub he could also allow himself the luxury and the pleasure of observing developments for perhaps fifteen or twenty minutes. As he reached the door of the saloon bar – perhaps only ten seconds after the explosion – he heard a shrill scream from the direction of Mandy's house. Overcoming his initial reaction of alarm, he calmly opened the door and stepped into the pub. There were a number of what he assumed to be regulars inside and their conversation, plus the door, must have covered the noise of the scream. He ordered a whisky with ice cubes, paid for it and added a good dash of water. He took a sip, looked for a "Gents" sign and was about to head for it when a series of approaching hysterical screams heralded the bursting open of the pub door and the appearance of Mandy Drake.

There was blood on her white jersey and tears of terror and horror ran down her cheeks. In her arms she held a spaniel puppy, whose whimpers rose to a crescendo at the sight of so many unfamiliar faces. Part of its face was blackened with burnt fur and Corbett could see that blood was running from its nose and lower jaw. The conversation froze as Mandy wailed tremulously.

"Help me! Please help me! They've blown up Sammy!"

The shocked regulars crowded round her. "What happened? Poor little bugger!" "Who were they?" "Did you see them?" "Are you all right?" The concern and the questions tumbled out as the landlord said, "I'll call the police."

For a few brief moments Corbett was horrified at what he had done. He hadn't meant this to happen. Then Mandy's voice rose above the hubbub, "I was in the bathroom and there was this big bang. Sammy screamed and when I got downstairs there was smoke everywhere and he looked like he was on fire."

In an instant Corbett's horror turned to anger. Silly bloody bitch. It was her fault. It was she who was murdering the English language, not him. If she'd only spoken it as it should be spoken none of this would have happened. Her fault. Her bloody fault. He downed his whisky and headed for the Gents. As he peed he found that his hands were shaking. From shock or from anger? It was all the same to him. Anger then. He returned to the bar, looked at his watch and murmured to anyone who might notice him, "Is that the time? Gotta go. Sorry about the dog."

Outside he changed the baseball cap for a ski hat and hurried round the corner to the spot where he had been lucky enough to park the car in Heath Street, halfway up the hill. Carstairs wagged a welcoming tail and received another Bonio in reward. Corbett sat in the driving seat and consumed a beef sandwich and a banana. They comforted the cold feeling in the pit of his stomach, which he knew was not caused just by hunger.

Corbett drove on up the hill, round the roundabout at Spaniard's Corner and retraced his route down Heath Street and onto the Finchley Road, where he turned right past Lord's Cricket Ground and into St John's Wood Road. He parked fifty metres beyond the next target address, delivered the thunderflash and envelope and was nearly back at the car when the explosion occurred. He was pleased to find that this one was bang on his count of thirty seconds. He drove back round Hyde Park, stopping briefly to change hats and to exchange the anorak for the raincoat before carrying on west along Kensington High Street, Hammersmith and Fulham Broadway down to Putney Bridge. Crossing the bridge, he drove up Putney High Street, turned left into the Upper Richmond Road, and, after about half a mile, right into what would lead into Keswick Road. There he delivered his ninth thunderflash of the night, noting that the lights in the house were on. Another satisfying explosion, again on his count of thirty, saw him approaching the car and he was already unlocking the door when he heard a shout from the target house. "You bastards! You fucking bastards! Where are you?"

In his wing mirror he saw a figure run out of the gateway into the road. Without turning on the car lights so as not to reveal his number plate, he gunned the engine and accelerated away to a squeal of tyres on tarmac. He saw the figure set off in pursuit, but fortunately at the road junction there was no oncoming traffic and he was able to turn quickly into the road that would take him back to the Upper Richmond Road, flicking on the car's headlights as he did so. A little tight and he felt his heart beating strongly. Such language from a business pundit who was quoted in a respectable paper like the *Financial Times*! Tut, tut! And fuck you too, he thought to himself.

Corbett headed west along the Upper Richmond Road towards Kingston, turned left up Queen's Road and then right into Richmond Hill where the tenth and final London thunderflash would be delivered. Stopping just past the address he again changed headgear and approached the front door, envelope and thunderflash at the ready. When he reached the door he found, to his intense annoyance, that the letter box had been boarded over. Obviously the occupants – Tracey Carroll from the National Lottery – and her partner did not want to receive any more dog turds. He thought for a moment, went back a few metres down the path and picked up a medium-sized stone. Returning quietly to the house, he put the envelope on the doorstep, weighting it down with the stone, struck the thunderflash, placed it fizzing by the envelope but not too close, and retired at a fast walk to the road, still counting. As he got to the car he heard a lovely bang, so much louder than when muffled by a door. How appropriate that one of the National Lottery draws was named

"Thunderball". As he headed for the A24 and the countryside to make the remaining seven hand deliveries, Corbett glanced at the car clock and saw that it was 11.15 p.m. H hour plus four hours, fifteen minutes. Excellent.

* * *

Rayner thanked Betty for a delicious dinner, which they usually ate on their laps in front of the television when he was home in time; he cleared the dishes, loaded the dishwasher and washed and dried the saucepans and glasses (which Betty never allowed him to put in the dishwasher for fear of them getting chipped or cracked), before settling on the sofa next to Betty in front of BBC Newsnight and lighting an after-dinner cigarette.

"How many today?" Betty asked her usual question.

"Nine," he lied, relieved that his name was not Pinocchio.

"Well done," Betty said, not believing a word of it. "Keep it under ten, and see if you can get it down to five or six this week."

"I'll try," he replied. "If there's not too much stress going on."

Betty smiled. "You thrive on stress. You'd be bored without it."

"Hmm. True I suppose," said Rayner. "But the nicotine intake tends to go up. Anyway, this week's been a quiet one. Which reminds me. I called Holloway today. In a spare moment."

Betty responded excitedly, "Oh good. And ... ?"

"Nothing I'm afraid. The Governor was away at some conference. But they promised she'd call me back later in the week." Rayner saw the disappointment in Betty's face. "Well, it's better than nothing." At that moment the telephone rang.

Rayner sighed, "Not now, surely," and picked up the receiver. The time was 10.45 p.m.

Working on a shoestring budget, with only Zoë and him, plus PC Roberts, as permanent members of the ASIF investigation team, Rayner had arranged for any incidents occurring out of hours to be reported to London Metropolitan Central and relayed to him from there if it was urgent.

"Yes, Rayner here." The woman's voice at the other end of the line was not familiar to him.

"Detective Sergeant Healey, Sir. Met Central."

"Yes, Healey. Go ahead."

"ASIF incidents, Sir. Several of them."

"Details please." In a way Rayner was pleased that the escalation he had forecast seemed to be taking place. So much for the Commissioner deciding to look on the bright side in order to protect his bloody bottom line.

"Six in the Kensington and Chelsea area, Sir, and one in Hampstead."

"What kind of incidents?'

"Explosions, Sir."

"Explosions?" Rayner's face tightened.

"Yes, Sir."

"How big? Inside or outside?"

"We're still getting details. Mostly inside, we think. Not that big so far as we can tell from what we've got at the moment. No fatalities reported yet."

"Anybody injured?"

"Reports are still coming in, Sir. A dog hurt in a Hampstead pub. Nothing else yet."

"A pub? In Hampstead?" Rayner was surprised. There was no pub on his ASIF list.

"That's what they said, Sir."

"Right. Do you know the addresses? Names of occupants? Are they the same as the last ones? Are there any new ones, apart from the pub? Did they get the same note?" Rayner put urgency into his tone.

"I'm sorry, Sir. I'm not familiar with the case."

Rayner's anger flared. "God dammit. Not familiar? Why the hell not?"

"I'm just on the duty shift, Sir." Healey sounded half defensive, half apologetic.

"Didn't anyone brief you?"

"Not really, Sir. I was just told to call your number if there were any ASIF incidents. That's all. Sorry, Sir."

"All right, Healey," said Rayner, reining in his annoyance. "Do you have my mobile number and my car radio contact?"

"Yes, Sir."

"I'm going to my office. Should be there in, say, an hour. Between now and then you can get me in the car with anything urgent."

"Right, Sir."

"And, Healey, get hold of PC Roberts. Tell him to stand by. I'll pick him up on my way. And call Detective Sergeant Henderson for me. Fill her in with what you've told me and tell her I'll see her in the office as soon as she can make it there."

"I'll do that straight away, Sir."

"Thank you, Healey. And just one more thing. Has anyone taken any action to warn the other people on the ASIF list? Or sent any surveillance teams?"

"I don't know. Sorry, Sir."

Rayner sighed inwardly. "Okay, Healey. Thanks for calling." He put down the receiver.

Betty came in from the kitchen carrying a cup of coffee.

"Sorry, love. What a shambles."

"You'd better drink this before you go."

"Thanks." Rayner took the cup. "So much for a quiet week. If only the Commissioner had given me an extra hand. We could have been following this lot up already. As it is ... " he drained the cup. "I'd better be off."

Betty handed him his overcoat and briefcase. "Drive carefully. The roads could be icy."

"I will. And I won't forget Step by Step." He gave her a hug and a peck on the mouth and she waved him off from the front door as he drove down the short drive and turned into the road.

Rayner picked up PC Roberts from his house in Kingston, apologised for spoiling his night and was in the office by midnight. A call to Met Central brought a report of two more incidents – one in St John's Wood and the other in Putney. He acknowledged the information and arranged for any more ASIF-related calls to be put through direct to him.

Zoë arrived five minutes later and at once proceeded to call the various relevant police stations dealing with the incidents. It was a time-consuming task as she tried to organise the fragmented information into something concrete and to sort out the facts from the conjecture.

Rayner was guessing, but he reckoned it was worth a shot. He and Roberts first contacted the seven Home Counties stations to check whether there had been any incidents yet reported from the addresses outside London. The replies were negative. Good. There might still be time to head off this ASIF person or people, or even to apprehend him or her or them as they approached one of the addresses on the list. Rayner knew he was making some big assumptions; the first that any further attacks would be made that night; the second that they would be made on the same people as before. If the London incidents were anything to go by, the second assumption should be right. He would have to wait and see about the first one.

To each police station he gave instructions for surveillance teams to be sent to each of the relevant addresses. He listened to the predictable protests about other responsibilities and lack of resources and used rank and a sense of urgency to overcome as many of the objections as he could. Then he and Roberts began to call the potential targets to warn them that they should expect a possible attack with explosives of some kind within the next few hours. While not wishing to alarm them (none of the incidents that had already occurred had resulted in injury or serious damage), the police recommended that if they had relatives or alternative forms of accommodation nearby they should leave the house. If not, they should preferably remain upstairs or, at least, away from the front hall. In no circumstances should they attempt to take offensive action or to apprehend any attacker in the interests of their own safety. Rayner didn't expect their calls to be popular and the responses from the potential targets were mixed, ranging from annoyance at being woken up at this time of night to protests at being left to fend for themselves and to leave their houses unprotected, and what were the police doing about it? Two newspaper columnists, one in Chessington and one in Dorking interrupted his attempted warning to tell him that he was too late; the horse had already bolted. They had only just telephoned the police a few minutes earlier and were now standing in a smelly, smoke-filled hall clearing up the mess. Damn, Rayner thought. Too bloody late. In both cases he asked the columnists to leave the mess until the forensic people arrived. No, he couldn't say precisely when that would be, he was glad that no one had been hurt, yes, he agreed that after the earlier incidents insufficient precautions had been taken to prevent these repetitions and again he was sorry that their sleep had been disturbed. Then he called the addresses in York, Chester and Sunderland to repeat the process. He was relieved to find that no northern horses had bolted and was surprised to hear the Labour MP actually expressing appreciation for the warning. "I realise the police have a lot on their hands. Thanks again for calling and good luck." Blimey, thought Rayner. Anyone would think he was after my vote.

It was one o'clock before Rayner and Roberts had finished their emergency calls. For the time being there was nothing more they could do, bar waiting for news or developments. Zoë looked up and told them that so far as she could gather a total of around two thousand metres of roads had been cordoned off in the London areas where the incidents had occurred; and another report had come in of an explosion in Richmond Hill. Rayner could imagine the scene, repeated in ten different locations in the capital: police barriers; signs and entry-barring tapes all over the place; sirens possibly; police cars with lights flashing; ambulances too perhaps, just in case; residents and neighbours wrapped up against the cold standing in the street alongside passing rubberneckers. A lot of people would be short of sleep tonight. Talk about stable doors and bolting horses. He just hoped the whole mess would be cleared away before the morning rush hour.

For the next half an hour Rayner, Zoë and Roberts continued to field the intermittent inflow of calls. Still no fatalities. The Hampstead pub had not been a target. The victim lived a few houses down the road, Mandy Drake, the weather presenter on ITV. It was her dog that had been injured and she had run to the pub for help.

Zoë, who was taking the Hampstead call, suddenly waved at Rayner and said, "Hang on a moment." Then, to Rayner, "Description, Sir" and switched the phone to speakers. "Right. Go ahead," she said, not quite succeeding in keeping the excitement out of her voice. Despite himself, Rayner's heart leapt with hope.

The Hampstead policeman explained that the pub landlord had reported a stranger who had come into the bar a few minutes before the girl. He had not behaved suspiciously. He had ordered a whisky, drank it, had a pee and left. He was only there for two or three minutes. Yes, he'd been there when the girl came in carrying the dog. Probably nothing to it, but the landlord had thought it worth mentioning. Yes, there was a description. Male, Caucasian, about 5' 10", probably in his sixties. Wearing a red anorak, blue baseball cap and trainers. That was all. Rayner nodded.

"Thank you, Hampstead," said Zoë, and then to Rayner, "Well, Sir?"

"It's something," he said. "Maybe a start, maybe not. Circulate it anyway. You never know."

Zoë returned to the phone to circulate an all-stations description in relation to the ASIF incidents. A minute later Roberts fielded a call from Putney – another description. The attacker had been seen just as he was getting into his car, but at a distance and it was dark. The householder had thought he was of medium height and definitely wearing sports shoes of some sort. He seemed to be wearing something like a woolly hat and a longish coat, possibly a raincoat. No, the witness had not seen the number plate. The car had driven off too fast.

"Bugger," said Rayner, and signalled to Zoë to add this description to her all-stations call. "Sounds as if we're dealing with a team of them. Or," he added thoughtfully, "a pro."

* * *

In his rather nice Queen Anne house near Guildford, the *Daily Telegraph* columnist gave his wife a summary of the call he had received from the police. Dog turds were bad enough, but explosives? What the hell was going on, and why were they being singled out? Anyway, they'd better give their daughter Penny a ring and ask whether she could put them up for the night, or what was left of it.

His wife disagreed. Why didn't they just stay where they were? It was cold outside. Why should they disturb Penny and John and their kids, and anyway why go to all the hassle of getting up, getting dressed and driving twelve miles on a winter's night when for all they knew nothing was going to happen? The police weren't sure were they?

The columnist was tempted to agree with her, but thought it would be better to be safe than sorry. The police had talked about explosives, after all.

His wife had an idea. Why not try to grab them, give them a blast from the shotgun, or thump them with a golf club? But the columnist ruled this out. No heroics. Her safety came first. And, in any case, in these days of political correctness and the European Court of Human Rights they would probably find themselves arrested, charged and locked up if they took any action that might be ruled as unreasonable, even if it was in self-defence. This was what the country had come to. He would write about it in his column the following week. And finally, they didn't know how many of them there might be. He picked up the phone and called their daughter.

* * *

By one o'clock Corbett had delivered all but one of the remaining thunderflashes. He didn't know exactly what game the police might be in the process of playing in reaction to his salvo No. 3, but he knew that, so far at any rate, he was ahead of them. There was only one address still to be done, the Queen Anne house near Guildford. He remembered the longish drive leading to the house from the road and knew that he would need to be wary, even if he was still ahead of the police. But it was late at night, the newspaper columnist was probably tucked up snugly in bed and his trainers would make no noise on the drive, which he knew was tarmacked rather than gravelled.

He drove past the entrance to the drive without stopping, turned at a road junction two hundred metres further on and drove back again, parking on the verge. There was no sign of a police presence or suspicious activity. He decided against leaving the car's engine running. His story, if he needed one, would be that he had broken down and had waited for several minutes in vain in the hope of flagging down any passing traffic for help. His mobile phone was on the blink, so finally, with the greatest reluctance considering the time of night, he had decided to ask whether he could use the house's telephone. The alternative would have been to spend the rest of the cold winter night in the car. He thought it would sound convincing enough.

Wearing the camouflage smock and grey baseball cap, Corbett walked up the drive towards the house. There were no lights on. They were probably asleep. Suddenly he found himself flooded in bright light. At first he thought it was an external automatic security light but then he realised it was the headlights of a car. Shit! Police car? Or what? He froze, lifted his hand to protect his eyes from the glare and shouted out, "Hello!?"

A voice answered from the car. "Who are you? What do you want?" Corbett advanced slowly and smiled an apologetic smile.

"I'm awfully sorry. I've broken down just outside your drive." He continued to spin his yarn as the columnist got out of the car and approached him. "I'm so glad I didn't wake you up. Could I possibly use your phone? There's an all-night garage on the Horsham Road."

The columnist eyed him up and down. Corbett tensed himself in case of trouble but smiled innocently.

"I'm really sorry to impose on you. But the alternative was either a two-hour walk to the garage or spending the night in the car. Unheated too, with the engine not working."

The columnist hesitated and then made up his mind. The man seemed open enough, harmless enough. "Tell you what," he said. "We're going that way. We'll run you there."

Corbett thought quickly. The last thing he wanted was to be dumped at a garage eight miles away, leaving a perfectly sound car containing Carstairs, plus several changes of clothing for the police to find.

"That's very kind of you, but I'd prefer not to leave the car. It doesn't lock properly and I've got the dog in the back."

"Okay. Stay with the car if you'd prefer. We'll tell the garage you're in trouble. Any idea what's wrong?"

"Not really. The engine just died on me. Electrics probably. There's plenty of petrol."

"Fraid I'm no good with engines, but I'll have a look if you like."

Corbett laughed. "I'm afraid it'll be the blind leading the blind." He made to turn back towards the road. "I'll stay with the car then and keep my fingers crossed. Are you sure the garage is on your way?"

"No problem," said the columnist, returning to his car.

"Many thanks again." Corbett walked to the road and stood on the verge as the columnist drove out. He gave them a wave, while watching the car's rear lights fade away in the distance and disappear from sight round a corner. Then he went to his own car, opened the bonnet to give the impression of a problem and gave the columnist three minutes, just in case he had decided to stop and sneak back on foot to check whether Corbett's story was genuine.

After three minutes nothing had changed. Corbett shrugged. Well, why not? This is what he had come here to do, after all. He strolled back up the drive and delivered the thunderflash and envelope through the letter box. Pity there was nobody in to enjoy the bang.

Corbett got home half an hour later, noting a police car as it came towards him and disappeared in the direction of Guildford. With the exception of the three northern addresses, salvo No. 3 had been delivered.

He gave Carstairs a five-minute wander round the garden and another Bonio when they went indoors. He poured himself a large whisky and sipped it as he ate the last sandwich. He was tired but too keyed up to try to sleep yet. He allowed himself a rest from the television and sat back to review the day.

With the benefit of hindsight he had, perhaps, been rash to deliver the thunderflash at the Guildford address. Although he had got away with it, he had been seen for some time lit up all too clearly by the car headlights. If it came to it he could be identified. Damn! Idiot! He should have driven off straight away and perhaps even dropped into the all-night garage to tell them that he had fixed the problem and demonstrating at the same time that he had absolutely nothing to hide and was altogether a very nice guy to save them the trouble of a wasted journey to go to his aid. The trouble was that he had been so relieved at having got away with his unexpected meeting with the columnist that he had allowed it to cloud his judgement. Rather than an innocent motorist, he and his face would now be associated with the thunderflash. Or would they? After all, he could have been perfectly genuine, his visit could have been coincidental, he could have driven off and the guy with the thunderflash could have turned up later on. He pondered this possibility for a while and concluded that it was probably wishful thinking. Damn again! Looking back over the rest of the evening, he was confident that the Putney target would not have seen his face, though there was a possibility that he might have noticed what he was wearing. Then there was the pub in Hampstead. But why should anyone there have reason to link him with the explosion at Mandy Drake's house? Whoever was responsible for Mandy's thunderflash would surely have put as much distance between himself and the explosion as quickly as possible. He wouldn't have wandered into a pub only fifty metres away, would he? One thing was certain. He'd have to get rid of the headgear and anoraks and raincoat. He'd do that first thing tomorrow.

Later, having gone to bed after a second whisky, he tried to sleep but without success. He found himself thinking about Mandy's dog and her tear-stained face and the blood on her jersey. Then, as he began to drift, he had images of Annie, the first for a long time. What would she make of all this? She'd go bananas. She'd probably think he was stark staring mad. But he wasn't. He was only trying to save the English language.

CHAPTER SIX

By nine o'clock the following morning, Rayner and his team had pieced together the details of the London incidents. The Home Counties reports were still coming in. Forensic had already come through with their analysis of the debris caused by the explosions – all identical; cardboard, heavy duty; thunderflash, probably Mark IV, almost certainly military; the same ASIF message, again, cut from *The Times* in manila envelopes scorched in places but intact. Looking at the large map of London on Zoë's wall, Rayner could see each of the addresses attacked, each marked with a red flag. Attached to the flag was the time of the attacks, or at least the time when they had been reported. Ten of them, between 8.30 and 11.30 p.m. Did this mean they were up against a gang? Or could one individual have done it within that time frame? Two descriptions, one from Hampstead, one from Putney. Same height. Different clothes, apart, possibly, from the shoes. Two CCTV shots, both indistinct, which might have been of the same person. One car, described but not identified. Not much to go on yet. Not enough to draw any conclusions. And they were still no further on with whatever or whoever ASIF was.

Rayner yawned. There was nothing he would have liked more than to get home and go to bed. He had stretched out in an armchair for an hour on Zoë's instructions, but had probably not managed to snatch more than half an hour's sleep, disturbed by ringing telephones and conversations from Zoë or Roberts. As soon as he had heaved himself up from the armchair, at around 4 a.m., Zoë and Roberts had taken their turn for a snatched snooze, but he didn't suppose they had managed any better then he had.

Coffee and bacon sandwiches, organised by Roberts, had helped to restore some energy at 6.30 a.m., but Rayner knew it would be a long time before his desire to get home to his own bed would be fulfilled.

First on the agenda was to unscramble all the cordoned-off streets. Not that he would have cordoned them off in the first place but, he supposed, given the circumstances at the time, Met Central had little alternative but to play it safe. Well, on the basis of forensic's analysis, he felt confident enough to back his judgement that the whole of London was not about to go up in smoke from a series of huge bangs from thousands of kilos of Semtex or hundreds of suicide bombers in the wake of a few thunderflashes. He rang Met Central to suggest that they give the go-ahead to remove the cordons and stand down any emergency teams still in situ.

Then he rang the Commissioner, who should have arrived at his office by now. Rayner had better things to do than to waste time with a personal visit.

"Well you've got your escalation," the Commissioner snorted. "What a bloody shambles. Traffic's snarled up all over London. The mayor's been on to me; and the Home Secretary."

Rayner told him that he had just given the go-ahead to remove the cordons. He didn't bother to say that they had not been his idea in the first place. For all he knew they had been ordered by the Commissioner himself.

"Well, at least that's something," said the Commissioner. "And now, what about the perpetrator, or perpetrators? Are you any closer to him ... or them?"

Rayner briefed him on the incidents of the previous night and the action he had taken. The reports that had come in from the Home Counties had yielded no useful new information save that any surveillance teams that had been sent to the target addresses had arrived too late. The attacker or attackers had been ahead of them. He forbore from referring to their last meeting when his request for surveillance teams had been rejected. Nor, he noticed, did the Commissioner care to bring it up either. Finally, he mentioned the one bright point – the two descriptions they had received, either of two separate assailants or of one wearing different clothes and the all-stations message that had been sent out. Not much, he agreed, but it was a tiny step forward.

"I'm tempted to bring in MI5," said the Commissioner. "They're in charge of counter-terrorism now. And ASIF might mean something to them."

Rayner had known that this proposal might come sooner or later, but hoped that he could postpone the Commissioner's decision for as long as possible.

"I've already tried them on ASIF," he said, "and it meant nothing to them. As for their taking over the case, well ... on the basis of some dog turds, Sir?"

"But we're on explosives now," the Commissioner replied.

"Just a few bangers. No fatalities. No damage to speak of. A nuisance, I grant you, Sir. But ... terrorism?"

The Commissioner hesitated. Rayner hoped that the last thing he would want would be to seem to be panicking unnecessarily, or, worse, to be made to look foolish.

"All right. You can keep it for the time being."

"Thank you, Sir."

"But any further escalation ... "

Rayner seized the opportunity to interrupt. "Surveillance teams, Sir?" He could almost feel the reluctance in the Commissioner's reply.

"Oh, very well, if you must. But try to keep all this in proportion."

Rayner made sure that his voice concealed his delight. "I will, Sir. Oh, by the way, I almost forgot. No thunderflashes reported at Downing Street."

"So I should bloody well hope," said the Commissioner.

* * *

Half an hour later, Zoë fielded a call from the Surrey police. Taking notes hastily, she thanked them and updated Rayner. The columnist to whom Rayner had spoken last night had left the house as advised to spend the rest of the night with his daughter. On his return this morning, forty minutes ago, he had found a police car outside and the debris of an explosion of some kind in his front hall. Plus the usual ASIF message.

"Just like the others then," sighed Rayner. "The surveillance car must have arrived too late."

"Ah, but this one's different, Sir. He saw the assailant. Not only saw him, but spoke to him."

"Good God!" said Rayner.

Zoë gave Rayner the details, plus the description. Clothing different from the Hampstead and Putney witnesses, but height and age the same, appearance similar to the pub landlord's description, plus ... the trainers.

"Right," said Rayner. "Get him for me, please. I'd like to speak to him myself."

A minute later, Zoë put the call through to Rayner, who reintroduced himself to the columnist and asked him to run through exactly what had happened. Rayner listened, with Zoë listening in on the other line. From time to time Rayner nodded and grunted his acknowledgement.

Eventually – "And you just left him there?"

"He wanted to stay with his car."

"The car. Did you see his car?"

"Sorry, no. We turned in the opposite direction. The columnist's voice was defensive. "He seemed perfectly genuine. Maybe he was. Maybe it was someone else ... "

"I don't think so, Sir," Rayner interrupted. "Your description of him tallies with others we've received."

"Perhaps I should have tried to nab him." He sounded apologetic.

"Not at all, Sir," said Rayner, wishing that the columnist had done precisely that. "The safety of you and your wife comes first. Talking of which, if it's all right with you we'll be keeping your house under twenty-four-hour surveillance from now on."

"Do you think he'll be paying us another visit then?"

"I don't know, Sir, but if he does we'll be waiting for him."

Rayner ended the conversation and turned to Zoë. "Right, I'm satisfied that all this is the work of one man. We'll go with that. Agreed?"

"Agreed, Sir." Zoë's nod was repeated by Roberts.

* * *

Corbett had finally slept and was woken by the radio alarm at 7.45 a.m. He went downstairs, let Carstairs out, made himself a cup of early morning tea, let Carstairs back in and took his tea back to bed with a bundle of morning newspapers. The radio was tuned to the BBC's *Today* programme and Corbett lay back to enjoy the 8 o'clock news. He was not disappointed. The news headlines reported a series of explosions in London and the South East. No casualties had been reported, but rush-hour traffic had been severely affected in several parts of the capital. The police were investigating but were not yet ready to make any statement about the incidents. The newspaper headlines were predictable and their exaggerated drama ranged from "BLASTS ROCK LONDON" in the *Daily Mail* to "EXPLOSIONS SHOCK CAPITAL" in the *Telegraph* and "TERROR STRIKES IN LONDON" in *The Mirror*. *The Sun* went for the sob story with a colour photograph of Mandy's dog accompanied by a headline caption, "SAMMY SHOCKED IN SAVAGE ASSAULT". Mandy was holding the dog in her arms and Corbett noted that she had had time to apply make-up and change her white blood-stained jersey for a red, lower-cut version. Most of the leader columns raised questions about Britain's, and particularly London's, vulnerability to terrorist attacks and expressed relief that by pure good fortune there had been no injuries (apart from the dog). Hypocrites, thought Corbett. They would have loved dozens, even hundreds of casualties. "Small earthquake, no one killed" was never going to sell a lot of newspapers.

He got up, shaved and bathed, put on his gardening clothes and boiled himself an egg for breakfast. After breakfast he began to build up the garden bonfire on which he would get rid of the clothes. A good soaking of petrol guaranteed sufficient heat to do the business and he added several loads of garden debris for good measure. Then he thought about the piles of newspapers in the drawing room. He would need to get rid of them too. And the thunderflashes. He might as well blast a few more molehills while he was at it. Two birds with one stone. He had been seen, after all. It was highly unlikely that the police might pay him a visit; his description, if they had one, would fit thousands of people all over the country. But you never knew. Best to get rid of everything. He would keep the notebooks though. These contained hours of painstaking research and would be useful in the later stages of his campaign.

After an hour of tending the fire and a thorough turning of the ashes with a garden fork, Corbett was satisfied that he had got rid of the evidence. He would give the ashes time to cool and would then load them into rubbish bags, drive them down to where a secluded public footpath followed a fast-flowing stretch of the river Arun and get rid of them there. There would be no trace of them by the time the river reached the sea at Littlehampton.

Over a cup of coffee he read the morning papers more closely and noticed that Mandy's frantic story in the pub had been re-quoted in several of them. "I came downstairs and it looked like Sammy was on fire." He wrote the quotation in his notebook and added another tick to Mandy's name. Then he put on the surgical gloves, took out another thunderflash from the barn and wrapped it in bubble paper. Using *The Times* as usual, he cut out and pasted the ASIF message and then, after some thought, added, "PRIME MINISTER, YOU ARE NOT FIT TO SPEAK IN THE HOUSE, LET ALONE GOVERN THE COUNTRY. BE THANKFUL FOR YOUR SECURITY SCREEN". He placed the thunderflash and message in an envelope, added a first-class stamp and stuck on the label addressed to 10 Downing Street. This all took an hour or so, by which time he judged that the ashes would be cold. He piled the newspapers into the boot alongside the rubbish bags containing the ashes and set off on a half-hour run to dump the ashes in the river, feed the papers into the paper bin at Billingshurst and post the letter in Pulborough. He was back home in time for lunch. He was hungry. He peeled some potatoes, diced them and parboiled them for a couple of minutes. He opened a tin of corned beef, sliced it and put it in a frying pan with some melted butter, adding the diced potatoes. While the hash began to brown nicely he fried two eggs in another pan, then, when it was crisp, poured the hash onto a plate and tipped the eggs on top. A feast fit for a king or for the guardian of the English language. To hell with cholesterol. After lunch he would settle down in front of the television, no doubt to be entertained by views of cordoned-off streets, traffic jams and Mandy's cleavage. At the same time he would start on his Christmas cards. Or perhaps start work on salvo No. 4.

* * *

Rayner prowled up and down studying Zoë's wall. Spread along the ten metres were Corbett's three salvos, the dates, the addresses to which each had been delivered and the names and occupations of the targets, including sex, age, colour of hair and anything else that might help to link them in some way. Two television weather presenters. A National Lottery presenter. An actress (Zoë had wanted to put Fortunata under a heading entitled "celebrities" but Rayner had vetoed that on the grounds that the woman did not qualify, though he had to agree with Zoë that she hardly qualified under the heading of "actress" either). A TV quiz show host. A sports commentator. Two TV foreign correspondents. A newsreader.

Plenty of linkage there, with television appearances of one kind or another running through all of them. A radio show compère. Then the five newspaper correspondents. Linked with each other as well as with the others on the list, under the heading of "media". The lone sportsman, with no apparent connections with any of the others. Two chief executives of companies listed on the Stock Exchange, plus a retired company chairman, under the heading of "business". A Labour MP. And the Prime Minister.

Under "suspect" were the three descriptions of Corbett. Corbett's three salvos were shown side by side in a pattern of possible escalation. Note -> Note + turd -> Note + turd + thunderflash -> Note + ??? Three maps – of London, the South East and finally the whole of Great Britain – were spread on another wall. Alongside were two more headings – "ASIF" and "Motive". The spaces below each were blank.

It was still only mid-afternoon, but Rayner and Zoë were beginning to flag after their all-night session. Rayner had sent Roberts home to catch up on some sleep in case he was needed with the car later. Rayner hoped he wouldn't be. Fortunately, courtesy of the Commissioner, who had finally acceded to Rayner's request, DC's Rawlinson and Hooper would be joining them in an hour, attached indefinitely from Met Central. They would take over the night shift and field any reports from the surveillance teams. Rayner was aware of his responsibilities, including the financial ones, of which he knew the Commissioner would remind him with monotonous regularity. As well as his core team of five in the office, he had nineteen surveillance teams, six people in each, plus thirty-eight cars. Luckily Downing Street could take care of itself. His demands on the time of forensic and Mark Telford's IT team would be costed and allocated back to this investigation. He just hoped that the man they were looking for wouldn't decide to widen his list of targets, thereby adding to the Commissioner's costs. On the other hand, as he examined Zoë's wall, he knew that they still weren't any closer to their man. Rayner was going to have to accept further escalation, whatever that might turn out to be. So, he thought grimly, was the Commissioner. The ball was in the ASIF court and there was nothing they could do about it.

Rayner was not only tired, he was also depressed. He tried to hide it from Zoë but knew that she was in the same boat as she watched him pace up and down. She half smothered a yawn and stood up to join him.

"Not much I'm afraid, Sir. Sorry."

"It's not your fault, Zoë. Not anybody's fault, apart from that Guildford columnist. Why the hell didn't he just grab him?" Rayner's frustration was plain.

"You did warn them all not to take any risks, Sir."

"I know, I know. Well you have to, don't you. But surely someone with a bit of gumption ... and the car. He didn't even see the bloody car."

"So near and yet so far." Zoë tried to sound sympathetic. "It looks like it's going to be a long haul."

"As if, Zoë," said Rayner absently as he surveyed the wall.

"As if, Sir?"

"Yes. You're the best assistant it's ever been my pleasure to work with. But every now and then your grammar really makes me wonder ... "

"As if, Sir!" Zoë was urgent now.

"Yes, that's what you should have said instead of like. You said 'it looks like' but you should have said .... "

"As if," Zoë repeated the two words with a half smile, which turned to startled astonishment as Rayner seized her in a huge bear hug and swung her off the floor in excitement.

"You've done it! You've done it. As if! As if! As if!" He put her down and grinned. "God what a fool I've been! What a bloody fool!"

"Me too, Sir," said Zoë as she straightened her clothes.

"All of us! Me. You. Roberts. Mark Telford and all his IT people. The Commissioner! It was staring us in the face. We jumped to the conclusion that it was four separate letters, four separate initials and we all went along with that, and we've wasted God knows how much of our time and everybody else's in a wild goose chase trying to find out what they stand for. They're not four separate letters at all. They're two words. And you, Zoë, whom I should have recommended for promotion years ago, you are the one who cracked it."

"Only by accident, Sir."

"By bad grammar. Sorry to say so, but that's what it was. That lovely, beautiful bad grammar of yours."

"Shall I take that as a compliment, Sir?"

"You can take it as anything you like," said Rayner exuberantly. "You can carry on with your bad grammar as often as you like. As if. As if."

"Now that we've cracked it, Sir ... "

"You cracked it, Zoë."

"What does it mean? What's it telling us?"

Rayner paused. "I don't know. Not yet. Before we go any further let's just check those ASIF notes. Before we go on another wild goose chase."

Zoë opened a filing cabinet and took out a sheaf of papers. "Here, Sir," and she put them on the table. Together they studied them.

"There you are," said Rayner. "No wonder. Clipped from *The Times*, all capital letters, irregular intervals between them, no wonder we thought they stood for something. But look. Here ... and here. Definitely two separate words. And another one here. How did we miss it?"

"We just weren't thinking."

"No, we weren't," agreed Rayner. "But now we'd better start thinking. And fast. Good question, Zoë. What message is our man trying to give us?"

"What message is he giving to the people he sent it to?" Zoë corrected him.

"Thank you, Zoë. What's he trying to say to ... them?" Rayner looked up at the names listed on the wall.

"Well, for a start," Zoë said, "he's sending the same message to each of them. Accompanied by turds and then by thunderflashes. So what's he got against them?"

"And what do each of them have in common?" Rayner continued. "What have they done to him, or to someone, that's got up his nose? Assuming they have got up his nose."

"Turds and thunderflashes? And who knows what next? They've got up his nose all right. But why and how?" Zoë frowned. "What do they have in common, apart from all having received the same message. Why 'as if'? What have the Prime Minister and Fortunata or Mandy Drake got in common?"

"The Prime Minister's deficient in the tits department, that's for sure," said Rayner. "Or, for that matter, what does the Labour MP for Sunderland East have in common with, say, a quiz show host? They must have some link, otherwise why send them the same message?"

They both considered the names on the list again. "TV, newspapers, radio and so on, that's easy enough. They're all in the media, one way or another. But where do three businessmen come in? Not to mention a tennis player and two politicians? There's got to be a fit somewhere." Zoë shrugged her shoulders in frustration.

"What do they actually do?" Rayner mused softly.

"I'm not with you, Sir. We know their occupations."

"Yes, yes. But what do they actually do? Those TV people for example."

"Entertain?" tried Zoë.

"Entertainment? Is that what you call it? But anyway, not really. Not the weather presenters when they're forecasting rain. Nor the newsreaders. And you can't say that politicians entertain us. So entertainment's not the link." Rayner pursued his theme. "Those businessmen, they represent shareholders, don't they? Or they're supposed to. Politicians represent people too - the voters. There's a connection there."

"Between business and politics," Zoë agreed. "But the media people, TV or press, aren't in that particular chain."

Rayner continued to think out loud. "These TV types. They're not all entertaining us. But they're talking to us, aren't they? They all talk."

"So do a lot of people," said Zoë. "So do we. But we haven't had turds or thunderflashes put through our letter box. Nor ASIF messages."

"They're informing us," Rayner exclaimed. "That's what they're doing. The TV lot, whether they're telling us about the weather or the news or the state of affairs in some foreign country, they're informing us, communicating with us. The press the same. Politicians the same. You can call it spin but they're still communicating with us."

"And the businessmen?" Zoë queried.

"They're captains of industry, or fancy themselves as such. They're talking about the price of commodities or of sterling, they're telling us costs are too high or profit margins too low or something. Imports or exports and so on. And they're communicating with their shareholders and potential investors too, either directly or in press statements or interviews or speeches at the Institute of Directors."

"Which leaves the tennis player," said Zoë.

"Bugger the tennis player," retorted Rayner after a pause. "But I tell you what. I bet you he writes some column on the sports pages somewhere. Or gives interviews or something. I bet you he's talking to people too."

Zoë reflected. "It makes sense," she said.

"Maybe. It makes as much sense as anything else in this investigation. The common denominator between all these people is communication or information. One way or another they're all in the communication business." Rayner made up his mind. "Right. That's what we're going on. Communication."

"Fair enough," said Zoë. "What next?"

Rayner renewed his pacing. "They're all communicating either with the spoken or the written word. The subjects they cover are varied, reflecting their different occupations. So the common denominator is not what they communicate but how. What do you think?"

"Pretty good, Sir."

"Right. So our man's sending them messages about how they communicate. Okay?" He went on as Zoë nodded. "We assume that, for whatever reason, he doesn't like how they communicate, doesn't like what he hears or reads. If he liked it he'd be sending flowers and chocolates, not turds and thunderflashes. So ... ?" He looked at Zoë questioningly. "So what doesn't he like? What's got him so angry that he's prepared to indulge in criminal behaviour in order to make his point?" Zoë frowned again. "And in order to make his point he uses two words. As if. What's wrong with as if?"

"Or what's right about it?" queried Zoë. "What do you mean?"

"There's nothing wrong with 'as if'," said Rayner. "'As if' is right. Which means that something else is wrong. When I corrected your grammar a few moments ago, which I shall never do again," he added, "I was in the middle of telling you that in the context of what you were saying 'as if' was right and 'like' was wrong."

"Yes, Sir," said Zoë. "Can you give me an example?"

"Well, for a start, what you said. You said, 'it looks like it's going to be a long haul'. The correct phraseology would have been 'it looks as if it's going to be a long haul'. See?"

"I think so." Zoë sounded doubtful.

"Try another," said Rayner. "You've got a hangover. Your head feels like it's splitting. Wrong. Your head feels as if it's splitting. Right. It looks like it's going to rain. Wrong. It looks as if it's going to rain. Right. Although, to complicate things, 'it looks like rain' would be permissible. See the difference?"

"I suppose so," said Zoë. "But ... Does it really matter, Sir?"

Rayner thought for a moment. "Well, there's a right way and a wrong way. Some people may not think it important. Not nowadays. So perhaps to them it doesn't really matter. But to our man I'm guessing that it matters very much indeed."

"So we need to check it out?"

"It's only a theory. But I think, if it's accurate, that it'll give us a chance of getting under our man's skin. Of reading his mind. Putting ourselves in his shoes. Maybe even knowing what he's going to do before he's thought of it himself. But, yes, we need to check it out. Sorry."

Zoë's heart sank. She knew why Rayner had said "Sorry". Whenever he apologised in advance for something it normally meant that an awful lot of research and legwork was lurking just round the corner.

"First," said Rayner, "Let's get an artist's impression of our man. Can you fix that? Our artist will need to see the landlord at the Hampstead pub and the Guildford columnist. It'll be interesting to see how they compare."

"I'll arrange it, Sir." Zoë knew that until this case was solved Rayner would keep a copy of the resulting likeness on his desk as he tried to get into their man's mind.

"And, by the way, did we get hold of the military about any missing thunderflashes?"

"Yes, Sir. I spoke to the MOD earlier today. They'll make the usual enquiries and keep us posted."

"Good. Now the next thing." Rayner mentally checked the list of items he wanted to be covered. "Let's get in two TV sets, plus video and DVD equipment. I hope we don't need more. Then we'll need to get in touch with each of the TV channels. Fingers crossed that they record all their programmes. I'd like them to put together, on as many videos or DVD's as it takes, all the TV appearances made by the people on our list over a period of, let's say, the last three months. Radio too, if necessary."

"Three months, Sir?" Zoë repeated.

"Yes. Let's hope that'll be enough to give us what we're looking for. Fancy watching three months' worth of weather forecasts, Zoë? And three months' worth of the National Lottery and the news and whatever else they come up with?"

"Not much," said Zoë.

"Nor me," said Rayner. "Then we have to get hold of the newspapers these columnists write for and ask them for copies of everything they've written over the same period. Also any interviews, or whatever, that they've held with the businessmen, the tennis player and the Fortunata woman. How long do you think all that'll take?"

"Search me, Sir", Zoë said. "I don't know how they keep their records."

"Tell them all it's urgent. Top priority."

"Of course, Sir."

"I'm afraid we'll be home later than I'd hoped. Can you survive for as long as it takes to get those requests through?"

"I'll do my best," said Zoë, picking up her telephone. "I'll start with the TV channels."

"I'll do the press," said Rayner. "And let's make sure we get an estimate from them as to how long it'll take to deliver what we need. Any estimate they give you, try to get them to halve it."

Rayner went into his office and started to make a list of the calls he needed to make. He completed the list and started to pick up the telephone but it rang before he could do so. The caller was the Governor of Holloway Prison. Damn, thought Rayner. That's all I need.

As the Governor asked how she could help him, he was sorely tempted to say that she had chosen a bad time to call; but he thought of Betty and forced himself to forget ASIF for a moment. So he introduced himself and briefly explained the Step by Step Reading Plan and Betty's hopes that after successful trials at other prisons it might be given a chance at Holloway. After a pause he could detect the lack of enthusiasm in the Governor's voice as she confirmed that she had heard of the scheme and then proceeded to run through the list of reasons why it would not be easy to apply it in Holloway. The list contained all the objections that Betty had already described to him, which he acknowledged with periodic grunts, hoping he would sound sympathetic. Somehow he needed to convince the Governor that he understood her problems, while at the same time persuading her that Step by Step Reading was a cause that merited support. It was an exercise that required all his patience after what had already been a long day.

Then the Governor changed course. "I must say, Chief Superintendent, I'm rather surprised that you should be spending your time on this kind of thing. From all the reports of what happened in London last night I would have thought that the police would have had their hands full." She gave a sarcastic laugh. "Shouldn't you be concentrating on catching criminals rather than worrying about whether they can read or not?"

Rayner stifled his anger and confirmed that he was indeed busy on the very case to which she had referred, but then reminded the Governor that it was she who had called him.

"So it was," she replied. "I'm so sorry. Perhaps this isn't a good time?"

Rayner sensed a tone of satisfaction in the apology. He clearly was not going to get any further at this stage; but he would try for a rematch at a later, more convenient date.

"Actually it isn't." Rayner put as much friendship into his voice as possible. "Perhaps I could call you back when things aren't quite so hectic."

"Of course."

"Maybe I could look in on you one day when it's convenient for both of us. It's a long time since I've been to Holloway."

"You'd be more than welcome. Just give me some advance notice. I imagine we have the usual ratio of illiterate inmates. You probably put some of them here yourself."

Rayner thanked the Governor and rang off. He would have to tell Betty that he had got nowhere; but at least the door was still open. He sighed and lit another cigarette. He was tired and had used up most of his diplomatic skills for one day; but more were going to be needed. Mentally he switched over to his reserve tank, looked at the list of calls he had to make and reached for the telephone again.

CHAPTER SEVEN

The media people were surprisingly cooperative. Zoë thought this was a good example on the part of the police of how to make friends and influence people. Rayner, more cynical than his assistant, put it down to the media's ever-present hope that there might be a story in it somewhere. One way or another they received what they had asked for before the end of the week. Rawlinson and Hooper were briefed by Rayner and settled down for the Friday night TV-watching shift. They would be supported by two more officers on temporary loan from Met Central. There was an awful lot of material to watch; eight hours of weather forecasts alone.

Before Rayner and Zoë left that evening for a well-earned decent night's sleep, Rayner had tried to make light of the work that lay ahead. "You couch potatoes should be in your element," he told them. "When you've finished with the weather you can start on *Match of the Day*. Look what we've got specially for you." He picked up some videos and examined them, "Arsenal - Liverpool, Man' United - Chelsea, Aston Villa - Pompey."

"We already know the results," moaned Hooper. "And Pompey lost."

"Just consider yourself lucky you're not walking the beat somewhere. And no sleeping on the job." Rayner gave them his parting shot, before leaving to head for home.

Once there, Rayner gave Betty a summary of his conversation with the Governor of Holloway. "Now you know what Step by Step Reading is up against," she said, and Rayner nodded grimly.

"They don't like change," he replied. "And they don't like what they regard as interference. They need to be taught about lateral thinking. Once they can begin to think outside their own narrow paradigms they can be won over; but it'll take time. And if that's true at the Governor level it's even more so when it comes to prison officers." He yawned deeply. "Leave it with me, Betty. I'm not going to give up on this."

Betty stroked his arm affectionately. "I know you won't," she said. "But right now it's time for a drink, supper and for you an early bed."

The following morning, a Saturday, Rayner and Zoë were in the office at 8.30a.m. with Roberts. They would take it in turns to watch the videos and, to ring the changes, read the countless copies of newspaper articles piled high on the table. Thoughtfully the press people had produced only the relevant articles, so there was no necessity to thumb through page after page of broadsheet or tabloid trying to find them. Rayner knew that they could just as easily have done their reading and video watching at home, but he judged that the importance of undisturbed concentration, coupled with a show of solidarity with the team, made it preferable for them to carry out the task in the office. He promised Betty that he would spend Saturday night in his own bed but the planned outing on Sunday would be off.

As the long weekend hours passed, the team's notebooks gradually began to fill up. Had they known it, they were surprisingly similar to the format in Corbett's books. Quotes and ticks for every time one of the victims had used "like" instead of "as if". Periodically, Rayner would peer at the notes being taken by Zoë and Roberts. He had already checked Rawlinson's and Hooper's and their teammates'. He was pleased to see that they had made no errors, although from time to time he did find that they had included what he called the American teenage "like" – "I was 'like' wow!" and so on. These minor slips did not worry him unduly. He didn't suppose their man enjoyed reading or listening to them either. He had to assume that the night-shift team had not missed any incidents. Gradually the piles of newspaper cuttings changed shape. The stacks of unread material unmistakably grew smaller, while those containing the articles that had been read grew correspondingly larger. The latter were brightened where the ungrammatical uses of "like" had been highlighted in red.

It was boring, painstaking work. Roberts had the excellent idea of starting a sweepstake on which of the twenty names would be the winner with the most ticks against their name. They each put in a fiver and Rayner was amused at the excitement that was sometimes generated when the lead changed hands. By the time they went home on Saturday evening, Mandy Drake was in the lead, followed closely by one of the tabloid columnists. Tracey Carroll was lying third and the Prime Minister was trailing the field with only one tick to his name.

By lunchtime on Sunday, Rayner decided to call it a day. He had enough data to satisfy him that his theory was sound. Although there were still some recordings of quiz shows and documentaries to be viewed, plus probably two or three hours' worth of radio to be listened to, all the newspaper articles had been read. The number of ticks against the names on the list had continued to grow with the exception of the Prime Minister, who had still only scored once. "Must have fallen at the second fence," said Zoë.

The winner of the As If Stakes was Roberts with Mandy Drake, who had coasted home by five ticks. Zoë, who was on the second-placed Tracey Carroll, complained that the rules were unfair. Her National Lottery runner only appeared on Wednesdays and Saturdays, whereas Mandy Drake was in the starting stalls nearly every day, sometimes more than once. On the basis of average ticks per appearance, Tracey should have won. She appealed to Rayner who responded that, after a stewards' enquiry, the result would stand. Roberts scooped the pool but the others knew that they would receive their fivers back in liquid form on some occasion in the foreseeable future. That evening when Rawlinson and Hooper arrived, Rayner smiled at the look of relief on their faces when he told them that their video watching duties were over. "But make the most of them while you've got the chance," he said. "The sets go back to Met Central in the morning."

On Monday morning a report from Downing Street security, delayed for some unexplained reason, told Rayner that the Prime Minister too had received a thunderflash but mailed rather than delivered through the letter box of No. 10. Having only recently completed his tax return, Rayner regretted that the banger hadn't actually gone off or, better still, been misdirected to the Chancellor of the Exchequer at No. 11.

Rayner was looking forward to the next part of his plan. It had been five days since the thunderflash incidents. He wondered how much time he had to work with before the next attacks, whatever form they might take. He guessed that if his escalation theory was correct the next series of incidents would be worse than thunderflashes. In fact he was almost certain of it. Human lives could well be at risk the next time. Even if he and his team were not yet far enough ahead to apprehend their man – and he feared that to do that they would need Lady Luck to be on their side – he could still try to head him off. If his guess was right, their man had to be stopped, even if they had not actually managed to track him down. His plan would stand or fall on whether he was reading their man's mind correctly. But time was not on their side.

He rang Mandy Drake, introduced himself, hoped that she and Sammy were recovering from their ordeal and asked whether it would be convenient for him to visit her at home as soon as possible. Mandy agreed and by 11 a.m. Rayner and Zoë were on their way up the Finchley Road. Mandy welcomed them into the small hall, where Rayner noticed scorch marks on the wallpaper just above the skirting board a couple of metres from the front door. In the drawing room Sammy was lying in a basket in front of the fake Adam fireplace and they made a fuss of him while Mandy brewed up some instant coffee. She was pretty enough, even without her make-up, and Rayner thought that in her jeans and a pale blue roll-neck jersey she looked a good deal more attractive than in the warpaint and scanty clothes she wore when presenting the weather.

After the usual niceties, Rayner put his request to Mandy. It was a delicate task, involving, as it would need to, explaining the grammatical complications of the English language to someone who, Zoë's researches had revealed, had only managed to obtain two 'O' level passes, one in geography, the other in art.

"We'd like you to do something for us, Miss Drake," said Rayner, sensing correctly that Mandy was not often addressed as "Miss Drake" and took it as a compliment.

"Something for the police?" asked Mandy, looking surprised.

"That's right, and also for the other people who've received these ASIF messages."

Mandy gave a shudder and looked at Sammy in his basket. "It was horrible," she said. "Sammy looked like he was on fire. Can't you catch him, whoever it was who did it?"

"That's where I hope you can help us," said Rayner, and he gently began to outline his theory and, as he had done with Zoë, to explain the difference between "like" and "as if". As he gave the same examples as he had given Zoë, Mandy seemed puzzled.

"But nobody at ITV has complained."

They wouldn't nowadays, thought Rayner and then continued, "Oh I'm sure they haven't. It's not really important and they're not the ones who did that to Sammy after all. But the man who did do it ... well, we think that to him it is important."

"So what exactly do you want me to do?" asked Mandy.

"In future, starting as soon as possible," said Rayner, "we'd like you to say 'as if' instead of 'like' when you're doing the weather. If you can, even try to create an opportunity to do so."

"But I can only say what's on the monitor," she replied. "The weather's on a very tight time schedule."

"Of course. I realise that. But I'll have a word with your producer too. 'As if' needn't take any longer than 'like'. This evening, for example, if it's going to be a sunny day in the South of England tomorrow, you can say, 'it looks as if the South will have a sunny day tomorrow' instead of 'it looks like the South will have a sunny day tomorrow'."

"Is that all?"

"That's all, although if you can find more opportunities to do it, so much the better. You might be able to do it for, let's say Wales, or even the North of Scotland. Easy, you see."

"Oh I can do that all right," said Mandy, and then added, "I think."

Rayner promised he would be at the studio that evening to hold her hand and didn't forget to make another fuss of Sammy before their departure.

* * *

Corbett had spent the weekend working on the letter bombs. These would be the components of salvo No. 4. He had read the newspaper reports about the thunderflashes and watched the TV coverage. He hoped that he had put the wind up the people on his list. First just the ASIF note to create awareness. Then the turds to annoy. Then the thunderflashes to frighten. But he had no evidence of success, apart from the TV interview with Mandy Drake. He discounted the panicky press headlines. Those were just marketing tactics. Nor had he seen any indication that the ASIF message had struck home. In his ongoing vigil of TV watching, radio listening and newspaper reading, most of his targets had continued to offend. They needed to be taught a lesson. So he had decided on letter bombs. These would be designed to hurt. Awareness, annoyance, fear, injury. That was the route he would pursue.

Having reached his conclusions, he set about constructing the appropriate instrument. Locked away in the barn, perfectly legally, were the remains of the business he had sold, including the demolition components. He had already used some to blow up several large tree stumps. He knew that they represented sufficient materials to make up to one hundred letter bombs – or a single absolutely gigantic, monster one. He would dearly have liked to go for the monster. It would be fun. But he wasn't doing this for fun. He was doing this to save the English language.

First he began to work on the prototype. Not too big. He didn't want to demolish buildings or kill anyone yet, just injure them. A lost finger perhaps. A scarred face. It all depended how close they were to the bomb when it went off. He would design it to ensure that anyone who was very close would get ... well ... more than something to think about.

In the barn he knew he had two boxes of detonators, two boxes of one-ounce primers and twenty kilos of plastic explosive, consisting of eighty sticks, each about the same size as a stick of the Brighton rock his parents used to buy him on half-term outings from his prep school. Each stick weighed two hundred and fifty grams. By itself the plastic explosive (PE) was perfectly harmless. You could throw a stick of it around, even light it like a cigar. You could mould it just like plasticine, although if you did it would give you a slight headache which might last for twenty minutes or more. It was the tiny detonator, helped by the primer, that gave the plastic its explosive properties.

He decided that he would make the prototype using one hundred and twenty-five grams of PE. Not too little, not too much, like the old Erasmic Lather shaving soap advertisement. That would fit snugly into a small to medium-sized cigar box. He had purchased thirty of these from a variety of tobacconists in London during the past month.

Going into the barn, he withdrew the materials he needed for the prototype. He cut the stick of PE in half with a Swiss Army knife. The knife slid through the cream-coloured substance with ease. Putting on a pair of thick gloves he kneaded it into the shape he wanted. Carefully he xxxxxxxxxxx the xxxxxxxxxx into the shape and inserted the xxxxxxx into the hole in the middle. He wound the xxxxxxxxx round his forefinger until he was satisfied with its strength and consistency and attached it to the xxxxxxxx. Using a xxxxxxxx he gently eased the xxxxxxxxx into the xxxxxxxxxx and cut a strip of masking tape with which he taped the end of the xxxxxxx to the lid of the box, giving enough but not too much freedom of movement to allow him to xxxxxxxx the xxxxxxxx. Then he gently closed the lid. The bomb was assembled.

Before testing the letter bomb, Corbett got out the rest of the thunderflashes and prepared a number of molehills for detonation. Any passers-by whose curiosity was aroused by the explosion of the letter bomb and who might come snooping would only find old Alan Corbett waging his ongoing war with the gentlemen in velvet. Then he placed the bomb in the middle of the lawn. Using the tip of a six-metre length of bamboo, which he had cut for the purpose, he readied himself to lift the lid of the cigar box. It opened a small crack, then a centimetre, then two centimetres, then three. At just over four centimetres the bomb went off. The bang was not much louder than the one made by a thunderflash but the effect of the blast was much more dramatic. The bottom of the box fractured into splinters which lay embedded at the bottom of an indentation six centimetres deep and fifteen centimetres wide in the earth. The lid and four sides of the box each flew outwards for a distance of six metres, one coming to rest close to his feet. The two small metal hinges made an audible and menacing whistling noise before they buried themselves in a nearby grassy bank.

Corbett was satisfied with the result. Everything had gone like clockwork. However, he felt that the blast was a little on the large side. It might do more than just injure whoever opened the boxes. He didn't want that to happen. Not yet. He decided that he would need to reduce the size of the charge to one hundred grams. He spent the rest of the afternoon giving the moles a hard time.

The rest of the weekend was spent assembling the twenty bombs and inserting the ASIF notes. He would include one for the Prime Minister even though he knew that it would be intercepted by the Number 10 security squad. They had only received the turd and the unstruck, unexploding thunderflash so far. With any luck a nice bang would give them something to think about and keep them on their toes.

He wrapped each cigar box in bubble paper. He didn't want any jarring or banging to disturb the detonator and set off a premature explosion. He taped the ASIF message, now concealed in a stout Manila envelope, to the bottom of each box. Then he parcelled each box up neatly in brown paper, sealed the parcels with sellotape and added the address labels. For this salvo he had printed the labels in capital letters and used a different, larger typeface. Instead of the targets' names he had printed "The Occupier". Using his colour laser printer he had printed another label in large red letters – "2006 CENSUS" and in smaller letters – "Important documents for completion by householder". He stuck these on the top left-hand corner of the packages.

Early on the Monday morning he put the boxes in the boot of the car and drove to London, parking by Hammersmith Post Office. He went to the parcels counter with one box and paid the amount required for first-class post. He then purchased sixty first-class stamps, sufficient for the other nineteen parcels and returned to the car, where he stuck the stamps on each package. He had already checked that each parcel would fit through the slot in a standard letter box and spent the next two hours posting them in different parts of London. By lunchtime he was back home and salvo No. 4 was on its way.

That evening, having nearly completed writing his Christmas cards, Corbett and Carstairs sat down as usual for their TV-watching stint. Despite the successful mailing of salvo No. 4, Corbett was depressed. His success in terms of disrupting the lives of his targets and achieving ample coverage in all parts of the media was all very well, but he still had not seen a jot of evidence to indicate that anyone was taking any notice whatsoever of his ASIF message. They were all continuing to offend in the same old way. So were many others, and his list of reserve targets was growing daily. What was wrong with these people? Wasn't the message clear enough? Why weren't they asking themselves – as if what? Why weren't they making the connection between his ASIF note and the words they themselves spoke or wrote? Were they thick or something? Perhaps he should have extended the message that he had enclosed as part of salvo No. 4. Perhaps he should have spelt it out. Perhaps he should have added the word "like" with a cross against it and put a tick against ASIF. But that would make it too easy for them. Besides, he had already spelt things out at length in countless earlier letters to the media and others, all to no avail, which was why he had decided to launch his current campaign. In any case, on further reflection, any longer message with the letter bombs was probably going to be pretty badly shredded if the effect of the prototype explosion on the cigar box was anything to go by. This didn't worry him overmuch. They would know where the bombs had come from. Although, in fact, they wouldn't. All would naturally depend on how many bombs were actually delivered and how many might be intercepted by any mail surveillance system the police might have set up. They must have set up something, he thought, but with luck it would be limited to watching the respective addresses. He hoped that his census form decoy label might help at least some parcels to get through any net that may have been established. No, salvo No. 4 was not the time or place for any extended message. Time enough to work out something that could accompany salvo No. 5.

The evening wore on. He went through *Holiday 2005*, *Changing Rooms* on BBC1, *Celebrity Relics*, *University Challenge* and *Never Mind the Buzzcocks* on BBC2, *Tonight with Trevor McDonald* and *Who Wants to be a Millionaire* on ITV and a programme about immigration on Channel 4. All the remaining slots were films or endless sitcoms, which he didn't bother to watch because his targets could not be held responsible for what was written by the scriptwriters. During the evening he added a number of ticks against the names in his notebooks, while drinking two whiskies and enjoying his supper.

At 10.30pm it was the ITV News and he turned up the volume as the newsreader – not so far an offender – reeled off a series of stories ranging from a suicide bombing in Tel Aviv, to a capsized passenger ferry in Indonesia, floods in Bangladesh and a government paper on fining schools if pupils were caught smoking behind the bicycle shed – a paper that drew the usual criticism from a human rights "spokesperson". Corbett wondered what it would take for the Government to produce another paper on all the other things that used to go on behind the bicycle shed in his day, but supposed that the human rights spokesperson would defend the rights of twelve- or thirteen-year-olds to go at it hammer and tongs, whatever 'it' was.

Then, at last, came the weather and Mandy Drake. Corbett made ready with his notebook and pen. He thought that it would only be a matter of time before one day her appearance would be heralded by the same kind of ghastly fanfare and idiotic applause that Tracey Carroll got on the National Lottery. He was confident that Michael Fish's replacement by Mandy Drake was only the thin end of the wedge.

Mandy was, for her, looking rather decorously restrained tonight. Her neckline wasn't nearly as low as Fortunata's had been in *Never Mind the*

Buzzcocks. So far as he was allowed to see by the camera angle her skirt length was almost down to her knees. Good heavens! Wonders never cease! Up came the map of Europe and away went Mandy, waving vaguely at the symbols as a warm front coming up from Morocco advanced towards a cold front moving down from the direction of central Russia. Then the map was replaced with one of the British Isles with cold winds blowing in from the North Atlantic as Mandy burbled on. And then the miracle happened.

"So it looks as if the West and South West could be in for a windy night tonight," she said. "And with the cold front threatening from Northern Europe and Scandinavia it even looks as if we might be in for some snow as we come to the middle of the week."

Corbett couldn't believe his ears. Or his eyes. Or anything. She had said, "as if". Not once but twice. She hadn't said "like" at all. How he wished he had been videoing the programme so that he could have rewound it and watched it again and listened to that lovely girl saying those beautiful words again, and again and again. He shook his head in disbelief, but he knew it was true. He hadn't imagined it. As if! As if! Oh happy, happy day. He found his eyes brimming with tears of joy and his voice broke as he cried out to Carstairs, "She said it! Carstairs, she said it!"

Corbett was over the moon. It was working. In those few vital seconds, with him, Alan Corbett, as the orchestrator, aided of course by good old Carstairs, and with Mandy Drake, of all people, as their instrument, a tiny foothold had been established, which would soon become an ever-expanding bridgehead in the counter-attack that would eventually lead to the victory of the English language over those who, for years, had been seeking to destroy it. It was, to quote the greatest Englishman, not the beginning of the end, but at least the end of the beginning.

He must celebrate. Of course it was early days yet. But he was sure, supremely confident, that it would be only a matter of time before the swallow that was Mandy would be joined by others. The newspaper columnist swallows, the newsreader and quiz show host swallows, the Tracey Carroll swallows, all would soon be winging their way and soaring and swooping over England's green and pleasant land. He began to hum 'Jerusalem' as he poured himself a celebratory whisky. He didn't even mind the possibility that the flock might be joined by the occasional cuckoo, such as Fortunata. Yes, he thought, Fortunata might well turn out to be a cuckoo, although you never could tell. After all, look at Mandy Drake. He lifted his glass to his lips. And then he remembered the letter bombs.

"Oh my God!" he whispered, and then again, loudly enough to make Carstairs jump, "Oh my God!" Panic. Panic of the first order. "Bloody hell! Shit! Shit! Shit!" It was Mandy's bomb that filled his mind. The others ... well, they had not yet earned their redemption. The latest salvo was on its way, even now. There was nothing he could do to bring it back. The package was probably sitting in some Post Office sorting office somewhere in Mount Pleasant or wherever they had sorting offices nowadays. Even now it might be lying on a large pile of letters or parcels destined for the North London districts. Perhaps at this very moment it was being loaded into some Post Office van earmarked for delivery within Hampstead itself.

He picked up the telephone to call Directory Enquiries. It took him some time to find the number, which had changed as a result of the Government's decision to turn what had been a service for telephone users into a series of competing enterprises designed to make a profit. Eventually he found a number, and, as he punched the buttons, he wondered whether he was calling someone in Bombay. To his surprise he got a Scots accented voice quite quickly and gave Mandy Drake's name and New End address. The voice gave him the related number which he scribbled down. Looking at his watch he was amazed to find that it was still only 10.45 p.m. It seemed a lifetime ago since he had seen Mandy's divine countenance shining forth upon those clouded hills. She would still be at the studio. Or on her way home but not yet there to take his call. The telephone would ring in an empty house, perhaps waking Sammy, sleeping on whatever he slept on. Damn! But then, Corbett thought, there would be an answering machine. He would leave a message. A simple one. "A package is in the mail to you and should arrive tomorrow, or at the latest on Wednesday. Do not open it. I repeat, do not open it." Then he kicked himself. She'd have a mobile phone. Must have. Her answering machine would be bound to give him the mobile number. Bound to. Excellent. With luck he could talk to her personally, thank her for helping him to save the English language and apologise for the mistake about the letter bomb. Right!

He picked up his telephone and punched in the first four digits of her number. Then he stopped and replaced the receiver. Fool! Utter fool! What the hell was he thinking of? Phone calls could be traced, recorded automatically nowadays, couldn't they?

All this world of technology. Forget it. There was no way he could call from the house, from his own number. Nor by using his own mobile. A public call box then. He mustn't let Mandy down. He thought for a moment. It was years since he'd needed to use a call box in the area. He thought there was one in the village, outside The Fox. But that was really a bit close to home. He would try Billingshurst. There must be one there. By the station, or in the centre somewhere. Pity to leave a warm fire on a night like this, but it had to be done. He put the guard on the fire and summoned Carstairs to join him. Carstairs had had quite a lot of disruptions to his routine lately and was equally reluctant to leave his spot, but finally heaved himself up and followed his master. With luck there might be a Bonio in it.

Corbett drove to Billingshurst and found a call box by the station. Good. But then he discovered that it didn't take coins, only phone cards. He didn't have a phone card and there was nowhere he could hope to buy one at 11 o'clock on a Monday night. Cursing the modern world, he headed for the village centre. There he found another call box. The glass of the door was broken but he went in and was delighted to find that the machine took coins. He lifted the receiver and tried to feed in some coins. Jammed. Then he realised that the cord of the receiver was no longer attached to the machine. Cut. Vandalised. God!

He'd try Horsham. He was getting fed up with this but he had to make that call. He drove along the straight road to Five Oaks, negotiated the roundabout at speed and headed for Horsham. After a couple of hundred metres he realised that the headlights of the car behind were closing on him. For no particular reason, save that he was in a temper of frustration, he put his foot down. The driver in the car behind did likewise and Corbett was shocked when his pursuer turned on a flashing blue light. Bloody hell! At the roundabout the police car drew alongside and signalled to him to pull over. Hell's bells. Of all the times for this to happen; and after he'd been so careful for all these weeks. He drew up on the verge and lowered the window as the officer approached.

"Good evening, officer." He tried to sound as friendly and conscience-free as possible.

"In a hurry, Sir?"

"Well, yes, I am as a matter of fact. I've got a very urgent phone call to make. The phone at home's on the blink for some reason, so I've already tried two call boxes in Billingshurst, only to find that one only takes phone cards, which I don't have, and the other's been vandalised. So I'm hoping for better luck in Horsham." What could be more reasonable?

"Urgent call is it?"

"Yes, very." Corbett decided to leave it at that rather than come up with a web of lies for which he was not prepared.

"Would you mind stepping out of the car please, sir?" Damn. This guy was going to start making life difficult.

"Certainly. No problem." Corbett got out of the car. This was going to be bad news.

"Follow me, please." The officer was perfectly correct and polite but Corbett noticed that he had dropped the 'sir'. He followed him to the police car, from which the other officer handed him something. The first officer held up the breathalyser and asked Corbett to blow into it. Damn and hell. With two whiskies spread over two and a half hours, followed by the food he had eaten, he might have got away with it. But the third whisky, the celebratory one – he just hoped against hope.

"Well over the limit," commented the officer as he held the machine up and examined it. "I must ask you to accompany us to the police station."

Corbett sighed. "Look, it was an emergency. Okay? I had a couple of whiskies at dinner. If I'd known I was going to have to drive, of course I wouldn't ..."

"Get in the car, please," said the officer, opening the door of the police car.

"What about my car?" Corbett asked anxiously.

"We can't allow you to drive when you're over the limit. I'll drive it."

"But the dog's in the back." Corbett was pleading now.

"It'll be all right with me. What's its name?"

"Carstairs."

"Right."

The officer gestured Corbett into the police car and got into Corbett's himself. Carstairs hoped that this stranger knew that the Bonios were in the glove compartment.

At Horsham police station Corbett was tested again and the test confirmed that he was indeed over the limit. A check of their records by the station duty officer revealed the name of Corbett, Annie.

"Yes," Corbett replied to the question. "That was my wife. And the chap that killed her will probably be out in a few weeks, if he isn't already."

If he was expecting any sympathy he didn't get it.

"In that case," said the arresting officer, "you should know better than to drive your own vehicle when you're over the limit."

Corbett had no choice but to accept the overnight hospitality of the West Sussex police. His initial panic had subsided. This was nothing more than a setback. A night in the cells, in due course a visit to the magistrate's court, a fine and a few points on his driving licence - nothing that would put the campaign to save the English language off course for long. He was just sorry about Mandy. He hoped that the letter bomb would be intercepted one way or another. And he would make it up to her somehow - send her some flowers or something. He had been tempted to raise the question of his urgent phone call. Surely you were entitled to make one call if you were being detained. To your solicitor. He could have called Mandy's number and, if she still wasn't in, left a message that would not have aroused the suspicions of any policeman who might have been listening. "Don't open it," or something similar. Short and sweet. But he realised that the call would be traced back to the police station; and, although it might be amusing if, for a time, the West Sussex police were put on the list of letter bomb suspects, he knew that eventually the call would be traced back to him. When the arresting officer asked him about his urgent telephone call Corbett merely shrugged and said, "Too late now."

As his master spent the night in the cells, Carstairs enjoyed an early Christmas in the police station canteen. He didn't think the arresting officer was unsympathetic at all. Sausage rolls!

CHAPTER EIGHT

Early the following morning Corbett was told that he was free to go and that he could, in due course, expect a summons for exceeding both the speed limit and the permitted level of alcohol in the bloodstream. With just a mattress, blanket and, in the morning, a cup of tea to speed him on his way, his sojourn had been somewhat less enjoyable than that of Carstairs, who wagged a happy tail as two policewomen said goodbye to him at the door of the canteen. It was too early to achieve anything other than to drive home, where a shave and bath and a decent breakfast helped to restore Corbett's damaged dignity.

He had given up on the idea of calling Mandy Drake and could not, in any case, do so from his own home. He would send her some flowers with an appropriate message. When the newspapers were delivered he ran his eye over the front pages and half hoped to see some headlines such as "MANDY DRAKE SAYS 'AS IF'" or "WEATHER GIRL ACTS TO SAVE ENGLISH LANGUAGE", but that would have been asking too much. It was too early for the newspapers to show anything about the letter bombs, which were probably only on the point of being delivered. He turned on the radio but there was nothing that related to the fourth salvo.

A few minutes before the shops were open he took Carstairs for a quick walk and then drove to Billingshurst where he knew there was a flower shop which provided an Interflora service. He had used it a number of times since Annie's death. There, after some thought, he chose a dozen red roses for Mandy. They cost the earth at this time of year, but he didn't want his gesture to be a cheap one. The message card did not permit more than a brief message, so he restricted himself to "THANK YOU FOR LAST NIGHT'S WEATHER, BEAUTIFULLY PRESENTED, PARTICULARLY 'AS IF'. WELL DONE! YOU ARE HELPING TO SAVE THE ENGLISH LANGUAGE. KEEP IT UP." Then he added a PS – "SORRY ABOUT YOU KNOW WHAT". There was no room for any more. He paid in cash, made sure that the shop girl could read his writing, gave her Mandy's name and address and returned to the car. All being well the roses would be delivered that afternoon. Whatever came out at the other end of the Interflora process would not be in his handwriting. He doubted that the Billingshurst shop would retain his own handwritten card for more than a day or so.

* * *

That afternoon Mandy was in, but she didn't get the roses or the message. They had been taken away for analysis by the same police officer who had taken away the letter bomb earlier that day. After being questioned, the Interflora delivery man had been allowed to go on his way. Rayner had initially been dismayed to get the report that a suspicious package had been delivered with Mandy's morning mail, and even more upset when he heard what the package contained. Was his theory wrong? Had he misread his man? Then he realised that the package must have been posted the previous day or earlier, well before Mandy had demonstrated her mastery of the English language during last night's weather programme. He kept his fingers crossed that his theory, on which he had decided to base his whole strategy, still held good.

Not one letter bomb got through to its intended target. Rayner was delighted as he and his team received report after report from London, the Home Counties and finally from Chester, York and Sunderland. When an irate Commissioner telephoned about a letter bomb addressed to the Prime Minister, and what the hell was he going to do about it, Rayner was able to explain that the Prime Minister was in good company and that their surveillance strategy had paid off.

"That's all very well," the Commissioner shouted. "But what the hell are you doing to stop these things happening by apprehending whoever's doing them?"

"Sir, we have stopped these things happening. Thanks to the precautions we have put in place. There's been no loss of life. No injury even. In this case our first priority must be to protect the potential victims, and we've done that."

"And the criminals? The terrorists? They're still roaming free."

"We're pretty sure that there's only one of them, Sir. A little patience and

I guess he'll make some mistake, perhaps come into the open. We'll get him sooner or later. It'll just take time."

And a little luck, Rayner thought. He just hoped that their luck had not been wasted when the newspaper columnist in Guildford had not seized his chance. He agreed to meet the Commissioner that evening.

Half an hour later Zoë fielded the report about Mandy's Interflora delivery. The package had been examined and found to be clean. It contained an interesting message too. She arranged for the flowers and accompanying message to be brought straight round to their office and twenty minutes later she and Rayner were examining them. It was a pity about the roses, or what was left of them. Each bud had been taken apart by the forensic people. In the box were merely a dozen crushed stems and a pile of red petals.

As they read the message Rayner's heart leapt. "Yes!" he exclaimed. "We were right."

They went into action straight away. Priority was the call to Interflora and, through them, the flower shop in Billingshurst. The proprietor answered the phone and Rayner received his greatest disappointment of the case to date. Ruth had been on duty that morning, while the proprietor was on her way back from Nine Elms. Ruth must have taken the order to which Rayner was referring. Could Rayner speak to Ruth? No. Ruth had left at lunchtime to go on holiday. She wouldn't be back until Christmas week and the proprietor hoped that she would keep her promise to be back then; it was so difficult to get reliable young people nowadays. Damn! And damn again! Did the proprietor know where she was going on holiday? No. Skiing somewhere but she didn't know where. The Alps, she thought. Somewhere high given that it was so early in the season. France? Italy? Germany? Austria? Switzerland? She couldn't say. Rayner sighed in resignation. Another witness, who had seen their man that very day and who would surely be able to give them an accurate description, had vanished into the Alps for ten days. They could try to trace her but there were an awful lot of resorts in the Alps. It would probably be just as quick to wait for her return.

He pressed the proprietor further. Did she have a record of the order? Yes she did, let's see, yes, here it was, 9.30 that morning, passed to Interflora in Hampstead. Did she, by any chance, have the message card that went with the order? Hang on, she'd have a look, it might still be here as they hadn't cleared up yet. Ah, yes, here it was. Rayner read her the message and she confirmed that it was the same as the one in her hand. Not at all the usual type that one saw. And oh yes, it was handwritten, in capitals. Yes, of course she'd be happy to give it to the police. Glad to have been of help.

Rayner thanked the proprietor and rang off. At least they had a consolation prize. They would be able to examine a specimen of their man's handwriting, even if it was in capitals. The suspect's handwriting but, as yet, no suspect. Talk about putting the cart before the horse.

While Rayner was speaking to the flower shop, Zoë and Roberts began ringing each of the other eighteen targets. Zoë had asked Rayner whether she should also put a call on the same subject through to the Prime Minister. Rayner thought they might leave that to the Commissioner. After finishing with the flower shop, Rayner joined the others in ringing the names on the list.

They managed to contact only six of the names first time. The others were either out, not at their desks or busy. Messages were left with the unobtainable ones to call Rayner urgently.

The task of explaining Rayner's theory and what he wanted the targets to do was, to say the least, delicate. They were, after all, being criticised for the way they spoke or wrote English. The six people they did manage to contact reacted in different ways. One columnist simply didn't believe Zoë when she explained the grammatical errors contained in some of his writings. Zoë was ready for him and read out some of the offending phrases in the articles, with the relevant dates. He was shocked, not only that he could have been guilty of such malpractice but also that the copy editor should have let him get away with it. Having deftly shifted at least part of the blame to the copy editor, he gladly agreed to comply with Zoë's request. He could absolutely see the point of "spiking your man's guns", and, come to think of it, of "raising the standards of our newspaper's English". Another columnist, who wrote for the *Guardian*, objected strongly to what he described as police criticism and interference with his work. In a superior tone he explained that English was a living language and that all languages needed to evolve or die. This was one of Rayner's calls and he rolled his eyes to the ceiling as the columnist rattled on. Were the police advocating censorship? He'd have something to say about that in his column tomorrow. Instead of telling him how to do his job, perhaps the police should start doing theirs and catch whomsoever it was who was causing all this trouble. He emphasised the whomsoever to demonstrate his knowledge of grammar.

"Of course we can't compel you to write anything, Sir," Rayner rejoined firmly. "It's just a suggestion, which we hope will lead to a cessation of these unpleasant and frightening incidents, until we apprehend the perpetrator. What you decide to write is entirely up to you."

The *Guardian* columnist hummed and hawed a bit and said he'd think about it. Rayner was tempted to suggest that he would be welcome to ignore the police's advice and to wish him luck with any more dog turds, thunderflashes or letter bombs that might drop through his letter box, but decided that, when dealing with the media, diplomacy needed to be the order of the day.

To each of the people they reached, Rayner's team expressed the hope that they would seize every opportunity to speak or write phrases that included the words, "as if", and warned them to do their utmost to ensure that the word "like" did not crop up by mistake. The quiz show host and a foreign correspondent asked when they should start this procedure, to which they received the reply, "Now, today or as soon as possible." One of the corporate executives asked how long he needed to keep up what he described as "this charade".

"Indefinitely, Sir," replied Zoë, "unless you want a repeat of the recent incidents, or worse. And after all, Sir," she added, "it is the correct use of the language." Rayner smiled when he heard her turn from poacher to gamekeeper.

Later that evening Rayner had his meeting with the Commissioner. He told him the details of Mandy Drake's Interflora flowers and explained the requests they had made or would be making to the nineteen names on their list. He was confident that if they complied with police advice the incidents would cease, citing the message to Mandy as proof that his theory held good and that the plan would work. The Commissioner blanched at Rayner's suggestion that he should give the Prime Minister a lesson in the niceties of English grammar but eventually agreed that, on the basis of the Mandy Drake precedent, it would make sense to do so. He also, though with some reluctance, endorsed Rayner's decision not to spend time, money and resources trying to trace Ruth from the flower shop and in doing so implicitly assented that Rayner and his team should keep the case at least for the next ten days.

Then the Commissioner changed the subject. "By the way, Mike, what's all this about teaching prisoners to read?" He continued without giving Rayner a chance to reply. "I ran into the Governor of Holloway the other day. She said you're pushing some project or other ... "

"Step by Step Reading," said Rayner.

"Yes, that was it. What's got you mixed up in that kind of thing?"

Rayner explained Betty's involvement in the project and began to describe how Step by Step worked and what benefits it might bring, but the Commissioner cut him off.

"Yes, yes. That's all very well but we can't have you wasting your time – police time – on that kind of thing. There are plenty of bleeding hearts and liberal do-gooders out there telling us and the prison authorities how to do our jobs. Leave it to them. They love that kind of thing. Our function is to put criminals inside. What happens to them after that shouldn't concern us."

"But don't you think...?" began Rayner, but again the Commissioner cut him off.

"Leave it, Mike. If you want to get involved in these things informally in your own time, Okay, although if you do I'll begin to wonder if you're going soft. But in police time ... Get the message?"

A tight-lipped Rayner confirmed that he had got the message. On the way home he forced himself to put the Commissioner's remarks behind him and to concentrate on ASIF. He worked out the allocation of the calls to the remaining names on their list and hoped that by the end of the following day all twenty of them, including the Prime Minister, would start to mend at least some of their ways when addressing the nation. He also made a note to send Mandy Drake a dozen red roses.

When he got home he decided not to tell Betty about his session with the Commissioner. She would be upset and start worrying about getting him into trouble and then he would start feeling sorry for himself. Right now there was no time for that.

* * *

During the remainder of the week, Corbett's television, radio and newspapers vigil brought him what he equated with Nanki Poo's modified rapture. There were, of course, many ongoing examples of the misuse of English. People were still splitting infinitives, turning nouns into verbs, putting apostrophes in the wrong place, calling themselves chairs and describing girlfriends or boyfriends or even spouses as 'partner'. Examples of spin and political correctness continued to flourish. Banks and other providers of services or goods to consumers still called their services or goods 'products' as if they were making widgets. So all was still not well with the English language. But where his twenty offenders were concerned there was rapture indeed. Led by Mandy Drake, the examples of 'as if' replacing 'like' were sometimes coming so thick and fast that he could hardly keep up with them. Two columnists had used it four times in one day. So had the newsreader. Tracey Carroll used it twice on the Saturday National Lottery draw. Even Fortunata and the sports commentator had managed it. It was incredible, a complete volte-face. He and Carstairs had managed it. The notebooks were brimming with GOOD THINGS.

No mention had been made of any letter bombs in the media, so he assumed that none of these splendid people had been harmed, which was fine by him. Even the Prime Minister had joined the party. In *Today in Parliament* a question had been put by the MP for Sunderland East – "Would the Prime Minister agree with me that, in view of the restrictions recently put in place in respect of immigrants being permitted to enter this country, many of my constituents, particularly those with roots in the Indian subcontinent, are justified in feeling as if they and their loved ones still overseas are being treated as second-class citizens?." To which the Prime Minister had replied – "It sounds as if the Honourable Member for Sunderland East has misunderstood Government policy in this matter. The restrictions in no way apply to immigrants who wish to come to this country in order to join members of their family who already have United Kingdom citizenship". What a double act! What a triumph! It was all working like a dream.

The first thing must be to send a thank-you note to all of them along the lines of what he had written to Mandy, although he wouldn't go so far as sending flowers too. He would cut out the letters from *The Times* as usual. He hoped he was not jumping the gun. It would be too bad if they reverted to type, but they deserved to be thanked and his encouragement might in itself ensure that there would be no falling by the wayside. After some thought he decided to send them "LIKE : wrong. AS IF : right. WELL DONE. KEEP IT UP. THANK YOU."

The next thing would be to see whether these incredible developments would spread to people who had not had the benefit of receiving his four salvos. He would need to examine the names on his reserve list and start monitoring them. Perhaps he should also start planning the next step. After all, persuading people to say or write "as if" instead of "like" was only a drop in the ocean. He would have to consider which other examples of sloppy English were doing such damage to the language that they would need to be dealt with. God knows, there were plenty to choose from.

However, in the meantime he had to deal with the one person who either had not understood the messages or had decided to ignore them. The sole remaining offender out of the twenty original names wrote a column for the *Guardian*, and boy, was he offending! Not only was he still transgressing, with a recent average of three incorrect 'likes' per column – up from one per column a month ago – but also his latest contribution had been titled, "My Right to Write What I Like". Under the guise of an article about the government's election policies, he brought in all the old trendy chestnuts about how important it was for a language to evolve in order to survive. He stressed the need for change in order to reflect contemporary society and multiculturalism and even cited American as the ideal example of how a language should develop. Corbett shuddered. The last straw was one of the examples the article contained, suggesting that the use of 'like' instead of 'as if' was now perfectly acceptable and that 'as if' was probably and rightly destined to vanish from the English language. The whole article went against everything that Corbett held dear; and the example given was an affront, a direct challenge to him as Defender of the English Language. Painful though it was, Corbett forced himself to read the article a second and then a third time. As he did so it became quite clear that this *Guardian* guy was deliberately throwing down the gauntlet. Right! If that was the way he wanted it. Over the next few days the *Guardian* letters column might reveal the reactions of the paper's readers to what had been written, but, as far as Corbett was concerned, it could only mean one thing. This was war.

* * *

When Roberts passed the *Guardian* article to Rayner, the Chief Superintendent first raised his eyebrows, then whistled and finally brought his fist down onto the page in anger. This *Guardian* fellow was not only an arrogant, conceited barrack-room lawyer, he was also a fool. He was asking for it. Despite himself, Rayner almost began to feel sympathy towards their ASIF man as he had come to think of him. He was delighted to see that all the other columnists had followed police advice and so too had the other targets, according to the TV and radio reports his team had given him. He felt confident enough to lift the house and postal surveillance but thought it prudent to wait two or three days in the hope that their man may send them a note similar to the one he had sent with Mandy's flowers. If that happened it would provide further comfort and confirmation of his gut feeling that he was reading ASIF's mind correctly. So far as the *Guardian* columnist was concerned, however, Rayner had no compunction in ordering surveillance to be discontinued forthwith. He overcame the slight twinge of guilt which, as a policeman whose job was to prevent crime, he felt when he gave the order. The *Guardian* man would deserve whatever was coming to him.

Within the next forty-eight hours, all Rayner's hopes were fulfilled. Eighteen thank-you notes were received, all identical, all cut out from *The Times*, and all mailed from London, Surrey and Sussex. Even the Prime Minister got one. Rayner and the Commissioner exchanged mutual congratulations. The one exception was the *Guardian* columnist. As the hours passed with no report on the last person on the list, Rayner was on tenterhooks. He was hoping that the report, when it came in, would be of something appropriate, something rather dramatic or even grisly, but not something that would cause his conscience as a police officer to lead to further feelings of guilt about lifting the surveillance too early on the columnist's house.

* * *

The dead rat was Carstairs' idea. He had carried it, tail wagging, to Corbett and placed it proudly but gently at his feet. It was one of the largest rats Corbett had ever seen. "Carstairs, that is a very good idea indeed," he said as he lifted the creature up gingerly with his garden fork and examined it more closely. It was a pity it was December. In summer the rat would have ponged a good deal more and might even have had a few nice maggots wriggling in it, but December was too cold for that. It was just a dead rat. But, in the circumstances, and because he hadn't thought of anything better, it would do. It was, for the time being at least, a fitting response to the challenge from the *Guardian* columnist. Corbett tied a note round the rat's neck, and within two hours had delivered it safely and without incident through his opponent's letter box. The accompanying note was short and sweet: "GET STUFFED. ASIF."

Rayner was rather pleased about the rat when the report came in. Not bad, he thought; and then, before he could help it, good for you, Mr Asif.

It was less than an hour before the columnist was on the line. Ranting would have been an understatement. Rayner heard him out with silent enjoyment and then took pleasure in regretting that at present there were insufficient manpower resources to meet his demand for police protection. When the columnist promised to speak to his MP about all this, Rayner thought it was a pity that he didn't live in Sunderland East, while explaining that if he followed police advice when writing his column any future unpleasantnesses could, he was sure, be avoided. The columnist promised him that he would hear more about this before slamming the phone down.

That evening Rayner and Corbett, unwitting allies in the war against the *Guardian* columnist, were unaware that they had another ally in the form of the columnist's wife. It was all right for him, she shouted. He hadn't been there. It was she who had picked up the bloody dog turd, and now a dead rat, not him. And no! The fact that he had been there when the thunderflash had exploded didn't make any difference. She had had enough.

"I'm not going to let that bastard get away with it," the columnist said.

"So what are you going to do? Find him? Catch him? The police haven't been able to. What makes you think ... ?"

"Okay. We'll move house. Sell up and move somewhere else."

She fixed him with a look that would have stopped a basilisk in its tracks. "Oh no! No way! If you want to run, go ahead. Without me. I'm staying right here."

"But I'm only thinking of your safety."

"The only thing you think about is your effing column. All right, if it's me you're thinking of, why don't you do what the police suggest?"

"No one tells me what to write," he retorted from his high horse. "Never have. Never will."

She saw the opening and struck immediately. "I'm not telling you what to write. I'm telling you what not to write."

"Ah," he said.

Two days later Rayner in his office, and Corbett in bed with his morning tea, turned to the *Guardian* ahead of any other newspaper. They both read the column titled, 'Feminism and the Woman's Role in the Home'. Rayner went through it from start to finish and smiled grimly. Well, well! He's chickened out, he thought. Another victory for our man. Corbett didn't regard it as a victory. The article contained no phrase that could have included either 'like' or 'as if'. Coincidence? Not after the, 'My Right to Write What I Like' article. A draw then. The jury was out, and that is where he would leave them, until the columnist reoffended.

CHAPTER NINE

Rayner's pride, shared by his team, at having succeeded in putting an end, at least temporarily, to the ASIT incidents, was tempered by the fact that they were really not much closer to getting their man. He had almost certainly been seen near Guildford. He was seen, but only at a distance, in Putney. He had possibly been seen in Hampstead. He might have been seen in Sunderland. He was definitely seen in Billingshurst, but the girl who could identify him would not be back from her skiing holiday for another four days. Even then they would only have another description, which would presumably match those they had already received from the other witnesses. Rayner knew from past experience that descriptions and the picture-fits produced by police artists and technicians often did not lead to an arrest, even when widely circulated. Even if an identifit turned out to be remarkably accurate, it was no more than a one hundred per cent precise picture of a needle in a haystack. The CCTV images did not bring much to the party. Eleven so-called sightings had been reported in London already. None had led anywhere.

Zoë and he had discussed the possibilities in the hope of narrowing down the geographical area on which they should focus. Their man could, of course, be living somewhere in London. That was where most of the incidents had taken place. They decided to rule out the North of England. This was a risk, they knew that, but one had to go by gut feelings once in a while. The pattern of mailings, plus the incidents outside the London area, pointed to Surrey or Sussex, with Hampshire coming in as an outsider. Throw in the Billingshurst flower shop and they felt that the probabilities, rather than just gut feeling, pointed to Sussex and, for choice, to West Sussex. So what was the population of West Sussex? Half a million, give or take? Divide that by two for the different sexes. Two hundred and fifty thousand. Assuming the witnesses' descriptions were accurate as to age, how many sixty-year-old men might there be in that number? Ten per cent? Twenty maybe? That would boil it down to between twenty-five and fifty thousand potential suspects.

"That's not too bad, Sir," said Roberts. "About the size of a decent football crowd."

"Thanks very much," replied Rayner. "So all we do is go and watch a football match in West Sussex and hope our man's a football fan."

"Oh I don't think it's as bad as that, Sir." Zoë sounded almost cheerful. "It's better than sixty million, which is what we started with. Twenty-five to fifty thousand? How many of those read *The Times*? If their national circulation numbers are to be believed, it's read by about two per cent of the population. Four per cent if two people read the same copy. That narrows our numbers down to between one thousand and two thousand. Then," she added excitedly, "how many of those own a big dog? Ten per cent? Twenty per cent? That means we've narrowed it down to only one or two hundred people."

"And there he is!" cried Roberts, pointing out of the window. "And he's got his labrador with him!"

They all laughed, and Rayner was glad to be part of a team that could try to look on the bright side. After a pause, "Lady Luck. Where are you?" he said.

* * *

Quarter Master Sergeant Ginger Evans, Royal Marines, stroked his moustache and continued to fret. An hour ago the adjutant had shown him a police enquiry about some missing thunderflashes Mark IV. Twenty of these had been used in a series of incidents a few weeks ago, one of which had even included Number Ten Downing Street. The enquiry had been passed down from the Ministry of Defence to all military establishments, and, as usual, Territorial Army units had received it later than their regular counterparts. Were any units deficient in their supplies? Had any thunderflashes Mark IV gone missing or might they, in one way or another, have fallen into the wrong hands?

Ginger knew that the adjutant regarded the enquiry as merely a routine one and that no supervised stores check would be initiated. If Ginger said that there were no thunderflashes unaccounted for the adjutant would take his word for it. But, and it was a big but, what about old Alan Corbett?

Surely Alan couldn't be the guy who, according to the media, was responsible for blowing up half of London? Alan, of all people? And why? If Alan, or anyone else – and it must be someone else; it couldn't be Alan – wanted to blow anything up they wouldn't use thunderflashes, would they? What would be the point? A thunderflash wouldn't blow in a door, let alone a safe. So what were they trying to achieve, whoever they were?

Alan Corbett had wanted the stuff for his moles. That was fair enough. Ginger thought that, properly positioned, a thunderflash could be pretty effective against moles. Let's hope that was what Alan had used them for and not for something else.

Ginger had three problems that he was mulling over. Number one was that there was no way he was going to report that he was short of one box of fifty thunderflashes Mark IV, let alone that he had given them away. Nothing to be gained from an honourable confession. He'd get a reprimand – minimum. Maybe something worse in view of how the thunderflashes had been or might have been used. Problem number two was that he didn't like dropping a mate in it, particularly if the mate was totally innocent, as Ginger was sure Alan must be. And, of course, if Alan had been doing something bloody silly there must be a good reason for it, and Ginger didn't want to go dropping him in it. Problem number three was that Ginger didn't like terrorists. He'd been up against them in Kosovo and in Belfast, where he'd lost a couple of mates, courtesy of the Provisional IRA. Way back, the IRA had even blown the legs off the Commandant General. No, Ginger definitely didn't like terrorists, and if, by any chance, there might be some kind of terrorist connection with his thunderflashes – well, he couldn't ignore that.

Ginger thought that the best course of action would be to ask Jakey Dobbs's opinion. Jakey knew Alan a lot better than he did and was already aware of the thunderflash transaction that had taken place, so there was no risk there. Yes, calling Jakey would be the best idea and with luck Jakey would just tell him to forget it, in which case that is exactly what he would do.

So Ginger called Jakey Dobbs and told him his concerns. Jakey laughed out loud. "Alan Corbett blowing up half of London? Using thunderflashes? Come off it. Forget it Ginger." And that is where Ginger would have left it but for the fact that Jakey added one more thing. "After all, if Alan really wanted to blow up anything, even half of London, what would he need thunderflashes for? For a start they're not effective and secondly he's got plenty of explosives of his own, I imagine." Jakey laughed again.

"Alan's got explosives?" a startled Ginger asked.

"Unless he's finished them. Or got rid of them."

"How come?"

"That was his job. He had his own business, redeveloping brownfield sites. But he had to demolish the buildings first. Knew his stuff too. Should have seen him on Bagshot ranges, dealing with unexploded mortar bombs. Bloody good he was."

Ginger didn't ask Jakey the question that immediately flashed in his brain like an alarm bell. But after putting down the phone he asked himself. If Alan Corbett already had explosives of his own, what the hell did he want thunderflashes for?

Ginger Evans spent the rest of the morning wondering what to do next. He wished he'd never called Jakey Dobbs. He should have just told the adjutant that all the stores were accounted for and that would have been that. He could have forgotten the whole thing. But not now. Not after what he had heard from Jakey. Now he had to do something. After further thought, he found the telephone number in the unit address book and telephoned Alan Corbett.

"Alan, how goes it?" Ginger kept his voice light and carefree.

"Sorry, who is that?"

"It's me, Ginger. Ginger Evans."

"Ginger?" Ginger could hear the surprise in Corbett's voice. He'd never telephoned him before.

"Yeah. How did the bangs go?"

Corbett froze for a moment. "The what? Sorry Ginger. It's a bad line."

"The bangs, Alan. Those thunderflashes."

Christ! Corbett felt a surge of panic. Ginger knew. How the hell did he know?

"The thunderflashes?" He wracked his brain for something else to say. And then, as Ginger was in the process of asking his next question, Corbett's panic was replaced with a wave of relief as he suddenly realised what Ginger was getting at.

"The moles, Alan."

"Oh, the moles. Sorry Ginger I was thinking of something else. Miles away." He put some badly needed mirth into his voice. "I think the moles have decided to raise the white flag. Or at least bugger off somewhere else."

"Use them all, did you?"

"The thunderflashes? Yes. Gave the moles a real pasting. Those Mark IVs were just the right thing. Thanks very much Ginger, for your help. Much appreciated."

"I was just wondering why you wanted to use thunderflashes. Instead of the real thing." A pause. "You know, whatever you used in your business."

Corbett frowned. Was Ginger asking too many questions? He made light of it. "Oh that's all gone," he said. "In any case, I wouldn't want to waste it on a few moles. Anyway Ginger, what can I do for you?" He hoped there was another reason for Ginger's call, rather than just these awkward questions.

"Oh, nothing really. A few of the lads were planning a bit of a knees-up in the Sergeants' mess next Thursday. Wondered if you'd like to join us."

"That's the day before Christmas Eve, isn't it? Sorry Ginger. Can't make it."

"Oh well, just an idea. Too bad. Okay, well Merry Christmas anyway mate."

"Thanks Ginger. Merry Christmas to you too. See you in the New Year. Cheers mate."

Corbett put the telephone down with relief and found his hands shaking. What the hell was all that about? He hoped he'd handled it all right. Yes, of course he had. No need to start jumping at shadows. It was only old Ginger.

Ginger Evans stroked his moustache again. He didn't like it. He didn't like it at all. There was no escaping it. Alan Corbett had sounded rattled. It wasn't just his imagination. Thinking of something else was he? Miles away? You bet your life he was. Whatever he was thinking of, it wasn't moles. Bugger it! Now what?

When it was knocking-off time, Ginger Evans made up his mind. Taking his usual route to London Bridge station, he stopped at the pub on the corner and ordered a pint of bitter with a whisky chaser. He needed the chaser for a bit of Dutch courage. The pint took him five minutes, the chaser five seconds. At the station he found an unoccupied telephone booth and fed his phone card into the machine. Sorry mate, he thought, as he dialled 999.

Rayner was at home when one of the team's night shift called to tell him that Bermondsey police had passed on a report of an anonymous call about some thunderflashes. Yes, the caller had said that they were Mark IV. He had given the name and address of someone who might, as he put it, help the police in their enquiries. "Of course," he had said, "there's probably nothing in it, but I thought it worth mentioning." Then he had rung off. The call had been traced to London Bridge station. The name given was Alan Corbett. The address was in Rudgwick, West Sussex.

"Want us to follow it up, Sir?"

"No, not yet. We'll let it lie for the moment. Just ask Met Central and West Sussex to check their records to see if anything's known. Keep me posted. Thanks." At last, he thought. He just hoped he wasn't counting his chickens.

"Betty," he said, "I hope I'm not jumping the gun, but something tells me that this case will soon be over."

"So I should hope," Betty replied, and added, "Before Christmas please."

The following morning Rayner and Zoë looked to see what they had got. There was at least something. Alan Corbett, sixty-three years old. That fitted. Overnight stay in the cells at Horsham not long ago. Drink-drive case, plus speeding. No problems. Well behaved. Due to be up before the beaks sometime in January. Owned a black Labrador – Aha! – called Carstairs. Wife killed by a hit-and-run driver the year before last. Retired. Used to own a property development business. Nothing else.

"Well, at least we know him," said Rayner. "This hit-and-run business. Any motive there do you think? That must have hit him hard." He studied the fax. "The bloke that did it could be out by now."

"Horsham's checking on that now," said Zoë. "But I don't see any connection. Do you? The Prime Minister? That Sunderland MP? Mandy Drake, and so on?"

"No, probably not." He looked at his watch. "Tell you what. How'd you like a trip to the country? Roberts?"

"Sir?"

"West Sussex. Rudgwick. Scenic route please. Oh, and we'll stop off in

Horsham on the way."

They were made welcome in Horsham and spent forty minutes being briefed by the West Sussex police. They had little to add to the summary they had faxed through earlier. Apart from the drink-driving and speeding, which the arresting officer admitted was probably just a case of bad luck on Corbett's part, they had nothing else on him. He seemed well off, nice house, two or three acres, two cars – a Range Rover and VW Passat, member of the local golf club, all in all a model citizen, the recent driving offence excepted. There were no other endorsements on his licence. He'd probably get off with a fine and, if he was unlucky, a disqualification for a month or two. Rayner asked about the accident to his wife. Had that affected him, changed him in any way? Not that the police knew. Might he perhaps be embittered against the police and the legal system for the defendant's light sentence, or against the world in general? They had heard nothing. Oh yes, and he had a shotgun licence and an explosives permit.

"An explosives permit?" asked Rayner in surprise. "What's he need that for?"

The Horsham police explained about Corbett's business.

"But if he's sold it, what's he still doing with explosives?"

It was all perfectly in order, came the response. The permit had been renewed annually by the business and by Corbett personally since the business had been sold. The stocks were checked with each permit renewal. A few kilos of plastic, some primers and detonators. He used them from time to time to get rid of tree stumps on his land, and sometimes gave a hand to friends who needed to clear stuff off their own. Any reductions in the stocks were always fully accounted for.

Rayner glanced at Zoë and shrugged. Well, you couldn't really blame the West Sussex police. They had their own procedures and so long as they were followed ... But he hoped there wasn't an Al Qaeda cell tucked away somewhere in the county. He made a mental note to revisit the subject later, perhaps on a countywide basis. Greater awareness of the realities of what the war on terror really meant. Tighter controls. But not just more red tape. The poor buggers had more than enough of that already.

In the meantime he accepted Horsham's offer to show them the location of Corbett's house. They followed the police car and thanked them when they slowed down and pointed it out. They didn't call on him straight away.

A pub lunch seemed in order. Rayner told Roberts to follow his nose and a few minutes later they pulled up in front of The Fox, which looked as good as any.

Rayner ordered a pint, Zoë a glass of white wine, and Roberts, as driver, an orange juice. They all settled for fish and chips.

Over lunch at a quiet corner table they discussed their approach to Corbett. They agreed that kid gloves would, initially at any rate, be the best policy. After all, he seemed to have a clean bill of health from the locals. A driving offence could happen to anybody. So far as this enquiry was concerned, all they had was an anonymous phone call linking Corbett with some thunderflashes. Were these the same as the thunderflashes they were interested in? Did the caller have some kind of grudge against Corbett? It could all be a coincidence or a wild goose chase. Corbett could be perfectly innocent. At the same time, he did live in West Sussex, which they had decided was their main geographical focus, and Rudgwick was only a few minutes' drive from Billingshurst and the flower shop. And he owned a black labrador. Finally, his age matched the descriptions they had so far received.

They agreed to take their lead from Rayner. If Corbett did match the descriptions, Rayner would gradually increase the pressure from a gentle opening. So much depended on how Corbett reacted to questions and on his general behaviour. If necessary Rayner would be the hard man, while Zoë would provide the softer approach. Zoë's job would also be to observe, look for any signs of nervousness or uncertainty or prevarication which might give Corbett away. Roberts would stretch his legs and stroll around the grounds, picking up what he could, without participating in the main interrogation. As they drove towards the house, Rayner naturally hoped that Corbett would turn out to be their man. But his feelings were mixed. Whoever had silenced the *Guardian* columnist with a dead rat couldn't be all bad.

The gates to the drive were open, but Rayner and Zoë elected to go up to the house on foot, leaving Roberts to park on the verge by the gates. Halfway to the house they were greeted by a black Labrador who advanced to a distance of ten metres from them barking and then stood wagging his tail. A man dressed in gardening clothes shouted from the bonfire he was tending fifty metres away. "All right, Carstairs, that's enough." He walked towards them and as he approached Rayner was disappointed. The man bore no similarity to the descriptions they had received. He was probably only in his mid-forties.

"Mr Corbett?" he enquired. The man shook his head. "He's inside," he said. "All right Carstairs. Good dog."

"Thanks," said Rayner, happy that his disappointment had been premature. He and Zoë, accompanied by Carstairs, knocked on the door, which was opened a few seconds later by a plump, red-faced woman with a duster and jar of furniture polish in her hand. Zoë opened her mouth to say, "Mrs Corbett?" and only Rayner's interposed, "Good afternoon," gave her time to remember that Corbett's wife was dead. She bit her lip in relief at her narrow escape as Rayner continued, "Is Mr Corbett in, please?"

"Mr Corbett!" the woman shouted and then, "Carstairs you stay outside till the floor's dried." Carstairs stopped on the threshold in disappointment as Corbett appeared from the rear of the hall.

"Mr Corbett?" tried Rayner again.

"Yes."

"Chief Superintendent Rayner, Sir. Metropolitan Police. This is my assistant, Detective Sergeant Henderson. May we come in?"

Zoë observed Corbett's reaction closely. Was it dismay or surprise? Or fear? It was impossible to tell at this early stage. The voice indicated surprise more than anything else.

"The police? Yes, of course, do come in. Thank you Mrs Downing."

The red-faced woman turned and disappeared through a doorway. Corbett made every effort to ensure that he sounded controlled and, so far as was possible, friendly. All along the line he had accepted that this was an eventuality for which he had to be prepared. He hoped he could handle it. He knew they would be watching him closely, looking for anything that might give him away. Any reflex, any tiny clue. Whatever he said would depend on what they asked. He wouldn't be calling the shots in that respect. But how he looked, how he behaved, how he conducted himself, these things were equally important in creating the right impression.

"It's not about that damned driving thing is it? I'll be pleading guilty by the way. Whenever the hearing is."

"No, Sir," said Rayner. "We're making some enquiries ..."

Corbett cut him off. "Thought not. You're a bit high-powered for that, aren't you? Chief Superintendent?" And, before Rayner could reply, "Can I take your coats?" Corbett tried to keep control for as long as he could.

"Thanks." Rayner and Zoë removed their coats and Corbett hung them on the coat rack by the front door.

"Enquiries. How can I help you?" and, again forestalling any answer to his question, "Why don't we go and sit down. May I?"

He led the way into the drawing room. Five television sets. He was ready for any reaction. Was it against the law to have five television sets in the same room? He was up to date with his licence payments.

Zoë looked at the TV sets in amazement but, taking her lead from Rayner, kept her mouth firmly shut and sat down on the sofa. Rayner made an instant decision. It was time to take control. Corbett wanted them to ask why he needed five TV sets in the same room. No way. He wasn't going to allow their man to divert him from the questions he had planned. He and Corbett sat down in armchairs facing each other.

"We're enquiring about some thunderflashes, Sir," said Rayner, adding the "Sir" to keep it polite. He could see the disappointment in Corbett's face as the expected question about the TV sets remained unasked.

"Thunderflashes?" Corbett repeated. "Good Lord!"

"Yes, Sir. They were used in a number of recent incidents in London and the South East. You may have read about it in the press. Or," Rayner glanced at the television sets, "seen it on the box."

"Oh that. Yes I did see something. But from what the media were saying I didn't realise it was thunderflashes they were using."

"They, Sir?"

"Well I assume it was they. IRA or Al Qaeda or someone like that. But thunderflashes. Not their style is it? From the way the media were going on about it, it sounded like Semtex or something."

"Do you have any experience of Semtex, Sir?"

"Me? Good Lord, no." Corbett's heart lurched a little. "Why do you ask?" The question and Rayner's reply would give him time to regain his calm.

"I was surprised that you went straight on from thunderflashes to Semtex. As if you knew about Semtex."

"Not at all. It was just a logical progression. From explosives to IRA to Semtex. That's the stuff they often use, isn't it?" Another question, which

Rayner ignored.

"And thunderflashes, Sir? Do you have any experience with them?"

"Oh certainly." No point in denying it. "I spent twelve years in the TA. Royal Marines Reserves actually. We used them frequently on exercise. Great fun, thunderflashes."

"And since you left the TA?"

"Oh yes. From time to time. I use them to keep the moles down. Bloody nuisance they are. A lot of them round here. Do you have mole trouble, Chief Superintendent?"

Again Rayner ignored the question. "When did you leave the TA, Sir?"

"About twenty years ago."

"The thunderflashes you use against the moles. These aren't just a few you ... saved up from your TA days then?"

"Are you asking where I get them?"

"Yes."

Despite his doubts about QMS Ginger Evans, Corbett didn't want to go dropping him in it. "Let's say I have my sources. From the old days. Things can go walkabout if you know what I mean. But if you don't mind I'd prefer not to mention my sources. Technically I suppose passing over a few thunderflashes might be regarded as misappropriation of government property, and I don't want to split on some old mates. Sorry. If I'm accused of an offence – handling hot thunderflashes – so be it. I plead guilty. But it was only to get rid of a few moles. Not to blow up half of London." He smiled confidently.

"Were these Mark IV thunderflashes, Sir?" Rayner continued patiently, making no comment on Corbett's 'between you and me' answer.

"Yes they were. They have a longer fuse than the other Marks, so you have more time to ..."

"To put them through a letter box and be well clear before they explode?"

Corbett didn't bat an eyelid. "Yes, I suppose that would be true if that's what you were using them for. But I was putting them down molehills, as I've already explained."

Fifteen all, thought Zoë. Corbett was having no trouble returning Rayner's service. She wondered what Rayner would do next. Rayner's next serve was an unexpected one.

"Ever been to Sunderland, Sir?"

Zoë could see that the change of tack had taken Corbett by surprise.

"Sunderland? Sunderland? Yes, come to think of it. Only once. A few weeks ago."

"What was the purpose of your visit?"

"The purpose of my visit?"

Zoë noted Corbett's technique of repeating the question in order to give himself time to think of an appropriate reply. He was pretty good. Then she observed him try to return serve with an attack of his own.

"I rather think that's my business, don't you?"

"The purpose, Sir?"

"Pleasure."

"Pleasure? In Sunderland?" Zoë nearly giggled at Rayner's genuine surprise.

"I was visiting a friend, if you must know."

"Does he ... or she live in Waterfield Road, by any chance?" The question seemed innocuous but both Rayner and Zoë saw it strike home.

"It was a male friend," said Corbett, desperately buying time. Was there such a place as Waterfield Road? He had made it up on the spur of the moment that day in Sunderland. It would be a stroke of unbelievably good fortune if it actually existed. He could almost feel them holding their breath, waiting to see if he would fall into the trap. He would just have to wing this one. "But I must have got the address wrong. Couldn't find it. Had to give it up in the end, and come all the way home."

"Not a lot of pleasure in Sunderland after all then," commented Rayner dryly.

"A completely wasted day," Corbett said, with a shrug and a smile. Phew! That was close. These police knew more than was comfortable. Then he took a punt. "But anyway, what's Sunderland got to do with these thunderflashes you were talking about?"

"There was an incident there too," said Rayner, referring to the turd but hoping that his comment might lead to something.

"Oh, I see."

"Involving a Labour Member of Parliament."

"Really? Lucky for him it wasn't Semtex then." Corbett tried to hide his confusion. Why Sunderland? He hadn't delivered Salvo No. 3 there yet.

Rayner pondered this response for a moment. "Do you have reason to dislike him, Sir? Or should I just take it that you don't support the Labour party?"

"Me? Vote Labour? That'll be the day." Corbett was pleased to have moved on from Waterfield Road. "But actually I quite like him."

"Really? Do you know him?" Rayner asked.

"No. But I saw him on *Today in Parliament* a few days ago. Spoke rather well, I thought. For a Labour MP." Corbett remembered how he had worded the question to the Prime Minister and felt that the least he could do was support someone who was a convert to the cause of saving the English language.

For a moment Rayner was at a loss. This guy kept taking the wind from his sails in the most unexpected way. It annoyed him but he enjoyed a duel. And he was beginning to respect, almost to admire, his opponent. The *Guardian* columnist's rat had already set that thought process in motion. It was time to regain control.

"Do you know Hampstead, Sir?"

"Not well." So they were on to Hampstead now. "I've been there from to time. There's a little theatre there, the New End, where they specialise in new productions. Occasionally they're quite good." Corbett was enjoying himself. "I saw a comedy there only the other night. *My Sainted Aunt*, or something like that. Very funny I thought. You'd enjoy it. But I think it's off now. You might catch it if it goes on tour or to the West End." He was glad that he had noticed the hoardings outside the theatre.

Damn the man, thought Rayner. Not only was Corbett taking control again but also he'd given himself a good explanation for having been in the pub next to the theatre. Rayner tried again.

"Do you know Mandy Drake?" He watched for Corbett's reaction.

"Mandy Drake? Why does that name ring a bell?" Corbett frowned and then brightened. "Oh, I know. Isn't she a weathergirl on the box? The sexy one?"

"Ever met her?"

"I should be so lucky," Corbett replied. "What makes you think that I might have?"

"She lives close to the New End Theatre."

"Oh. In that case I may have seen her on my way to the theatre. Or in the pub next door. But not knowingly."

"Ever corresponded with her?"

"No," Corbett lied. "What reason would I have?"

"Just wondered," said Rayner.

Then, in swift succession, Rayner hit Corbett with the names of Justin Harper, the Frank Bruno lookalike weather presenter, the quiz show host, the TV newsreader, the two foreign correspondents, Fortunata and Tracey Carroll. Corbett weathered the storm without flinching, responding negatively in each case with the exception of Tracey Carroll and Fortunata, whom he acknowledged as having seen on the box. Bloody hell! Was there anything these people didn't know? He decided to go on the attack again.

"Excuse me, Superintendent," he said, deliberately dropping the 'Chief'. "You've called in here to enquire about some thunderflashes. I've told you that I sometimes use them for perfectly valid reasons. And then you start reeling off a list of names of people whom I'm supposed to know, mainly TV celebrities so far as I can gather. I don't get it. What's the connection? I'm sorry but I think you're barking up the wrong tree."

"They were all involved in similar incidents," Rayner replied.

"Well I've never met any of them." Corbett tried to give the impression of trying to remain polite while beginning to feel irritation at the continued questioning. "I'm being as helpful as I can, but ... is this going to go on much longer?"

Zoë thought it was time to step in. "Excuse me, Sir, but may I ask a few questions?"

Corbett turned to face her. "Go ahead," he said.

"Why do you have five TV sets in the same room?"

"Ah, I was wondering when you were going to ask that."

"Just curious, Sir."

"I lost my wife about two years ago. We'd been married for thirty years. When you're ... suddenly alone ... well, you tend to find life a bit empty. Time on your hands. You know."

"I'm sorry, Sir."

"So I watch the box quite a lot. To kill time as much as anything. A lot of it's rubbish of course. But often you can't tell in advance. Not from what you read in the TV guides. So I have five sets, one each for BBC1 and 2, ITV and Channel 4 and one to surf the satellite channels. I have them all on at the same time."

"All on at once?" enquired Zoë, with raised eyebrows.

"It seems a bit strange I admit. But if I'm watching something I want to see, I have the others on at low volume and occasionally I find that on another channel there's something that looks better than the one I'm watching. So then I turn the volume up on that one. It means that I don't miss anything, you see. With just the one set, switching from one channel to another, you might miss something interesting." He laughed. "Silly of me, I suppose, but ... Well, it's a process I've got used to."

"And the newspapers, Sir?" Zoë glanced towards the pile of *The Times* on the carpet.

"What about them?" Corbett asked, hoping he was not betraying any anxiety. Fortunately he had put this morning's delivery on top of the pile of *The Times*. Beneath them a mere glance would reveal older copies, which he had not yet burned, with large sections missing, where he had cut out the letters to compose his last series of thank-you messages.

"You take *The Times*."

"Yes. And a lot of others too. Another way of killing time."

"Do you keep them for long?"

"Only *The Times*. It's good for lighting the fire, I find; although not as good as it was before it went tabloid. Also I like to have some back numbers to refer to. I write to them sometimes." He laughed deprecatingly. "Never got a letter published yet, though."

Rayner was grateful to Zoë for giving him the opportunity to gather his thoughts. He felt frustrated. Corbett had come through pretty well so far. Too well for Rayner's liking. He certainly hadn't crumpled when the list of names had been fired at him. He'd try him with some more, although he didn't expect the outcome to be very different. Before Zoë could ask another question he jumped in and reeled off the list of columnists' names, adding the corporate executives for good measure. As expected, Corbett didn't know any of them but recognised some of the names, including the man from the *Guardian*. Another blank.

Zoë took over again. "What do you find to write about?"

"Oh this and that," replied Corbett, smiling.

"Such as?"

"Well, it depends what's been happening. Government policy, country going to the dogs. That kind of thing. I suppose I'd be qualified as Colonel Blimp or Disgusted of Tunbridge Wells." He laughed again.

"In what way do you think the country's going to the dogs?" Zoë asked with a friendly smile.

"Oh, good heavens. Any number of ways. Political correctness. All those massive salaries and bonuses for the bosses and the City slickers. They're obscene. Standards of behaviour. Standards of English. Dumbing down." He pointed to the TV sets. "Plenty of examples in those. I could go on, but I won't bore you."

"You don't bore me at all," Rayner interposed, welcoming the opening he needed to put his theory to the test. "I'm sure many of your views are shared by plenty of people. Even in the police." He smiled warmly. "But tell me, in what way do you think that standards of English are dropping? Assuming you do think that. I happen to agree with you."

"Ah! An ally. Splendid." Corbett became enthusiastic. "What the hell do they teach them at school nowadays? Some of the teachers are as bad as the children so far as I can see. So much for 'education, education, education'. It's appalling, honestly."

"Turning nouns into verbs. I find that annoying", said Rayner. "Targeting things or people. Accessing something or someone. Since when were target or access verbs?"

"Oh God! You're absolutely right." Corbett was excited now. "It's those bloody Americans. Do you know? Webster's dictionary gives both of those as verbs, as well as nouns. And a lot more. If I had my way I'd burn every bloody Webster's dictionary in the world. The only one that should be allowed is the Oxford. And I'm afraid even that's getting a bit dodgy nowadays."

"Split infinitives. Sloppy speaking, dropping the 't', a kind of glottal stop language," Rayner contributed.

"Absolutely. And more often than not the offenders are people who should know better. I don't mind regional accents per se. Cockney, West Country, North of England. They enrich the language. But laziness or sloppiness, that's quite different."

"I'll tell you one thing that really gets me," said Rayner, raising the stakes. "It's when people say 'like' instead of 'as if' or 'as though'." He and Zoë watched Corbett like hawks.

Alarm bells pealed inside Corbett's head. He could feel the lurch in his stomach as if he had just jumped off a ten-metre diving board. He didn't know how long he may have been silent as the shock hit him. He frowned and tried to appear to be pondering Rayner's remark. He mustn't freeze. This was just a friendly discussion of his favourite subject. "Hmm. That's bad enough, but to me people who say, or even worse write, 'of' instead of 'have'. 'Would of'. 'Could of'. Who the hell educated them?"

That was enough. He had to put a stop to this. Trying to appear at once, relaxed, normal, when the tension was so unbearable, was more than he could take. Corbett looked at his watch and allowed himself - at last - a look of guilt.

"Good Lord. I'm so sorry. How rude of me. Here we are chatting away and I haven't offered you anything. A cup of tea? I normally have some at this time of day. Or coffee perhaps?"

He was appalled at the risk he was taking. The last thing he wanted was for them to agree. He would have to leave them while he went to organise whatever it was they might want; and while he was out of the room ... *The Times*, with the cut up pages, his precious and all-too-revealing notebooks in the drawer of the desk. It wouldn't take them long to snoop around. Unless he could just give a shout and ask Mrs Downing to do the necessary. But it was a risk he had to take. He couldn't stand a moment more of these questions.

Corbett didn't have to take the risk. Rayner looked at his watch. "That's very kind of you, Sir, but I think we've taken up enough of your time already. We'd better be going." He stood up and Zoë followed suit.

"Well, I do hope I've been able to help your enquiries," said Corbett as he led them into the hall and helped them with their coats. "And I really enjoyed discussing the drop in the standards of English. Nice to find someone who feels as I do. The language's future depends on people like us. Perhaps we might be able to have another chat sometime."

"I'm sure we will," said Rayner. "Here's my card if you'd like to get in touch." He handed him his business card and he and Zoë took their leave.

From the house Corbett watched them make their way towards the gate. He was exhausted, drained in both body and mind. He wanted to sit down, even lie down, but there was no strength left, not even to walk the few paces to the drawing room. He knew that even if he tried to turn around to make the effort his knees would buckle. So he just propped himself up against the window and waited to wave if they turned their heads for a last look at him. How had they found him? Oh, he had been seen that night near Guildford and, he supposed, in Sunderland. But he was just one face in a million. How had the police traced him to his own home? They had started off with thunderflashes, Mark IVs at that. Ginger Evans? Jakey Dobbs? But why? In any case, Ginger and Jakey knew nothing of the real reason why he wanted the Mark IVs. So far as they knew, he was going to be using them against moles, which he had done. Well, some of them anyway. The list of names they had reeled off ... Well, that was no surprise per se. All his victims had complained and the police had added two and two together, but that didn't explain how they had found him. What had impressed him was how they had made the link between thunderflashes and the English language, and yet, of course, that was precisely the link that he had wanted his victims to make. The important thing was that, given that they had found him, he hadn't put a foot wrong. Of course he was exhausted. Who wouldn't be after all that?

But he was not just exhausted. Within him there was a feeling of elation and triumph. As he began to take slow, deep breaths the feeling mounted. His fatigue was not that of someone who had just been grilled by the police. It was the fatigue of a one hundred metres sprinter who had just won Olympic gold. He had done it. He had been put through the wringer but had come out on top. He had taken everything they had thrown at him and had come out the winner. Not only that but also he had found an ally. He was sure of it. The Chief Superintendent understood how he felt about the English language and agreed with him. Oh sure, he had a job to do; he was a policeman after all. But he was on his side, there was no doubting that. Not an enemy but a worthy opponent. Better still was the background to this afternoon's events. People had taken notice of him. On the TV and the radio they were beginning to talk proper English again. In the newspapers they were beginning to write it again. They were no longer turning their backs on the English language or taking it for granted. They were showing it the respect it deserved. And all thanks to him, Alan Corbett. Soon, if he kept up the good work, the word would spread and, who could say, one day people would come to love the English language as much as he did. Were it not for the fact that Mrs Downing had not yet left, he would have burst into joyful song. Glory be! Swing low sweet chariot!

Rayner and Zoë walked to the gate in silence. When they reached the car, Roberts was standing beside it. He was holding a plastic bag and there was a look of excitement in his eyes. "You look pleased with yourself," said Rayner. "What have you got there?"

"Evidence, Sir," said Roberts proudly and held out the plastic bag.

"Evidence?" Rayner replied in surprise, and he took the bag and opened it. "Bloody hell, Roberts!" he exclaimed, wrinkling his nose. In the bag was a large dog turd. It was still warm. "Charming. Thank you so very much. Most kind of you." He passed the bag to Zoë, who pulled a face when she saw the contents.

"Used my initiative," said Roberts. "Saw the dog letting one go, so I picked it up when the gardener wasn't looking. It's fresh."

"So I noticed," observed Rayner sourly. "You might at least have gift-wrapped it."

"I thought, you know, that what with DNA and so on, forensic might be able to match it with the others. And if they can, well that'll be another nail in our man's coffin."

"Zoë, do dogs have DNA?" asked Rayner. "And if so, would it apply to turds?"

"No idea, Sir."

"Nor me. We'll see. Anyway, well done Roberts. I'll bear it in mind when I write your next performance appraisal."

At Rayner's suggestion Roberts dropped him at home before taking Zoë on to hers. He could keep the car for the night after delivering Carstairs' offering to forensic.

At home Betty welcomed him with a look of concern. "Darling, have you had a bloody awful day? You look wiped out."

"So would you if you'd spent the last hour sharing the car with a dog turd," said Rayner.

CHAPTER TEN

After leaving Corbett's house, Rayner and Zoë had discussed the events of the afternoon. Roberts and the turd had provided some much needed light relief, for there was no doubt that Rayner had not been happy at the way the interview had gone.

"Bugger him," he had snorted as soon as they got into the car. "Always answering a question with another question. Or with a bloody speech. God! If I'd been a barrister and we'd been in court I would have loved to have cut him short. The question, Mr Corbett. Answer the question."

Zoë had nodded in sympathy. "I did notice," she had commented. "He was very good at it. He did it deliberately, of course."

"Of course he did. Almost as if he'd been trained in anti-interrogation techniques. Perhaps he was, in the TA. He was pretty cool, I thought. Didn't really manage to trip him up at all."

"I thought you were close a couple of times," Zoë had said. "He wasn't expecting the Sunderland question. That worried him." Rayner had nodded in agreement. "And when you came up with 'as if' instead of 'like' I thought he very nearly dried."

"But he recovered well, though, didn't he? And Zoë, you were first class the way you moved from television to newspapers and then to what subjects he wrote to *The Times* about. That gave me just the opening I was looking for. But ..." he had sighed disconsolately, "I don't think we've got enough to nail him in court. Not yet."

"Don't you, Sir?"

"No. It's all circumstantial or inspired guesswork on our part. All he's confessed to is handling stolen property. We could bring him in for that I suppose, but nothing more. As for any other charges, a decent defence counsel would tear holes in our case in no time."

"What about the identifications, Sir?" Zoë had asked.

"What do you think?"

"Inconclusive, Sir."

"I agree. Our drawings show him with a hat on. I was trying to envisage him with one on just now. Difficult. Oh there are some similarities sure enough. Age, height and so on. But again, a good defence counsel could make a big thing about mistaken identity. No. It all depends on the girl from the flower shop. If she can give us a positive identification and confirm that he was the one who sent those flowers and that message to Mandy Drake we'd be on much firmer ground. Don't forget, he denied having corresponded with her. That could be his big mistake. Provided the flower shop girl comes up trumps. If she doesn't, I reckon we could be back to square one."

"Do you think he's our man, Sir?"

"Right now? My gut feeling would say yes. But if I was a member of a jury I'd have to give him the benefit of the doubt. However, having said that, I'm not going to take any risks. ... Roberts, drop into Horsham on the way. We'll get them to put a watch on him for tonight. Don't want him doing a bunk. We'll arrange a permanent tail tomorrow."

* * *

The following morning Rayner called the Commissioner to brief him and arrange for a twenty-four-hour watch on Corbett. He overcame the Commissioner's objections at the cost involved by reminding him that the surveillance teams on the nineteen victims had not only proved effective in terms of avoiding letter bomb casualties but had also recently been lifted, thereby reducing the pressure on costs substantially.

Then, with Zoë telephoning furiously, an emergency meeting was set up with the editors of all the national newspapers for later that morning and a similar one with the heads of each of the TV and radio channels for immediately after lunch. At the meetings Rayner summarised the details of the enquiry and put his request on the table. He was asking them to go out of their way to find opportunities to use the phrase 'as if' as frequently as possible and, for good measure, 'would have', 'should have,' 'might have' and so on. He wasn't asking them to manufacture news, but to use stories or articles covering almost anything they liked. News and current affairs where possible, of course, including sport, with appropriate editorial comments; and then feature items such as gardening, fashion, politics, entertainment, motors, finance, pretty well anything they liked. He expected questions and he got them.

"How long do we have to keep this up?" queried the editor of a tabloid.

"Keep up publishing decent English?" replied Rayner, and he didn't need to go any further amidst the general laughter that followed.

"Is this guy you're after some kind of nutter?" asked another.

"I don't know," Rayner said frankly. "And rather than waiting to find out the hard way, I'd prefer to apprehend him."

"Isn't all this ... what you're asking us to do ... rather like a sledgehammer to crack a nut? Or a nutter?" asked the editor of the *Guardian*.

"Perhaps. But, as I've just said, I'd rather be safe than sorry. So far we know that he's gone from a plain note to dog turds, to thunderflashes, to letter bombs. Luckily we were able to intercept the latter. What next? You ask me. If he's consistent he'll continue to follow a path of escalation. Just what that might turn out to be ... well, your guess is as good as mine. What I can tell you is that the twenty people who were the subject of his attacks to date have been left alone since they agreed to do what I'm now asking you to do. Indeed, they have received a note from our suspect, thanking them for what they've done. I hope that state of affairs will continue. But for all we know he may, even now, be setting his sights on twenty more targets. And another twenty after that. If, through the media, we can make him believe that he has achieved his objective, or is at least well on the way to achieving it, then there may be a chance that he will stop."

"When will you arrest and charge him?" asked the head of Channel 4.

"We don't want to jump the gun until we're as certain as possible that we have all the proof we need. The last thing we need is to fail to prove our case and that as a result he gets off. That would leave him free to get up to his tricks again, maybe come up with some new ones. Right now I'm in the process of putting a plan into action."

"A cunning plan?" the editor of the *Telegraph* interrupted.

"A very cunning plan!" smiled Rayner to more laughter. "And you, and what I'm asking you to do, represent an integral part of it."

The editor of the *Guardian* hadn't finished yet. "To me what you're suggesting smacks of appeasement. We'll be doing what he wants us to do. He will have won."

"What I'm asking you to do is designed to put him behind bars before he does anything worse," Rayner replied dryly. "If my plan, our plan with your help, succeeds, I don't think he'll feel that he's won anything. Unless, of course," he smiled again, "you continue to publish decent English. In which case ... yes, perhaps he would have won. We would all have won. And you, ladies and gentlemen, in your role of publishing and broadcasting more work in English than anybody else, will have contributed to that victory."

"Are you implying that you agree with what he's doing?" the editor of the *Guardian* continued.

"As a policeman I cannot approve of his methods; but as a lover of the English language I can't say that I disagree with his objectives. But far be it from me to tell you how to do your jobs. I'd just like your cooperation for what I hope will only be a few days. What you decide to do when we've wrapped up this case will be entirely your own decision. Fair enough?"

Both meetings ended congenially and Rayner thanked them all for their help. He had an extra private word with the editor of the *Guardian* to see if he could persuade his columnist to join the party. It would help a lot. The editor promised that he would see what he could do.

When he returned to his office, Rayner learned from a disconsolate Roberts that forensic had not come up with anything conclusive on the latest Carstairs contribution. It bore similarities to their other analyses but no more than that. Any analysis could only be as good as the materials it was analysing, and in this case it all depended on what the dog had eaten recently. All they could say with certainty was that the specimen had come from a large dog. We could have told them that, thought Rayner.

For the rest of that Friday afternoon Rayner and Zoë went over the case time and time again, studying Zoë's wall chart data as they did so. Rayner could not help feeling that this enquiry was different from any other he had handled. Under the 'motive' heading he had frequently read 'greed', 'gain', 'financing drug habit', 'jealousy', 'revenge', 'silencing witness', 'racist' and 'self-defence', covering offences from burglary or fraud to grievous bodily harm or murder. They had never had 'defending the English language' before.

Together they listed the evidence that they hoped would provide foundations that were solid enough not only to support their case but also to ensure a verdict of guilty. Three separate identifications from

Sunderland, Hampstead and Guildford. They hoped for a fourth more positive one from Billingshurst. Dog owner. *Times* reader. Admitted possession and use of thunderflashes. Possession, albeit with a permit, of explosives, which could be used to construct letter bombs. Denial of correspondence with Mandy Drake, assuming the Billingshurst flower shop girl came up trumps. A bee in the bonnet about the English language. That was about it. Throw in five TV sets in the same room, which might be construed as their man being a bit of a weirdo. They looked at one another and played devil's advocate. Nothing on their list could be held out as being illegal. A chum had slipped Corbett some thunderflashes and he had used them. Against the moles, he claimed. Hardly a capital offence. His denial of having corresponded with Mandy Drake could be explained away. It had slipped his mind. He didn't think sending flowers represented 'correspondence'. There had, after all, been no regular exchange of letters. Rayner and Zoë gloomily agreed that a good defence counsel could tear their case to shreds. A positive identification by the flower shop girl would help, but it wouldn't be enough. What they wanted was a confession. Rayner's plan would need to be activated. He would need all the skills that Mark Telford could provide.

Rayner called Telford and explained what he wanted. Telford agreed to put a team together to meet in the morning and resigned himself to another lost weekend – the last shopping weekend before Christmas. No one was going to be very popular at home. Rayner arranged with Zoë that they would meet early on Monday morning and go straight to Billingshurst. Then he headed for home for a conversation with Betty to which he did not look forward.

"The whole weekend?" Betty cried. "But you promised. There's so much shopping still to be done. And the tree. Won't they ever give you a free moment?"

"It was my decision, I'm afraid. It's no good blaming anyone else. If everything goes well, Mark and I may be finished by the end of Saturday. Or at least by lunchtime on Sunday. But I'm afraid that's not all."

Then he told her about Christmas Eve and, worse, Christmas Day. To Betty's protests he could only answer that he would almost certainly be back for Christmas dinner.

"Dinner? But we always have Christmas lunch. Have done ever since we were married." Betty was almost tearful now. "What about Ro and Richard? They know it's lunch. How'll they get home if it's dinner?"

"They can stay the night. We've got plenty of room."

"When are we going to open the presents then? We normally do that after lunch. After the Queen's speech."

"We can do it whenever you like. I'll be back by teatime with any luck. Why not have present opening with pre-dinner drinks? That'll be fine, won't it?"

Betty didn't reply and Rayner didn't try to force her. He expected the rest of the evening to be frosty – and he was right.

On Saturday morning the traffic was light and Rayner was in Mark Telford's office by 8.45 a.m. Mark welcomed him with a coffee, introduced him to the team and pointed out an ashtray, for which Rayner was duly grateful.

"Fill me in, Mark," Rayner said.

"We think it can be done," replied Telford.

"Great," said Rayner with a sigh of relief. "Any buts?"

"A few questions really."

"Fire away."

One of the team checked his notepad. "How long do you want it to be?" he asked.

Rayner had already considered the question. "I don't think we're likely to need more than two or three minutes," he replied. "But we may need to be prepared to go on longer. How long does it normally last?"

"About ten minutes."

"Okay. Let's make it the whole ten minutes, just in case. Sorry for the extra work, but I don't want to be caught out on a limb."

"Okay?" Telford asked the team. They all nodded. "Right," he said. "Next?"

Another team member raised a finger. "Do you envisage a full-frontal shot, talking to the mike and camera all the time? Close up? That kind of thing?"

"Not necessarily," Rayner replied. "I think we need to start with something like that, of course. Either posed and formal or moving around less formally. It's been a lot less formal in recent years anyway. Whichever's easiest for you. But after that I'd be quite happy to cut away. Newsclips of her and/or the family. Shots of other people. But with her voice-over. You know the kind of thing."

They nodded again. "Any particular theme?' one of the them asked.

"Well, Christmassy of course," replied Rayner. "And linking it to one or two world, or at least UK, events. I've nothing specific in mind, I'm afraid. Ideas anyone?"

"Jonathan's been giving some thought to that," said Telford. "Like to run us through it, Jonathan?"

Jonathan, a TV scriptwriter, explained his approach and read through his first draft. Concurrently, another member of the team flashed a series of storyboard slides from an overhead projector onto the screen on the opposite wall. After ten minutes Jonathan stopped and Rayner nodded his approval. "Not a bad start," he said. It was clear that someone had been burning a lot of midnight oil.

"Again?" Telford asked.

"Please," Rayner replied and lit a cigarette.

By the end of the morning they had gone through half a dozen separate drafts with a variety of the proposed slides, or visuals as the team member described them. Then, over beer and sandwiches, they discussed what they had seen. Gradually they picked and chose, discarding some items, favouring others, suggesting yet others that had not, so far, been included, considering linkage, fadeouts, timing and lip synchronisation where appropriate. By late afternoon they had reached agreement and Jonathan and the rest of the team departed to put the whole thing together. They were optimistic that, provided they didn't run into any unforeseen technical problems, they would be able to show Rayner and Telford the final draft the following morning. If it met with their approval they would have the finished article printed and ready for viewing on the Sunday afternoon.

"Bloody good bunch," said Rayner.

"The best," Telford agreed. "Assuming it turns out Okay, do you think it'll do the trick?"

"My career's on the line if it doesn't," replied Rayner.

* * *

Corbett spent the whole weekend in a haze of astonishment. There were frequent occasions when he almost felt that he should pinch himself in case he was dreaming. It seemed too good to be true; but it was true. Whether he was reading, listening or watching, the message was the same. In every newspaper, on the radio and on each TV channel there it was. Over and over and over again. As if. As if. As if. Not only that. On the radio he had heard, and on the TV quiz show he had seen and heard, the quiz show host clearly say, "I would have" and later "You should have" instead of 'would've and should've'. All his initial converts were behaving like lambs, bless their hearts. Even the *Guardian* columnist had finally joined the party. But there were so many others doing likewise. One by one he checked off the twenty names on his Number Two list in his notebooks and found, to his astonished delight, that they were all dancing to the same lovely tune. What was more, there were articles in the press written by people not yet on any of his lists, who were joining the campaign. In the *Mirror on Sunday* there was a photograph of a fifteen-year-old boy, grossly overweight, holding a football. The picture was captioned 'Obesity – Is it all in the mind?' with the boy quoted as saying, "People can say I'm fat but when I've got a football I feel as if I'm David Beckham". Page 3 of *The Sun* had a picture of a vastly mammary-endowed young lady saying, "I know it looks as if I've had surgery but they're all mine." On Match of the Day, as Arsenal scored their fourth goal, a commentator had said, "It looks as if it's all over for Man United." Corbett thought he knew how Chairman Mao must have felt. Talk about a thousand flowers blooming! Perhaps he should buy some new notebooks – coloured red. History was being made – thanks to him, Alan Corbett, and Carstairs, of course.

He leant down and patted the dog. That was the answer for the empty plinth in Trafalgar Square. He and Carstairs. Saviours of the English language. Who cared about the pigeons?

For a moment or two he did worry. All these marvellous things that were happening, all this proof of his success – had he done himself out of a job? Then he laughed out loud. Finished? It had hardly begun. There were still so many things that needed to be dealt with. All those nouns being turned into verbs. The estuary accent. And those clichés – 'know what I mean?', 'at the end of the day', 'bottom line', 'at this moment in time', 'in point of fact', 'move forward', just a few off the top of his head. The list was endless. And on the subject of 'off', what about 'off of'; and what about 'out the window'? Oh, he had plenty to keep him occupied. He knew he could do it. Success breeds success, after all.

He had a sudden thought. That police chap. He'd be pleased, wouldn't he? After what he had said about 'like' and 'as if' he must have noticed what had suddenly started to happen. Corbett went to the drawer of the desk and took out Rayner's business card. What about calling him to discuss these great events? Then he noticed that the card only carried the telephone number of Rayner's office. A pity, but perhaps just as well. Best not to disturb him at home during the weekend anyway. He'd try him at the office on Monday.

Corbett decided on an early night. After all the excitement he felt really tired. He sat with a nightcap and watched as Mandy Drake came on to present the weather. A cold north-easterly front was moving in from Scandinavia. It looked as if (lovely girl) Scotland and the North, down as far as East Anglia, could be in for some snow flurries before dawn. Then she pointed to Devon and Cornwall, and for one moment Corbett gasped in horror as he thought that the worst had happened. Speaking what he thought was just a little bit more precisely, and staring straight at the camera with a smile playing round her lips, Mandy said, "and for Devon and Cornwall tomorrow it looks like," a short pause, then "sunshine". Corbett could have sworn that as she ended the sentence she winked at him. Oh what fun life was. What tremendous fun.

* * *

On Sunday morning Rayner and Telford watched the final draft that the team had produced. Thoughtfully, it opened with fifteen seconds of a summary of the rest of the day's scheduled programmes before slipping easily into the actual presentation. Very realistic, thought Rayner. For the next nine minutes and forty-five seconds they looked at what Rayner almost believed was the genuine article. It was put together very well indeed and Rayner was generous with his praise as he and Telford applauded at the piece's conclusion. Telford promised that he would have two copies delivered to Rayner's office the following morning, labelled confidential, for his personal attention.

Rayner thanked them all profusely and acknowledged their good luck wishes before driving back home to Betty. As good as his word he was there in time for lunch and spent the afternoon putting up and decorating the Christmas tree without breaking any of the ornaments. He managed to get the fairy perched at the right angle on the treetop to Betty's satisfaction after only the third attempt and he broke all records by cursing only twice when fixing up the lights. All in all he was rather pleased with himself.

On Monday morning the car arrived promptly at 8.30 with Roberts at the wheel and Zoë at his side. Rayner ran through the events of the weekend and promised them both that they would be able to see the results of Mark Telford's team's efforts when they returned to the office later that day. They reached the Billinghurst flower shop at 9.15 and were welcomed by a suntanned girl of about twenty-four whom they rightly assumed to be Ruth. They introduced themselves and, after enquiring after her skiing holiday, explained the purpose of their visit.

They reminded Ruth of the date and nature of the flowers that had been ordered for Mandy Drake and of the accompanying message. Before they had even had time to ask whether she could describe the client, let alone show her the artist's impressions from the Hampstead and Guildford sightings, Ruth confounded them both by saying, "Oh yes, Mr Corbett. Such a nice bloke."

"You mean you know him?" Zoë exclaimed in surprise.

"Oh yes. He comes here quite often."

"I wonder why the proprietor didn't mention that," mused Rayner.

"Oh, she's not here often. Only when me or Rosie are away. She's got shops in Crawley and Godalming and down the road in Storrington."

"I see," said Rayner. "These flowers for Miss Drake. Has he sent her flowers before?"

"Not from us," replied Ruth.

"But he's a regular customer?"

"Quite regular. His wife used to come in quite a lot, before she got run over. Poor man. I think he misses her but he doesn't talk about it, of course. Says he likes to have flowers in the house 'cos it seems empty without them. But he doesn't know anything about flower arranging, so I make him up a bunch, all nicely arranged, so he can just put them straight in a vase. I told him he should go on a flower arranging course, but I don't think he's bothered."

"You're sure that it was he who gave you the order?"

"For Miss Drake's flowers? Quite sure."

They thanked Ruth for her help and went back to the car, with Rayner shaking his head. "Well I'll be damned," he said.

"What now?" Zoë asked, accompanied by Roberts', "Where to, Sir?"

"It helps, of course," acknowledged Rayner thoughtfully. "Much better than a one-off description. But does it make that much difference? We can prove beyond reasonable doubt that Corbett sent the flowers and the message that went with them. But there's nothing illegal in sending flowers to someone. And we can't prove any link between sending the flowers and sending the other things, either to Mandy Drake or to anyone else. The only thing we have to work on is his denial of having corresponded with her at all."

"So?" said Zoë. "We still go for a confession?"

"Yes," Rayner replied. "Let's drop in on him. Zoë, check with our surveillance people that he's at home."

Zoë put through a call and confirmed that Corbett was indeed in.

"Right," said Rayner. "Rudgwick, Roberts, please."

A few minutes later they arrived at the house and Rayner and Zoë walked up towards it. As they approached, the front door opened and they were greeted by Corbett, preceded by a tail-wagging Carstairs.

"Chief Superintendent! Sergeant ..."

"Henderson, Sir," Zoë provided.

"Henderson, of course. Sorry." Corbett was clearly not phased by their unexpected arrival. "Good morning! So nice of you to come. You got my message then?"

"Message?" asked Rayner.

"I rang your office, about an hour ago. They said you were out. And now you're here, so I assumed ..."

"What did you ring about?" Rayner interrupted.

"Well ... you know ... about all these things that are going on in the media. Marvellous things. You must have seen them."

"Oh ... yes, of course," said Rayner.

"I hope you're as pleased as I am. Particularly about 'like' and 'as if'. That was one of the things that really got you, I think you said. Come in. Come in." He led them into the hall. "Look, did you see this? Where is it?

Yes, here it is." He picked up some newspapers and turned the pages. "Look," he showed them the overweight boy and the page 3 girl. "Amazing, aren't they?"

"I take it you're not talking about her breasts," Rayner remarked.

Corbett roared with laughter. "Have you seen them? There are plenty more."

"I don't have a lot of time to read the papers," said Rayner as he read through the blurb. "But I did notice something similar in the *Telegraph*. Not the breasts," he smiled, "but the standards of their English. Perhaps someone's had a word with their editors." Zoë joined him in examining what Corbett handed them.

"Oh these are just a couple of them," Corbett went on. "It's been happening all over the place. TV and radio too. Even ..." He stopped as he realised that he had been on the point of giving himself away. He had been about to say, 'even people who aren't yet on my list'. He thought quickly. "Even in a football commentary." He told them about Arsenal and Manchester United.

"Amazing," said Rayner. "There's still hope for the English language after all. What's made all this happen do you think?" Go on, he thought. Tell me. Tell me. Claim all the credit you want. That's fine. But just tell me. Then I won't have to do what I plan to do. Then I won't have to bring your world tumbling down around your head. Please tell me.

"Absolutely no idea," replied Corbett. "But it really is quite something, isn't it?"

Oh you poor man, thought Zoë.

"Yes, it certainly is," Rayner agreed. Then, putting on a more formal tone, continued, "Mr Corbett, the reason for our visit is that we'd just like to go over a couple of points that arose when we were last here."

"Oh, yes. Of course." Beneath his apparent unconcern Corbett put up his guard. "I'd forgotten you didn't get my message. Go ahead."

"We've just come from Billingshurst." Aha, thought Corbett. "We talked to a young lady in the flower shop there."

"Ah, that would be Ruth. Or Rosie. Nice girls."

"She told us that not long ago you arranged for them to send some flowers through Interflora. To Miss Mandy Drake."

"Yes, that's right," Corbett said, unmoved. "A dozen red roses."

"Sir, when we were last here I asked you whether you knew her or had ever corresponded with her. You said 'no'."

"Did I?" said Corbett. "Don't remember. But if you say so, then I suppose I must have."

"But you now admit that you sent her a dozen roses."

"Yes. Of course." A bald admission. "But in my book that doesn't rate as corresponding with her. We haven't been exchanging letters or anything like that."

Rayner looked rueful as he heard the expected response. "But you sent her some flowers. Why?"

Corbett hesitated. "Well ... as an admirer, I suppose."

"You? An admirer of Mandy Drake?" Rayner didn't bother to hide his disbelief.

"I know it sounds silly, looking back on it." Corbett gave a half laugh of embarrassment. "But it was the night that she said ... oh, I forget exactly, but it was something like 'it looks as if it'll be a wet night in Scotland'. Nine times out of ten she would have said 'it looks like it'll be a wet night'. This time she said 'as if'. I was really surprised, and so glad that I happened to be watching her when she said it. I'd been thinking quite a lot about the English language at the time. I'd been reading that book by Lynne Truss. You know, *Eats, Shoots & Leaves;* and that other one by John Humphrys about mangling the English language. So ... I decided to send her some flowers."

"You decided to send her some flowers," Rayner repeated flatly.

"To ... you know ... thank her. For making my evening. And for contributing, just a little, you know, to improving the standards of English on the box."

Zoë broke in. "Did you send her a message with the flowers, Mr Corbett?"

"Yes, I did. Forget what it was now. Something about congratulations on your weather presentation. I think I did actually mention her using 'as if'. In case it was ... well ... accidental. I didn't want her to go forgetting it the next time. I was hoping she'd keep it up. And she has," he added. "Plus a lot of others. It's fantastic."

"According to the flower shop," Zoë continued, "you added a PS to the message. 'Sorry about you know what'. Is that right?"

"You know what. You know what." Corbett repeated, buying time.

"Yes. What did you mean by that?"

"Good question. What on earth did I mean by that?"

Corbett paused and Zoë asked again, "What was 'you know what'? What were you alluding to?"

"To what was I alluding?" Corbett corrected, appearing to be talking to himself. "A cold? Do you think she may have had a cold?"

"You tell me," said Zoë. "If it was a cold, why didn't you write 'sorry about the cold'?"

Corbett considered for a while. Then shook his head. "Sorry. My mind's a blank. I've got no recollection at all. Are you sure the shop's got it right? Maybe Ruth's mixing up my message with someone else's."

Rayner stepped in. "Sorry about you know what. Were you perhaps apologising for something?"

"But what would I have to apologise for?" asked Corbett in studied innocence.

"Possibly for sending her a letter bomb?" Rayner suggested softly.

"A letter bomb?"

"Or the thunderflash that nearly killed her dog? Or some canine excrement?" Rayner snapped the words out.

"But why should I ...? Sorry. You've lost me, Chief Superintendent."

Rayner stood up abruptly. He'd given Corbett his chance. It had been rejected. Rayner knew that he had no choice but to put his plan into action. "Okay, Mr Corbett. That's all for now." Zoë rose and joined him as he walked to the front door. Corbett followed.

"I'm sorry. I really think Ruth must have got it wrong. But I'll wrack my brains and if I come up with anything I'll call you if that would help." Corbett smiled helpfully.

"Please do, Sir," said Rayner as they stepped out of the house. Halfway down the drive he turned back. "Oh, and Merry Christmas."

"Thank you," said Corbett. "Merry Christmas to you too."

"Going away for it?" Rayner enquired as an afterthought.

"To my sister's. For lunch."

"She live far?"

"East Grinstead. Not far."

"So you'll be here until then? Just in case we need to get in touch?"

Rayner gave a friendly smile.

"Yes. We'll be here, won't we Carstairs," said Corbett, giving the dog a pat. "Keeping an eye on the media."

CHAPTER ELEVEN

When the police had gone, Corbett made himself a cup of coffee and sat down to review the position. They knew everything. They knew about each of his salvoes and each of the people at whom they had been aimed. They knew about the flowers and his message to Mandy Drake. Letter bombs, thunderflashes, dog turds, the lot. They clearly knew about his interest in the English language. But how much could they prove? Where was he at risk? Handling illicit thunderflashes, yes. He'd already admitted that. But only in respect of the moles. They had no proof that it was he who had put them through his targets' letter boxes. Ditto the turds. Ditto the letter bombs. Sending flowers? Not an offence. Forgetting the exact wording of his accompanying message? Not an offence. Perhaps he had slipped up in using the flower shop where he was known, but that was water under the bridge now and hardly a disaster. Presumably the columnist near Guildford would have given the police a description, but so what? He had been a passing motorist with engine trouble, which he had subsequently fixed. No proof that he and the thunderflash man were one and the same person. Being let down, he assumed by Ginger or Jakey, was a setback in that it had obviously led the police to him, but it wasn't lethal. The explosives? The police had not mentioned them but he assumed they were aware of their existence. The West Sussex force had issued his permit after all and he presumed that different police forces spoke to one another. But the explosives were perfectly legal and he had already made the necessary entries to his ledgers to account for the missing two kilos of the stuff that he had used for the letter bombs. So, no problem there. Even the motoring offence, which might so easily have been a crippling blow if he had been carrying thunderflashes or letter bombs at the time, was no more than a nuisance. He imagined he would be fined, have a few points put on his driving licence, and, if the worst came to the worst, face a driving ban for a month or two. None of that would be the end of the world and, with a perfectly clean licence up until now, he doubted that they would go as far as issuing a ban.

On the credit side, consider how he had succeeded! Wherever you looked the evidence was indisputable. His contribution to the well-being of the English language was undeniable. The fact that he couldn't publicise it and claim the credit didn't worry him in the least. The achievement was the thing. Future generations might not thank him for it but they would be the beneficiaries. It all went to show what one determined individual with a mission and a sense of destiny could do. Much work remained to be done but he was up to it; and, in spite of the fright he had had as a result of the attentions of the police, he was secure. Nobody, neither the police nor anybody else, could stop him.

Having burned the old copies of *The Times*, the only incriminating evidence that might put him at risk in the event of his being detained and the house searched was the notebooks. He would need to do something about them. What? Destroy them? No way. They represented his life's work now. Not only were they vital as a reference tool and as an aid to the work that remained to be done, but also they were a record that he alone, he, Alan Corbett, was responsible for the about-turn that was now being executed by the English language. He would never consider destroying them; but he should probably hide them somewhere until the heat was off. Until then he would have to make do with the backs of envelopes or something for any notes he needed to make for the next phase of his campaign.

He took the notebooks and put them in a plastic bag, making sure that it was completely watertight before securing it with sellotape. Then he emptied the mixed festive biscuits, which he had planned to take to his sister, out of their tin and replaced them with the precious notebooks. Then he wrapped the tin in another plastic bag.

Outside it was beginning to drizzle. He knew where he would put the tin. Slipping on an anorak, he went out and walked to the far end of the garden, taking a spade out of the barn en route. He reached the spot, well hidden from the road by the hedge and some shrubs. Sticking up from where the autumn leaves still covered the ground was a small wooden cross with a name roughly chiselled into it. It was the last resting place of Carruthers, Carstairs' predecessor. "Hello Carruthers, old boy," Corbett murmured. "Sorry to disturb you." He cleared the leaves away, marked out and removed a forty-five centimetre square of turf and dug a neat hole into which he put the tin. He covered the tin with earth, distributed the excess under a japonica bush, tamped down the turf and replaced the fallen leaves. No one would find the notebooks here. At his side Carstairs gave a sad whimper as he saw the tin, normally a potential source of goodies, disappear from view. "Good dogs, both of you," said Corbett.

* * *

While Corbett was hiding the evidence, Rayner and Zoë enjoyed a cup of coffee in the canteen at Horsham police station. On their way they had checked in with the unmarked surveillance car parked fifty metres from Corbett's gate and Rayner had impressed on its occupants the importance of their function during the next four days. Don't worry, the job would be over on Christmas Eve. They would be home with their families in time for the festivities.

Over coffee Rayner and Zoë briefed the Horsham station head and gave him a list of what Rayner would require. They would be bringing in their man, probably during the late afternoon of Christmas Eve. Unless they were going to be very pressed for space he should have a cell to himself. No, they didn't think he would be dangerous but that was no reason to take any chances. There might be a dog involved but Rayner or Zoë would try to make other arrangements for it. Rayner would give the suspect an opportunity to call his solicitor if he wished when they arrested him. If he wished to call from the station he should not be refused but in no circumstances should overnight bail be granted. He was to remain in custody until Rayner decided otherwise. Rayner hoped that would be later in the afternoon of Christmas Day, assuming that everything went according to plan.

Then the three of them went to the interview room. It was on the small side but large enough for Rayner's purpose. A CCTV camera was already in place. Rayner indicated exactly where he wanted the TV set to be installed. The station head confirmed that as well as the standard video and tape recorder already in the room for the purpose of recording interviews, a second video recorder would be concealed behind the filing cabinet and wired into the TV set. An officer would be instructed to ensure that the second video and TV would be turned on before Rayner, Zoë and the suspect entered the room just before 3 o'clock on Christmas afternoon. It would be arranged for the room to be free and available for any rehearsal that might be required on Christmas morning. Rayner noted the interview table and accompanying five chairs, and that the single ashtray was made of Bakelite and sufficiently small and light not to damage anything or anyone if an attempt was made to throw it.

Rayner and Zoë thanked the station head and returned to the car. Just over an hour later they reached the office where, on his desk, Rayner found the package marked for his personal attention. He opened it and read the attached note from Mark Telford wishing him luck on Christmas Day and a Merry Christmas to boot. He accompanied Zoë to the canteen and agreed that she and Roberts should join him after lunch to see what Telford and his team had put together.

After seeing the final version of the presentation, both Zoë and Roberts said that they would not have known that it was not the real thing without being told. Really good, was their verdict. Rayner agreed. It was seamless. Identical in every way to what it purported to be, except of course for those few carefully inserted changes to the script.

Afterwards Zoë with a frown asked, "What do you think it'll do to him, Sir? How's he going to react?"

"By confessing, I hope," said Rayner.

"Yes, Sir. Of course. But what else? Might it, you know, affect him mentally? Drive him over the edge or something?"

"I don't know," Rayner replied with a shake of his head. "That's the last thing I'd want to happen."

"Me too," said Zoë. "He's a nice bloke."

"I agree. But a nice bloke who gets so carried away with his fantasies that he's prepared to send letter bombs to twenty people, including the Prime Minister, aiming to injure or even to maim them, perhaps even kill. We can't allow that, whatever the motives."

"Of course not," Zoë said sadly.

"Anyway, I'm seeing Freud in half an hour." He mentioned the department's psychologist by his generally used nickname. "He'll have an opinion. Or three or four."

Half an hour later Rayner was giving Freud the entire case history and outlining the need for a confession from Corbett and the plan he had constructed in order to get one. Freud listened attentively, taking notes from time to time.

Eventually, Freud spoke. "Not having met him myself, it's more difficult to form an opinion. Tell me, forgetting the offences with which you're planning to charge him, how do you find him as a person?"

Rayner thought for a while. "Of course it wasn't an ordinary, everyday conversation. I was questioning him, after all. But, subject to that, I would describe him as courteous, charming, considerate ... actually a very nice guy. I like him. So does my Sergeant. But the trouble is ... he's done all these things. So far as he's concerned the end justifies the means."

"Quite. Well, from what you tell me I would say that his behavioural pattern is certainly obsessional, in this case about the English language. He's by no means alone in that, but others who may share his obsession don't usually express it by trying to frighten or even harm people. Normally a few letters to *The Times* would suffice."

"Yes," agreed Rayner. "But the difference is that the others just want to get their views, or obsessions if you like, off their chest. Whereas our man actually wants to do something about it."

"Exactly," agreed Freud. "Which is why, from what I've heard, I would judge that he may be suffering from a personality disorder which could be verging on schizophrenia. I'd have to examine him to give you a more precise diagnosis."

"As regards this split personality," said Rayner, "might there be a risk that some event might tip the scales, as it were? So that he might leave Dr Jekyll behind altogether and become all Mr Hyde?"

"It's possible. I take it that the event to which you refer would be what you are planning to do to him?"

"Yes," Rayner replied.

"In that case I would have to agree that there could be a risk. A substantial one. The shock, to his self-esteem as much as anything else, would be considerable. You would be depriving him of what he sees as his role in life. The least harmful outcome is that he would turn into a manic depressive. He would have nothing left in life to obsess him and occupy him."

"But if I could do it in such a way as to help him understand that there was nothing wrong with his chosen role per se but only in the way in which he was trying to fulfil it?"

"That would be the approach I would suggest," confirmed Freud. "But I can't forecast what his response might be."

Rayner thanked Freud for his time and advice as well as for his offer to interview Corbett when he was in custody. Rayner hoped very much that he would not find it necessary to take up the offer. That evening he voiced his concerns to Betty, whose annoyance at her disrupted pre-Christmas weekend had been softened by Rayner's success with the Christmas tree. He noted that under it there were already a number of parcels, neatly and colourfully wrapped, and knew that as usual the quality of the display would suffer when he added his own offerings to the pile. He was a believer in solidly reliable wrapping, helped by copious quantities of sellotape. The corners of his packages tended to be rounded and a bit knobbly, rather than neatly squared off. He wasn't into ribbons and bows. They weren't included in any Metropolitan Police training courses.

"I don't see why you, or certainly I, should waste our sympathy on this chap, especially as he's ruining our Christmas Day," Betty said after Rayner had told her what was troubling him.

Rayner didn't want to get into the Christmas lunch dispute again. "I just feel sorry about what I'm going to be doing to him. When he realises that what he thinks he's achieved is ... just ... so much thin air."

"You're only doing your job. He's the one who's been causing all the trouble, not you. You're getting soft in your old age."

"Perhaps I am," admitted Rayner. Then, with time having at least partly healed the wounds, he continued, "Do you know, the last person who said that was the Commissioner?" He told Betty of the Commissioner's accusation that he was wasting police time and of his dismissal of the benefits of Step by Step.

"The bastard," exclaimed Betty. "Accusing you, of all people; and talk about a closed mind. Pig-headed ... bone-headed ..." She gave up in exasperation and Rayner laughed.

"Maybe he's right," Rayner said. "Maybe I am going soft. Take this case. In all my career I've never come across one like it. On the wall in the office I normally look at the faces, if we've got any, of whatever villains we're investigating and enjoy the thought of their getting their just desserts. I started off feeling the same way about this one, but now, when I look at him, do you know? I find myself thinking that it's rather a pity that we've caught up with him."

"You'll get over it. When this case is over there'll be another one. And then you'll be back to normal. You'll see." Betty tried to sound comforting.

"I hope so," he said and decided that he wouldn't raise his concerns with the Commissioner when he saw him the following day.

Rayner's interview with the Commissioner was brief.

"Keep it short, if you don't mind, Mike," the Commissioner said, without looking up when Rayner entered the office. "I'm due at a Treasury sub-committee meeting in ten minutes. Amendments to next year's budget. Reallocation of resources and so on. And in Christmas week, of all times. I ask you." He sounded annoyed but, reading between the lines, Rayner could tell that his boss was only too pleased to be able to talk about the corridors of power in which he trod. "So?" the Commissioner continued, "Got him yet?"

Rayner brought the Commissioner up to date. He wasn't expecting any thanks or praise and he didn't get any.

"Taken you long enough," the Commissioner remarked when Rayner had finished. "It's all a bit of a mountain out of a molehill if you ask me. Bloody nutter. Wasting our time and our money."

"We'll be lifting the last surveillance team on Christmas Eve," said Rayner, knowing that that was the only thing the Commissioner really wanted to hear.

"About bloody time too. Right. Thank you, Mike. Let me know when it's all concluded."

On his return to his own office the look on Rayner's face was enough to make Zoë steer clear of him until he had gone straight out onto his balcony and angrily lit a cigarette. After he had returned to his desk, Zoë came into his office.

"About the dog, Sir."

Rayner smiled. The mundane matter of Corbett's dog was just the thing needed to take his mind off his meeting with the Commissioner and Zoë knew it. His smile reflected his thought that here they were, about to wrap up a time-consuming and costly case, and one of the things exercising their minds was the welfare of the suspect's dog. "Ah yes. Carstairs," he said. "Have you managed to fix anything?"

"Horsham already know him and say that one of their people will be happy to take him overnight. Longer if necessary."

"Fine. That's assuming that Corbett doesn't get the gardener and his wife to look after him. Whoever gets him will be honoured. It's not often that you get to meet a dog whose turds have been personally hand-delivered to nineteen celebrities and mailed to the Prime Minister."

The rest of the week passed uneventfully apart from three scares as the surveillance team reported that Corbett was leaving his house and getting into his car. Each scare turned out to be a false alarm as the surveillance car followed him to Tesco's twice and to the local golf club. After each trip he had returned home without making any detours. Rayner waited impatiently for Christmas Eve.

Corbett spotted the following surveillance car on his second trip to Tesco's. He couldn't be sure about it but his suspicions were confirmed when the same vehicle tracked him to the golf club. So they were keeping tabs on him. After an initial lurch of anxiety he thought - so what? If that's how they wanted to spend their time it was no skin off his nose. He could, he supposed, easily give them the slip and do a runner. But what was the point? Where would he go? Hole up somewhere? Flee the country? What about Carstairs? What about the English language? No! He would stay right where he was, in the comfort of his own home. To hell with them! What could they prove, anyway? On the basis of his earlier analysis - nothing. He would prepare for the worst and then sit it out. He didn't mind waiting; but what the hell were they waiting for?

CHAPTER TWELVE

It was drizzling and cold on the morning of Christmas Eve. After breakfast Corbett donned his raincoat and wellington boots and took a reluctant Carstairs for his morning constitutional. "It's for your benefit, not mine," said Corbett looking up at the sulphur-coloured sky. Any drop in temperature would turn the drizzle into snow, he thought. Twenty minutes along a muddy track was enough for Carstairs to be well soaked, while Corbett collected the usual mass of glutinous West Sussex clay on his boots. They turned back and on reaching the house were glad of the warmth of its central heating. Corbett dried Carstairs and wiped the worst of the mud off his paws, lower legs and belly before letting him in. Sitting down with a cup of coffee, Corbett perused the newspapers. The press were keeping it up. "As if" and several "as thoughs" were liberally scattered throughout the day's offerings, continuing to emulate the same high standards that had been set by yesterday's television programmes and this morning's radio. Last night he had been astonished to see and hear two "as ifs" in *Coronation Street* and another one in *Eastenders*. Extraordinary. It was spreading, there was no doubt of that. Even the scriptwriters of soap operas were becoming converted. In fact, he admitted somewhat guiltily to himself, it was almost beginning to get a bit boring. But then he smiled at the thought of the many new pastures that were still awaiting his attention. Why, he might even have a go at political correctness next, using the same methods. Perhaps he would start with the people who described themselves as "chair". What message should be put in his first note? "Man"? "Woman"? – depending on the sex of the recipient. Or perhaps "Table", but would they understand the message? He would have to think about it. Or maybe he should stick more closely to the English language campaign and go for people who turned nouns into verbs. There were certainly plenty of targets. Or what about something completely different, like the packaging industry? God. If anybody deserved a few salvoes it was the people in the packaging industry. Perhaps it was just that he was getting older, or perhaps it was the new-fangled ways they had of packaging things so as to make it virtually impossible to get at the contents. Only the other day it had taken a knife, a pair of scissors, a screwdriver and ten minutes to get at a new toothbrush, which had been so securely enveloped in thick plastic and cardboard that it might have come out of Fort Knox. How long would it be, he wondered, before the newspapers were reporting that old age pensioners were found dying of starvation, surrounded by packets or tins of supermarket meat or vegetables that they had been unable to open? To say nothing of the litter that resulted. Yes, the packaging industry would be a worthwhile target. Then he thought of the now almost daily use of the word "partner" to describe someone's husband or wife. It was bad enough using it to describe a live-in boyfriend or girlfriend, but now it had been extended to apply even to those who had the commitment and courage of their convictions to opt for marriage instead of being content just to shack up together and, as it was described in the good old days, to live in sin. Corbett was no prude. If people wanted to live in sin, so be it, but why should husbands and wives be tarred with the same brush by the application of the word "partner". Before Annie had died he had received some kind of bank questionnaire which had included a question about "your partner". He had completed the form, then torn it up and posted it back to the bank in the envelope provided. They had rung him up later about it and when he had explained the reasons for his actions the person at the other end had simply failed to understand what he was complaining about. But, he reflected, at least it had been a real live person, rather than a recorded message. Now that was another potential target. Recorded messages! Airlines, trains, banks, the gas board, the electricity people, the local council, just about every major company in the country, even Buckingham Palace for all he knew, they were all the same now. "If you wish to know the state of your account, press one. If you wish to take out a loan, press two. Thank you. If you wish to enquire about short-term overdraft rates, press three. If you wish to enquire about a long-term personal loan, press four." And so on and so forth. Press this. Press that. Oh, and, "If you wish to speak to a human being, press five." And then you were left for half an hour listening, if you were lucky, to a musak version of Beethoven's Fifth. No doubt it would only be a matter of time before you would be invited to press yet another button in order to select the tune to which you wished to listen while you waited for that elusive human being. Recently, when ringing what clearly turned out to be a call centre, Corbett had got into the habit of asking how the weather was in Bombay.

Over lunch, taken on his knees in front of the televisions, Corbett ruminated on the many things, so many things, that were wrong with the country and indeed the world. So much to do. So little time! Then he laughed. And he had been worrying about getting bored. But, for the time being, eye on the ball, Corbett. There's still the English language to be sorted out. We're not out of the wood yet. He settled down to monitor *Match of the Day* on BBC1 and racing on Channel 4. The other channels were showing films.

The car containing Rayner and Zoë, with Roberts at the wheel, was followed by a police car from the Horsham station. It was dusk as they approached Rudgwick and Rayner repeated his final thoughts to Zoë.

"So we'll give him a chance to come clean this afternoon. Agreed?"

"Agreed, Sir."

"If he comes clean then that will be that. We take him in, charge him and then let him out on bail. No need to hold him. And, more importantly, no need to sit him in front of the presentation tomorrow afternoon and destroy his little world piece by piece. If he promises to be a good boy and report regularly he can lead a perfectly normal life until he's due for trial. He can even go to East Grinstead for Christmas lunch with his sister."

"Let's hope it works out that way," said Zoë. "And there'll be no problem about the dog either."

"Much easier for all concerned," nodded Rayner. "No pain. No dramatics."

"Do you think he will come clean, Sir? Today?"

"No," replied Rayner. "I'm afraid I don't."

They stopped by the surveillance car where they received confirmation that the suspect was still in the house. Rayner thanked the team and released them from their vigil with his thanks and best wishes for a Merry Christmas. Roberts drove the additional fifty metres, followed by the police car, and both vehicles pulled up by Corbett's gate. Rayner and Zoë got out and, followed by two officers from the other car, walked up to the front door. Rayner would have preferred that Zoë and he carried this out alone but experience and arrest procedures dictated otherwise. The suspect was, after all, in possession of explosives and a shotgun. He had already shown that he was prepared to attempt to inflict grievous bodily harm in the form of thunderflashes and letter bombs. Although in Rayner's opinion he was unlikely to offer violence now, there was no point in taking unnecessary risk.

Corbett heard their knock on the front door, got to his feet and walked into the hall followed by Carstairs. He saw the two uniformed officers through the window. So this was it. His heart pounded. He took a deep breath. Here we go. He opened the door.

"Chief Superintendent! And Sergeant! Gentlemen." He gave a smile in welcome.

"May we come in, Sir?" Rayner's tone was formal but not threatening. Corbett was glad to note the 'Sir'.

"Of course. Another visit. And on Christmas Eve. Don't they ever give you some time off?" He led them through the hall into the drawing room. "What can I do for you? Basket, Carstairs." Carstairs sloped off obediently in the direction of the kitchen and Corbett was amused to see the look of surprise on the faces of the two uniformed officers as they took in the battery of TV sets facing them. "Still looking for your thunderflash man?"

"No, Sir," replied Rayner. "We think we've found him."

"Good for you. Sorry. *Match of the Day* and Channel 4 racing." He crossed to the TV sets and switched them off. "Didn't make my fortune today, I'm afraid."

"Mr Corbett, would you like to tell us all about it?"

"About what, Superintendent?"

"Please, Sir." Rayner's voice was gentle but firm. "We know it was you. I'd just like you to confirm that. It would make everything so much easier. For you and for the police."

Corbett stooped and picked up the poker. Out of the corner of his eye he saw his visitors tense and then relax as he stoked the logs and replaced the poker. "Cold out, isn't it?" he said.

"Please, Sir. Why not just tell us what happened?"

"Can't help you there, I'm afraid."

Rayner spoke with more urgency now. "Look, Mr Corbett. No one's been hurt. No serious damage done. I'd like to help you. But I need your help in return. The truth, Sir. That's all you need to tell us. If you cooperate, then I don't see why things should go too badly for you. I'll certainly do my best to see that they don't."

Rayner waited. Corbett made no reply and for a moment Rayner hoped that their man might fold. Then Corbett straightened up and gave a familiar friendly smile and Rayner's heart sank.

"This is your third visit to my house, Chief Superintendent. I've already answered all your questions as best I can. I'm sorry I still can't remember the exact wording of the message I sent with those flowers. I'm afraid I can't think of anything else that may help you."

Rayner studied Corbett in the fading hope that he might change his mind at the last minute. He gave him one more chance. "Won't you tell us? Please?" Corbett's silence filled the room. With it the tension mounted until the spell was broken by the noise of a shifting log. Rayner sighed in a mixture of exasperation and sadness. "In that case it looks as if I shall have to invite you to accompany us to the police station."

Corbett smiled. "Thank you, Chief Superintendent."

Rayner's heart lifted. Was it possible that at the last minute Corbett was going to give in. "Why thank me?" he asked.

"For a moment I thought you were going to say 'it looks like'. You didn't. You said 'it looks as if'."

"Mr Corbett, I have a warrant for your arrest." Rayner produced an envelope from his coat pocket. "And I must ask you to accompany me to Horsham police station where you will be formally charged."

"Fine," said Corbett and realised that his mouth had gone very dry. "I'll need to pack some things, I suppose. Is that all right?"

"Of course, Sir," confirmed Zoë. "One of the officers will accompany you."

"Of course. I quite understand. It's upstairs. Shall I lead the way?" He crossed towards the hall and one of the uniformed officers made to follow. Then Corbett stopped. "What about Carstairs? Am I likely to be away for long?"

Zoë answered, "One of the officers at Horsham will be happy to take care of him. Unless you'd prefer to make other arrangements."

"No. That'll be fine," said Corbett. "Thank you."

Rayner attempted to lighten the moment. "He'll probably eat better than you will, Sir."

"There's a Yuletide thought," Corbett replied with a cheer that he did not feel.

Five minutes later Corbett and the police officer returned, Corbett carrying a small holdall. "Just one thing before we go," he said.

"Yes?" asked Rayner hopefully.

"Christmas lunch tomorrow. My sister's expecting me. At East Grinstead. Should I ...?" he did not complete the question.

Rayner completed it for him. "If you'd only tell us everything, Sir, you could join your sister as planned." It was his last throw of the dice.

"But I've nothing more to tell you, Superintendent. Sorry."

"In that case, perhaps you'd like to ring her."

"Thank you. We wouldn't want the turkey spoiled, would we?" Corbett picked up the telephone and dialled a number. "Pen? Hi ... Fine. Well actually not fine. That's why I'm calling ... I'm feeling lousy. Some bug or other. Flu I suppose ... No, honestly I feel it would be best if I stayed here. Try to sweat it out ... No really. I wouldn't want to give it to anyone else ... I know, but one spoiled Christmas is quite enough and the way I feel now I don't think I could eat a thing anyway, let alone a full Christmas lunch ... No, no. I'll be perfectly Okay. I've got Carstairs and plenty of whisky. You've got enough on your plate already. Don't worry. Let's just hope it's only the twenty-four-hour variety ... No, no, don't do that. I'll probably leave it off the hook so I don't get disturbed. I'll call you when I feel up to it ... Sorry your presents will be a bit late ... What? *Sound of Music*? God I hope not. With luck they may be showing *Zulu*. Okay then. Not to worry ... Thanks and to you too. Lots of love. Bye." He replaced the receiver. "Right. That's done. Thank you."

"Why the story, Sir?" asked Rayner, impressed at how genuine the lies had sounded.

"No need to worry her more than necessary," Corbett replied. "Flu's one thing. Being arrested is another. Why spoil her Christmas? In any case, you don't know my sister. If I'd told her what was really happening she'd be banging on the doors of Horsham police station in no time, probably with half a dozen lawyers, her Member of Parliament and a bunch of friends shouting about habeas corpus and waving banners saying something like 'Free the Rudgwick One'. I'm doing you a favour, Superintendent, believe me."

"If you'd like to call your lawyer, you can do so from Horsham. But at this stage I must warn you that the police will not be recommending bail." Rayner spoke with a finality that precluded any discussion of the subject.

Corbett appeared indifferent. "I have no wish to spoil my lawyer's Christmas any more than my sister's. Carstairs will need some stuff. Shall I get it?" He turned to head for the kitchen, followed by one of the uniformed officers.

"We're in the wrong job," remarked Rayner to Zoë. "If we'd gone for the other branch of the law we might have had a less disturbed Christmas."

Corbett and the policeman returned carrying a dog basket, a packet of Smackos, a box of Bonios, a six-pack of Pedigree Chum and a dog bowl. Carstairs followed, carrying a slightly chewed plastic teddy bear which squeaked. "He was given that two years ago," said Corbett, "and it still hasn't lost its squeak." He turned to the policeman. "One Smacko when he comes in after being let out in the morning, a tin of Chum for breakfast, another tin for dinner and a Smacko and a Bonio at bedtime. Oh ... and half a Bonio for NAAFI break after his morning walk. I hope somebody'll give him a morning walk."

"I'll pass it on, Sir," assured the policeman.

"The officer who'll be looking after him lost his own dog quite recently," explained Zoë. "He said he was looking forward to walking a dog again." To her surprise her eyes were damp.

"Right," said Corbett. The heating's turned down. Fire guard." He put the guard in front of the fire. "Ready. I'm all yours, Chief Superintendent."

They crossed into the hall, turning off the drawing room lights as they left. One policeman carried Corbett's holdall, the other Carstairs' kit.

Corbett took down a dog lead from a hook and handed it to the policeman. "You'll be needing that," he said as they filed out of the house. Corbett turned on the alarm, double locked the front door and offered the keys to Rayner. "Will you be needing these? In case you want to search the house?"

Rayner shook his head. "They'll look after them at the station." Then he added, "Would we find anything if we searched the house?"

Corbett shrugged. "I can't answer that, can I? Not without knowing what you're looking for. But feel free. You can search the house as much as you like. I've got nothing to hide." He thought of the tin box at the end of the garden. "The only skeleton I have in the cupboard is the one of Carruthers, Carstairs' predecessor. And that's not in a cupboard. He's buried at the end of the garden."

That was a nice touch, he thought. Yes, he liked that very much. He mustn't let them get him down. Maintenance of morale. One of the main principles of war. That was the most important thing now. Maintenance of morale.

They travelled in separate cars, Corbett and Carstairs in the police car with the two officers and the driver. Corbett had proffered his wrists to be handcuffed but the policeman shook his head. "That won't be necessary, Sir," he said and Corbett felt that he had won another small victory.

In the other car Rayner, Zoë and Roberts drove in silence for a while. Eventually, Zoë remarked, "Well, you gave him every chance, Sir."

"Yes," replied Rayner. "I'm just sorry he didn't want to take it."

"Me too," said Zoë. "He just doesn't seem to care."

"That's the trouble," Rayner agreed. "He cares about his dog. And his sister. Even about his lawyer. Plus the English language, presumably. But he simply doesn't care about himself."

"Do you know what I think, Sir?" Zoë said thoughtfully. "I think he's been like that since his wife died. I think he cared for her. And then, suddenly, she wasn't there. He didn't have her to care for any more. And if he couldn't care for her he wasn't going to care for himself either. Some kind of self-punishment."

"You think he blames himself for her death?"

"Not exactly, Sir. But perhaps he blames himself for being alive."

"Not suicidal, surely!" Rayner protested.

"No, I don't think so. He just doesn't give a damn about what happens to him. You could call it unselfish in a way, I suppose. He thinks of other people but he needs someone to care for – really care for."

"And to care for him too."

"Yes."

"And the only one he's got is Carstairs," mused Rayner. "You'd better make damned sure that whoever's looking after him takes good care of him."

At the Horsham police station Corbett was taken through the reception and custody procedures. He was searched, as was his holdall. His house keys, wallet and small change were taken into safe keeping. He was allowed to keep his watch and the book on Wellington and the Peninsular Wars as well as the biro and writing pad which he had included with a change of clothing and toilet bag. He was shown into a small but, to his surprise, relatively comfortable-looking cell, containing a single bed with sheets as well as a blanket, a small writing table and upright chair, a wall light by the bed which could be independently operated and, to his relief, a washbasin and lavatory. At least the days of slopping out were gone in Horsham. After five minutes, during which he examined the brick wall, painted in a rather sickly green, the cell door was unlocked and he was taken into another room where Rayner and Sergeant Henderson were waiting. With them was another policeman who, Corbett assumed, was one of the locals.

"Sit down, please, Mr Corbett," said Rayner, indicating a chair. "I hope you find your accommodation acceptable." His voice was not unkind.

"Perfectly acceptable, thank you."

"Good. Now, Mr Corbett, we're not going to charge you straight away. We'd like to give you time to think things over ..."

"I don't need any more time, Chief Superintendent," Corbett interrupted. "I've nothing to think over, particularly as I don't know yet what I'm going to be charged with."

"The charges are likely to range from illegal possession of explosive devices, to conspiring to cause criminal damage, causing injury by explosive, sending an explosive device with intent, conspiring to cause grievous bodily harm and, in all probability, attempted murder."

"Blimey," said Corbett.

"Up to twenty counts on each charge," continued Rayner. "We are holding you in custody pending officially charging you, probably sometime tomorrow."

"Christmas Day," Corbett replied. "How nice."

"Mr Corbett," Rayner went on. "You have caused a great deal of trouble, you have taken up a large amount of the police's time, you have distressed a large number of people, you could have inflicted serious injury and, were it not for police intervention, even death to some of them. Have you anything to say?"

For a few moments there was silence as Corbett looked down at the table and Rayner prayed that the list of charges might just overcome this man's stubbornness. Then Corbett slowly raised his head and looked Rayner straight in the eyes. "Prove it," he said.

Rayner felt his anger rise but held it in check. He thought that in a way Corbett's bravado was a tacit admission of guilt. But it was also a challenge and nothing would be gained by rising to it. Corbett wanted a fight but Rayner wasn't going to give him one. What they needed was a confession, not a verbal punch-up.

"That's it for today, Mr Corbett. I'll see you tomorrow. Until then I ask you again to think things over thoroughly. You're in a very serious position. Are there any questions you'd like to ask me before I go?"

"When do we get to eat in this place?"

Rayner looked at the policeman. "Constable?"

The local man looked at his watch, doubtfully. "They get their tea at six o'clock," he said. "It's half past now. He'll have missed it."

Corbett's heart sank. Tea presumably meant high tea. The next meal would not be until breakfast, God knows how long away. He should have had a bigger lunch.

"Can you fix him up with something?" Rayner asked.

"Might be able to rustle him up a ham sandwich."

Rayner turned to Corbett. "Not exactly a feast, I'm afraid." He tried to make a joke of it. "I did tell you that Carstairs would be eating better than you."

"A ham sandwich will be fine," said Corbett.

* * *

They brought him the sandwich in his cell, served in a cellophane packet on a plastic plate. There was not much ham but a lot of bread. With it came a plastic mug of lukewarm instant coffee, milky, with sugar. Corbett took neither milk nor sugar but said nothing. He tipped the coffee into the lavatory and flushed it away. He sat at the table and munched the sandwich mournfully. This was all bad news. Very bad news. Not the attempted murder charges – he was still fully confident that the police would be unable to prove their case – but the evening meal. That was really bad news. It was still only eight o'clock. The whole night lay ahead. No pre-dinner drink. No proper hot meal. He thought of the fillet steak he had planned for dinner. No television to watch. Morale was definitely falling fast. He had to pull himself together. There was nothing to be gained by feeling sorry for himself. Think positively. The ham sandwich was better than nothing. For months he had been watching television, monitoring everything ceaselessly. Now he could take some time off. Sit back and relax instead of maintaining his constant vigil. Something of a holiday really. He had his book. That would help to pass the time. And he had his ace up his sleeve. Time to play it. That would certainly boost morale. He crossed to the washbasin. Making sure that his body was between the basin and the line of sight of anyone who might be observing through the peephole in the cell door, he opened his sponge bag and took out his toilet gear, including a bottle of aftershave lotion. It was not a very large bottle but he had felt that anything bigger might prove too interesting to an enquiring mind. He unscrewed the top and savoured the smell of the liquid. Whisky. Probably the most important of the preparatory measures he had taken when he had noticed that he was being tailed. Good Scotch whisky. Not a lot, unfortunately, but enough for two reasonable slugs. He poured a tot into the plastic mug and added water from the tap, only a little at first as he did not want to drown it, then, after a delicious testing sip, a little bit more. There was still enough whisky left in the bottle for a nightcap later. He sat back at the table, opened his book and sipped from the mug. Another victory. By no means a small one either. He was beating the system, and with luck the whisky might help him sleep.

* * *

At the front desk the duty sergeant looked up as the constable entered. "How's our visitor?" he asked.
"Sitting reading. No trouble."
"Did he enjoy his sandwich?"
"Dunno. He ate it."
"Did you ask if he wanted a drink?"
"No. If he'd wanted one I reckoned he would have asked, but he didn't," came the reply. "Maybe he's a teetotaller."

CHAPTER THIRTEEN

He had told them that the 81mm mortar was not a pinpoint weapon. It was an area weapon. But they had not listened. From where they had established the mortar troop's baseplate position in Bushey Park the range to the Rugby Union stadium at Twickenham was four thousand metres. From that distance the bombs fired by six mortars would produce a beaten zone of around three hundred by one hundred metres. Each bomb would produce a fragmentation area of around fifty metres from the point where it landed and anyone unprotected within that area would be vulnerable. But even if the main point of impact was bang on the kick-off spot on the halfway line, no bomb would necessarily land smack bang on it. The Prime Minister would probably be pretty well zapped but Corbett couldn't guarantee it one hundred per cent. The Prime Minister was standing on the halfway line. Why was he wearing black referee's kit? This wasn't a football match. He was declaiming very clearly but not loudly enough to be heard by everyone in the stadium, which didn't matter really because the stadium was empty, "I'm a pretty regular kind of guy," over and over again. Corbett heard his own voice giving orders over the radio. "Troop target, charge two, number one ranging, over." Jakey Dobbs' voice acknowledged the instructions back to him over the radio. "Four two hundred, zero lines, fire." Corbett's voice continued, but instead of Jakey's voice it was Ginger Evans', saying, "Six rounds rapid mortar fire, how are the moles, mate?" What the hell was going on? He looked up and suddenly saw that the stadium was not empty at all. It was full to bursting and everyone in it was holding up cards of white cardboard with ASIF printed on them in black capital letters and singing "Swing Low Sweet Chariot". And he was standing in the middle of the pitch wearing nothing but an anorak and underneath it he was stark bollock naked and the anorak had no zip or buttons and anyway it was too short to cover his dingly danglies and there were players in the England strip all over the place and he was looking at a maul and Dawson was whipping the ball out to Jonny Wilkinson only it wasn't a ball, it was an 81mm mortar bomb and he was trying to cover his nakedness but nobody seemed to notice and suddenly there was Carstairs with a ham sandwich in his mouth, making an outside break past two Frenchmen and heading unchecked for the try line but it wasn't a ham sandwich at all, it was a Mark IV thunderflash with the fuse fizzing and then the view was obscured by Sergeant Henderson in full uniform approaching him and saying, "Would you like a ham sandwich, Sir?" and how could he warn everybody that the time of flight of a mortar bomb was thirty seconds and that coming in over the South Stand from Bushey Park there would be thirty-six mortar bombs all due to land in the beaten zone during the next minute, and then in his earphones he heard himself shouting, "Cease firing, I say again, cease firing," to be followed by Rayner's voice saying, "Please think things over thoroughly," and then he realised that the ASIF cards were the lids of the crowd's lunch boxes except that they weren't lunch boxes at all, they were letter bombs and one way or another the whole thing was going to be a complete and utter bloody shambles because the Prime Minister was about to step into a huge runny poop which Carstairs had deposited on the halfway line.

Corbett awoke with a start. Artificial light was entering the cell from beneath the door so that he was just able to make out the shape of the walls and washbasin and table. For a moment he thought that his unfamiliar surroundings were part of his dream, before his conscious brain clicked into gear and he remembered where he was. Corbett did not often dream. When Annie had still been alive he would always remember the occasional dream and tell her as much about it as he could. Frequently they would laugh at some of the more outrageous ones. He wished she was here now, so that he could tell her about Carstairs' poop and the Prime Minister. She would have loved that. Thinking about Annie made him feel sorry for himself. Aware that he should keep the window on her memory closed, he put the thought out of his mind and switched on the light. His watch told him that it was just before 6 a.m. Then he remembered that today was Christmas Day. Merry Christmas, he thought, and then began to feel even more sorry for himself.

This would not do. He got out of bed, peed into the lavatory and then, after a moment's reflection, began to do some physical jerks. He started with a bit of shoulder rolling, followed by trunk twisting. These were the same as his habitual pre-golf warm-up exercises and gave him no trouble. Nor did the knees bending, during which he attempted to keep his back as straight as possible. Then he moved on to the dreaded press-ups, followed by the sit-ups and then, lying flat on his back and raising his legs slowly to a height of forty-five centimetres, he moved his legs astride and back together again before lowering them to the ground, equally slowly. He had not done any of the latter three exercises for as long as he could remember and he was astonished, shocked even, at the creaks and muscle-wrenching feelings that they produced. He regarded himself as reasonably fit for his age, what with golf and gardening and dog walking and rough shooting, but this was clearly not the case. Well, the workout would do him no harm as long as he did not overdo it. He would make a point of making this a part of his normal morning routine in future.

He finished the session with some deep-breathing exercises and then went back to the basin to clean his teeth and shave, using long slow strokes of the razor and going over the stubble for a second time. He was in no hurry. He had nothing else to do. When he had finished he looked at himself in the mirror and felt much better. The depression had left him. His present circumstances were nothing more than a small inconvenience, a temporary setback. By living his life minute by minute and not looking too far ahead into uncertainty, he could retake control. After all, compared with what he had achieved, this present discomfort was a very minor affair. He was in the process of saving and even resurrecting the English language. The road might be a bit bumpy on the way here and there but, so long as he did not take his eye off the objective, he could handle the occasional bump.

He dressed, feeling confident that he was ready to face whatever the day had in store for him, and was about to settle down to Wellington and the Peninsular Wars when he heard sounds of activity beyond the cell door. He checked his watch. It was 7 a.m. Could breakfast be in the offing? He was already missing his early morning tea. He listened at the door for a while but the sounds did not seem to be getting any closer. He went back to Wellington, disappointed. He realised that he was hungry. What did they give you for breakfast at Horsham police station? He looked on the optimistic side. After all, it was Christmas Day. Bacon and eggs? With some fried bread? Maybe even a sausage thrown in? What bliss! And perhaps some toast and marmalade, with a lump of butter which he could spread really thick. Never mind the cholesterol. Let's live a little! Then he looked on the pessimistic side. Porridge. Probably tepid at best. Bread and margarine and some kind of jam if he was lucky. And more milky coffee with sugar. Yuk!

When breakfast finally came it was something of a curate's egg, but without the egg. The tea was strong and hot with not too much milk or sugar. Just how he liked it. It was accompanied by two slices of Mother's Pride, thinly spread with butter and plum jam. At least it was butter. And at least it filled some of the void in his stomach. He wondered why they went to the trouble of spreading the bread for him themselves and then concluded that they did not trust prisoners with a knife, even a plastic one. He thanked the policeman and then remembered to wish him a Merry Christmas, trying not to sound sarcastic in view of the uninspiring breakfast. He received no reply. Ho hum! Never mind. Not the end of the world. He hoped Carstairs had got his morning Smacko and his Pedigree Chum. Then he found himself wondering what the Chief Superintendent was having for breakfast; and that rather pretty Sergeant Henderson. Perhaps she was opening Christmas stockings with her kids. Was she married? He must ask her. He couldn't imagine the Chief Superintendent opening Christmas stockings, though, even if he was married. Ah well! Back to Wellington.

* * *

Rayner had allowed himself a lie-in. It was Christmas Day, after all. He had set the alarm for 7.30 and had brought the mug of tea to Betty in bed, where he joined her with his own mug. They kissed and wished each other a Merry Christmas. Then they reached down and from either side of the bed produced a Christmas stocking which each passed to the other. It was a tradition, a silly one perhaps, but one that they both enjoyed. After the kids had left home Betty had suggested discontinuing it but Rayner would hear of no such thing. Both stockings contained more or less the usual things, which seldom changed from year to year. For Betty, a box of After Eight chocolates, a diary, a pair of oven gloves, two pairs of tights (which she normally took back to the shop after Christmas to exchange for ones that she preferred), two pairs of knickers (ditto), a paperback of some kind, some hand cream, a packet of nail files, an aerosol of hair lacquer, a miniature bottle of gin, an apple, an orange and, in the toe of the stocking a £2 coin. For Rayner, some razor blades, a toothbrush, a tube of smoker's toothpaste, a bag of gold foil-wrapped chocolate coins, a paperback, two pairs of socks, two pairs of underpants, a miniature bottle of whisky, a throwaway lighter and, against Betty's better judgement, a carton of two hundred cigarettes, which she had purchased at French prices and kept hidden in her wardrobe until Christmas. Plus the obligatory apple and orange, which would end up back in the fruit bowl on the kitchen table after breakfast. Each stocking filler was opened with curiosity and delight and comments that good old Father Christmas knew that, "that was just what I wanted."

* * *

Later that morning Zoë put on her police sergeant's uniform, as Rayner had requested. It felt unfamiliar after such a long time in plain clothes, but she was relieved that at least it didn't pinch in too many places. She agreed with Rayner's view that a display of full uniform should be part of their tactics to unsettle Corbett, who had never seen them in full fig before. But full uniform on Christmas Day! It really was a bit much.

"It must be very important," her mother said when Zoë came into the room. "Is it some kind of parade? You look very smart, dear."

"Just a meeting," said Zoë as she adjusted the rug round her mother's legs and checked that the wheelchair was close enough to the side table on which sat the remote control for the television, the mug of coffee and the plate of ginger biscuits. She glanced at her watch. Roberts would arrive any minute. "Now don't forget that the carer will be along in half an hour. It's Mary today. She's got the key as usual and she knows where your lunch is. It's shepherd's pie. Your favourite. We'll have something Christmassy together tonight."

"Yes, dear," replied her mother.

"And I'll be back as soon as I can. And then we'll open some presents and have a nice snug evening together. All right Mum?" She heard the car drive up.

"All right dear," replied Zoë's mother. "And can we have *Casablanca*?"

Zoë looked at the shelf of video cassettes on the wall. "I've already got it out," she said. "And if you'd like *The Maltese Falcon* while I'm out, I've got that out too. The carer will put it on if you ask her."

"Thank you, dear," said her mother. "Now don't you go worrying about me. You go and enjoy yourself. You do look smart."

"Okay, Mum," said Zoë as the doorbell rang. "Love you. See you later."

* * *

Carstairs crashed joyfully through the scrub to retrieve the stick which his new friend had thrown for him. He picked it up and carried it back, tail wagging. What a lovely morning it had been: a romp on his new friend's bed; lots of pieces of Christmas wrapping paper to tear up; a bone with a red ribbon round it, the same ribbon that was now attached to his collar. And as for breakfast, well! Not only the usual meat from the usual tin, but some chopped-up roast potato, some alphabetti spaghetti, a bit of ham fat and some broad beans. Five-star stuff. When they got back to his new home after their walk, Carstairs wagged his tail optimistically for his NAAFI break and then sat down looking as appealing as possible. And here it was. A NAAFI break to end all NAAFI breaks in the form of a large ham bone. He followed his friend out into the garden, where the bone was handed to him. He lay down on the wet grass and began to gnaw. He did not mind that the grass was wet. Everything in the garden was lovely.

* * *

Rayner, Zoë and Roberts arrived at Horsham police station just before midday. They made their number with the duty officer and were relieved, though not surprised, to hear that Corbett had given no trouble during the night. Rayner and Zoë went into the interview room, where Rayner produced the video and inserted it into the player. With the officer assigned to them they rehearsed the mechanics and timing three times, after which Rayner pronounced himself satisfied. The cameras and tape recorder were loaded and checked. Everything was in working order. They were ready to go.

At 12.15 Corbett was brought into the interview room. He started to say "Merry Christmas" but pulled up short when he saw Rayner and Zoë in full uniform. "I say," he exclaimed. "Look at you! The whole shooting match! Sergeant, you look absolutely ... gorgeous! Is all this in my honour, or is there some other special occasion? Or perhaps it's rig of the day for Christmas."

Zoë felt a blush coming on and turned her head away hoping that Rayner would not notice.

"Good morning, Mr Corbett," Rayner said dryly. "I hope you spent a comfortable night. Please sit down."

"Perfectly comfortable, thank you." Corbett sat facing them.

"Yesterday evening I expressed the hope that you would think things over in view of the seriousness of your position," Rayner continued. "Have you ... thought things over?"

"Yes," said Corbett.

"Is there anything you wish to tell me?"

"No."

"Is there anything you wish to add to your previous statements?" Rayner kept his voice level.

"I wasn't aware of having made any previous statements per se. So far as I'm concerned we've merely had a number of conversations. You asked me a lot of questions. I answered them, as best I could."

"Do you have any questions you wish to ask me?"

"Is Carstairs all right?"

Rayner ignored the reply. "Mr Corbett, you are now going to be formally charged. You are not obliged to say anything but it is my duty to warn you that anything you do say ..."

"Yes, yes," Corbett broke in, "will be taken down, etcetera, etcetera. Go ahead Chief Superintendent. I have nothing to say except that nobody seems to have told the Horsham police about providing hearty breakfasts for the condemned man."

"You're not condemned yet, Mr Corbett. You'll have to wait for the judge and jury to do that." Then Rayner charged him.

The charges were as summarised by Rayner the previous day. When he came to the end of the list, Rayner again asked Corbett whether he had anything to say and again Corbett said that he had not. Rayner told him that he would be remanded in custody pending the magistrate's court hearing in two days' time and Corbett nodded, making no comment.

Then Rayner relaxed and smiled kindly. "Well, that's the formalities over with, Mr Corbett." He looked at his watch. "It's lunchtime. I'm afraid I'm not up to date with what they give you for lunch here, particularly on Christmas Day. Can you enlighten us, Constable?" He looked at the local policeman.

"Turkey, I think, Sir," the man replied.

"Really? Hot or cold?"

"Oh, hot, Sir."

"You're in luck, Mr Corbett. Enjoy. I'll see you later this afternoon. Right Constable, thank you."

The Horsham policeman gestured to Corbett, who rose and was led out of the room. Back in his cell he eyed the plate of turkey with potatoes, sprouts and thick gravy. Well, beggars can't be choosers, he thought. As he ate he wondered how long they had cooked the sprouts. Then he wondered why Rayner had said that he would be seeing him later that afternoon.

Rayner and Zoë changed into their plain clothes, declined the duty officer's invitation to join him in the police station for Christmas lunch and picked up Roberts before strolling towards the Carfax where the notice outside the Brown Bear offered "Xmas fare with beer or wine" for £12.95. They went in and Rayner stated that, it being Christmas Day, the drinks and the lunch were on him. "And me driving as usual," said Roberts disconsolately. They declined the Brown Bear's offer of Xmas fare and opted for sandwiches instead. Rayner would not have minded the steak and kidney pie which was also on the menu, but bore in mind that he needed to keep his powder dry for Betty's Christmas dinner. Zoë would have liked something more sustaining than the BLT which she ordered, but she remembered that as the morning had worn on, her uniform had begun to feel somewhat tighter than it had when she put it on earlier. Roberts liked roast beef sandwiches, with plenty of mustard, as much as anything in the world. So he ordered two, and was glad to see Rayner paying up without complaint. They raised their glasses and wished one another a Merry Christmas again. Zoë added, "Break a leg this afternoon, Sir."

When his cell door opened at 2.45, Corbett was surprised to see Rayner standing there instead of the usual Horsham man. He noted that the uniform had been replaced by corduroys, a polo-necked jersey and a tweed jacket, but made no comment.

"May I come in?" Rayner enquired politely and, Corbett thought, rather incongruously in the circumstances.

"Be my guest." Corbett gestured to the chair and sat on the bed.

Rayner looked at the Wellington book. "Enjoying it?" he asked, remaining standing.

"Very much."

"So did I." Rayner paused. "How was lunch?"

"All right, I suppose," said Corbett.

"I had to restrict myself to a sandwich. My wife's cooking Christmas dinner so I'll need to put up a good show this evening."

"Lucky old you," said Corbett. "More fun than a police cell, I should imagine."

Rayner sat down and looked at Corbett steadily. "You don't have to stay here, you know. You could spend Christmas night in the comfort of your own home. Or at your sister's." It was half a bribe, half a plea. He wanted so much to save Corbett the pain and the humiliation that they had planned for him.

"Really?" said Corbett. "I was under the impression that I was stuck here until the hearing the day after tomorrow. And, no doubt, locked up somewhere else after that, awaiting trial."

"It doesn't have to be like that," Rayner replied quietly. "These ... silly ... unnecessary things you've been up to. If you'd just tell us what happened and why. Come clean ..."

"You're still asking me for a confession?" Corbett sounded almost accusing.

"Yes. Look, if you give us a statement confessing to the charges it will change things enormously. With an undertaking of good behaviour the police would be prepared to allow bail - straight away. And again at the Magistrate's Court. We can't drop the charges, of course, but given a confession we could probably reduce them, and then, at your trial, a plea of guilty would almost certainly mean that you'd get off with a pretty light sentence. Possibly even a suspended one. All you need to do to make that happen is to give us a confession."

"Why should I confess to something I haven't done?" asked Corbett.

Rayner hid his disappointment. The last thing he wanted was to destroy this man. But now he was left no choice. "Okay," he said. Then he added brightly. "I was on my way home but then I realised that I'd miss the Queen's speech on the box, so I thought I'd watch it here. Care to join me?" He mentally crossed his fingers as he waited for Corbett's answer. They could not compel him to watch if he did not want to.

"Why not?" Corbett replied, sealing his own fate.

"This way," said Rayner and he ushered Corbett out of the cell. He pointed down the now familiar corridor and brought up the rear. "Straight along and second on the right," said Rayner and as they passed the first turning he nodded to the policeman waiting at the end. The policeman nodded back and disappeared from view. Corbett hesitated at the door of the interview room and Rayner gestured to him to go ahead.

Zoë was already there, also in plain clothes. She gave Corbett a welcoming smile and pointed to a chair. "Come and join us," she said. "She'll be on in a minute."

Corbett nearly told her that he thought she looked much better in uniform, but decided that it would not be a very gallant remark to make. He smiled back at Zoë, thanked her and settled down in the chair she had pointed out. A local policeman was sitting in a third chair and Rayner sat next to Corbett but a few feet away from him.

On the television screen they were just coming to the end of the rest of the weather for Christmas Day and Boxing Day. Then some brief trailers of programmes scheduled for the evening and the next day followed. Rayner sat back to enjoy Mark Telford's masterpiece; except that he knew that he was not going to enjoy it.

An announcer said, "Her Majesty the Queen." The national anthem was accompanied by a shot of the sovereign's ensign flying above Windsor Castle. Rayner waited to see whether Corbett was going to stand for the anthem but he remained seated. Even for Corbett those days were long gone. There was a fade-out of the ensign, which was replaced by a picture of the Queen seated informally on a regency chair behind a writing desk. She was wearing a royal blue twinset with a pearl necklace and earrings. She began to speak. Corbett, Zoë and the policeman watched the Queen. Rayner watched Corbett.

"Nearly four years ago," she began, "my family and I, and many of you, celebrated the fiftieth year since my accession as Queen in 1952, the Golden Jubilee. A year later, 1953, was the year of my coronation and six years before that, in 1947, Prince Philip and I were married." The Queen's voice faded and they were looking at scenes of the coronation and of her wedding day as she continued to speak. "I have those and many other happy memories on which I can look back, and many of us will have memories of our own as we have lived out our lives. In doing so we, of course, realise that as we get older we shall have fewer years left to which we can look forward. And, because we are human and suffer from human frailties, which sadly are likely to increase with age, it is sometimes easy to feel like there is not really much to which we can look forward."

Rayner saw Corbett tense and quiver for a moment. Then his body relaxed slightly as if he couldn't believe what he had just heard, but his fists remained clenched and his knuckles were white. One down and eight to go, thought Rayner, and he wondered how many of the eight would be needed.

The Queen's face returned to the screen as she carried on. "If we sometimes have those feelings, we should perhaps bear in mind that less than one hundred years ago the average man or woman in this country could not expect to live much beyond what would today be regarded as early middle age. Today, thanks to the advances made by science, medicine and hygiene, we enjoy a far longer lifespan than our predecessors. And I do mean enjoy. In our later years our own enjoyment of what life still has to offer us can bring happiness not only to us but also to those around us." The Queen was replaced by a shot of Queen Elizabeth the Queen Mother at Sandown and Cheltenham racecourses, as her voice went on. "Even during the final years of her long and active life, my mother enjoyed herself to the full. She was so energetic that even her grandchildren told her that she should slow down because they sometimes felt like they couldn't keep up with her."

Rayner watched as the second blow struck home and Corbett's body flinched and then hunched as if he had been punched in the solar plexus. A gasp of shock escaped from his mouth in a hiss. He appeared to be trying to speak but no words came out. He was a man in pain. Rayner saw that Zoë was no longer looking at the screen but at Corbett. Was it his imagination, or did her eyes seem damp?

The Queen came back on screen. "I often feel that gathering together at Christmas time represents an important opportunity to renew the ties that bind the different generations and sometimes to strengthen or to repair them. For much of the year we are too busy to have the time to listen to others or to give them the attention that they deserve or seek or need. The young, at school or university, learning new things, facing the pressure of exams, the parents at work and maintaining the home and meeting the family's needs, the elderly, sometimes worried about making ends meet and about old age, are all preoccupied with their own concerns." Here it comes, thought Rayner. "The young have their own views on the world but feel like their elders don't want to hear them. To the parents what the young have to say sounds like they are being criticised. To the elderly and retired it seems like nobody wants to listen to them any more."

With the first of the triple combination of blows, Corbett's body coiled like a spring. With the second he was on his feet, shaking from head to foot. With the third he let loose what sounded like an animal cry of pain, rage and despair. "Noooo! Noooo! Stop it! Stop it! Noooo!"

Rayner's hand moved to the remote control to bring the agony to an end, but then he realised that Corbett was shouting not at him but at the Queen as she continued to speak Mark Telford's lines.

"I believe that the different generations should listen to one another and learn from one another." Her words were almost drowned by Corbett's continued howls of anguish, but Rayner almost knew them by heart anyway. "Despite our differences in age and experience it's not like the generations have nothing to offer one another."

"Stop it! Stop it! Stop it!!" Corbett was screaming now, his whole body wracked with paroxysms of agony and horror. Tears of frustration and misery were pouring down his cheeks. Grim-faced, Rayner heard Zoë's breaking voice added to the tumult. "Please, Sir. Please!" He saw that she too was crying openly now. He pressed the remote control "off" button and the screen went blank.

For a few moments Rayner let Corbett stand there. With the departure of the Queen the shouts turned to huge deep sobs of uncontrollable grief and Corbett's chest was heaving as he gasped for air. Rayner stood and, despite the risk of close proximity, put his arm round Corbett. "It's all right," he said. "It's all right."

For perhaps half a minute they stood there, with Rayner repeating his words of reassurance and tightening his embrace as gradually Corbett's body relaxed and he pressed it against Rayner's frame, and his sobs diminished to whimpers of unutterable desolation as he clung to his tormentor for comfort. Then, very gently, Rayner released his hold and withdrew a fraction.

"It's over," he said. "It's all over."

Corbett looked up slowly. "Did you hear her?" he moaned. "Did you hear her? Like! Like! Like!"

"It's all over," Rayner repeated.

"What the hell was she doing? Why? Why? Why? Who the hell does she think she is?"

"She's the Queen." Rayner's voice was gentle and soothing. "She was giving her Christmas message."

"But you heard her. It was awful. Awful. After all I've done. After all I've achieved."

"What did you do, Mr Corbett?"

Corbett was not listening. "Ruined. Wasted. Thrown away. All that work. All that effort."

Rayner repeated the question, but kindly. "What did you do, Mr Corbett?" Then he added, "What work? What effort?"

"The Queen. The bloody Queen, of all people!" Corbett's voice began to rise in anger.

"Now, now. Calm down. Everything's all right now."

"All right?" Corbett half laughed in bitterness. "A Queen who can't even speak the bloody Queen's bloody English. After all I've done." His voice broke in to another despairing sob. "After all I've done."

"What did you do, Mr Corbett?" Rayner asked the question a third time.

"You know. Of course you know. I was saving the English language. You saw it. The newspapers. The television. The radio. They were beginning to do it right. Speaking, writing. It was all thanks to me. You heard. You saw. You must have. I know you did. We talked about it. I was saving the English language. Wasn't I?"

"No," replied Rayner. He spoke softly, but the single syllable was like a death knell.

"No? What do you mean, 'no'? Are you suggesting it just happened by itself? No way. If it hadn't been for me they'd all still be writing or speaking ..." Corbett paused for a moment and then laughed. "Like the bloody Queen. It was me. I was the one. I did it."

For a fourth time Rayner tried. "Just what did you do, Mr Corbett?"

"I persuaded them. The worst offenders. And it worked. You've seen it for yourself."

"How did you persuade them?"

"Oh for God's sake," Corbett's impatience was tangible. "You know perfectly well how I persuaded them."

"Do I?" Rayner gave a last gentle prod.

"Of course you bloody well do. You arrested me for it, after all."

"Would you like to tell me how?"

"Oh God! If you insist. The turds. The thunderflashes. The letter bombs. You know. All that stuff. I did it. It was me."

"Thank you Mr Corbett. Would you be prepared to sign a statement to that effect?" Rayner did not allow any excitement to creep into his voice. He saw Zoë, dry-eyed now as she put a handkerchief back into her handbag, waiting anxiously for Corbett's response.

"Oh Christ!" Corbett gave a resigned sigh. "What the hell. Why not, if it makes your life easier. My bloody Christmas present to you, if you like."

"Thank you."

Rayner, Zoë and the policeman relaxed. Rayner nodded to the policeman, who rose and left the room.

"It was the only way, you see," Corbett continued. He sounded as if he was trying to reason with them. "The only way. I'd tried everything else. I'd written to *The Times* I don't know how often. They never published anything I said. So ... in the end ... the only choice was ... direct action. But it worked. Or it was working until ... How was I to know that the Queen ...? But it did work with all the others, didn't it?"

"No," said Rayner, and the death knell tolled again.

Oh God, thought Zoë, he's not going to go on, is he? We've got the confession. Isn't that enough? Can't we leave it at that? He doesn't need to destroy the man.

Rayner saw the look on Zoë's face and knew what she was thinking. He was tempted, sorely tempted, to take things no further. They had got what they wanted, on tape and on camera. Corbett's statement was being prepared now and, subject to any necessary amendments, he would soon sign it and that would be that. They could all go home, even Corbett. They would meet again when he came to trial.

But Rayner wanted more than that. He understood Corbett's aims. He even sympathised with them. It was the means that he could not condone and Corbett had to be made to understand and accept that. If Corbett believed that, subject to the small matter of the Queen, he was in the process of achieving his aims, then he would think that his means were justified. Rayner had to show Corbett that the dog turds, thunderflashes and letter bombs had, in fact, achieved nothing. If he did not disabuse him now, Corbett might feel that but for police intervention he could have achieved more. His life would be centred on resentment, not at his punishment but at his assumption that the police had prevented him from completing his mission. Who could tell where that state of mind might lead? Further offences? A life empty of anything but resentment? A pointless life that no longer had any meaning, or worse, any value? A life that, in that dangerous state of mind, Corbett might choose to end? Rayner knew that he had to be cruel to be kind.

"Please sit down, Mr Corbett," Rayner said.

Corbett sat, still in shock, haggard now from what he had just been through.

"What do you mean? Of course it worked." His voice contained uncertainty now. "What I did ... well it may have been ... wrong ... by your yardstick but you saw the results. Right across every arm of the media. No one can take that away from me. Not even you."

"I can," said Rayner. "And I will." He put up his hand as Corbett made as if to interrupt. "No. Please listen carefully to what I'm going to tell you."

Then Rayner began to explain, and, in doing so, to bring the whole edifice of Corbett's fantasies tumbling down. He explained how the victims of Corbett's campaign had no idea why they had been chosen. Whether it was just the simple ASIF message by itself, or whether it was accompanied by a dog turd or a thunderflash, it meant nothing to any of them. Nothing. Some nutter had it in for them for a reason that totally escaped them. He described how even the police, countrywide, including his team, were equally at a loss.

"We were barking up the wrong tree, you see, while your chosen targets weren't barking up any tree at all. We thought, we assumed, that ASIF stood for something. It could have stood for anything, although, given the current climate, we were inclined to the view that we were dealing with some kind of terrorist outfit. We concocted any number of organisations that it might stand for. Arabian Society of Islamic Fundamentalists. Arab Socialist Invasion Front. You name it. We were wracking our brains and using up God knows how much computer time, but we didn't turn up anything at all. We even tried Aberdeen Supports Individual Freedoms." He laughed, partly at the memory, partly to try to jolly Corbett along. Corbett did not join in.

"Then, thanks to Sergeant Henderson here," Rayner gestured towards Zoë, "we realised that ASIF could be two words. As if. When you stuck the newsprint letters on the paper, you see, they were often spaced as if they were all together. But reading them as two separate words – as if – put a totally different perspective on things."

Rayner went through the task they had faced in trying to find what Corbett's targets had in common, the TV vigils, the newspaper readings, trying to find a link to add to the fact that the targets were all, in one way or another, media-related. What they had found was not the presence of the words 'as if' but their absence. They found plenty of examples of 'like'. And then they put two and two together.

"Then," said Rayner, "it was a question of taking a punt. The first person I tried was Mandy Drake, and you saw the results for yourself. We hoped that if she used 'as if' instead of 'like' on her programme, the attacks on her would cease and our theory would be proven, particularly if the attacks continued on the other targets who had not changed their ways. Of course we then had the initial upset with the arrival of your letter bombs. We feared that we were barking up another wrong tree until we realised that the bombs must have been mailed before Mandy did her stuff. Then your flowers and message arrived and we knew that our theory was correct. After that it was just a question of contacting the other targets and suggesting that if they didn't want to be pestered by any other unwelcome things coming through their letter box they had better improve their written or spoken English. You know the rest."

Corbett nodded, stricken.

Rayner continued. "So although at that stage we didn't yet know your identity, we were able to take the steps necessary to ensure that the attacks were discontinued. And it worked. It would be true to say that a by-product of all this was a considerable improvement in the standard of English within the media. But I'm afraid, Mr Corbett, that that was due to our actions, not to yours. If you believe that you and what you did had a direct impact on the English language you're kidding yourself. It was our intervention that did it, not yours. Although I suppose it would be true to say that if it had not been for your actions we would not have had to intervene, so that indirectly ..."

"So I've achieved nothing after all," Corbett broke in miserably. "Absolutely nothing."

"I'm sorry." Rayner sounded as genuine as he could.

"What a bloody shambles," whispered Corbett, almost to himself as much as to them.

"Actually," said Rayner, again trying to bring some cheer into the proceedings, "You can take the credit for one of them. That bloke from the *Guardian*. Nothing I could do would persuade him. He more or less told us to get stuffed." He paused, then added, "We loved the rat. It was brilliant. A great idea, wasn't it, Zoë?"

Zoë wrinkled her nose and then, thinking of the incongruity of it all, started to giggle. "I wish I'd seen his face when that arrived," she said. "That made him improve his English pretty quick."

To Rayner's and Zoë's intense pleasure a slow, half-smile crossed Corbett's face. "Carstairs should take the credit for that," he said. "It was his idea." Then he looked directly at Rayner. "How did you find me?" he asked.

"An anonymous phone call."

"Aha. I thought so." Corbett sounded bitter.

"Do you reckon you know who it was?" asked Zoë.

"A friend of mine. Or I should say a former friend."

"He was only doing what he thought was right," she responded. "And we would have caught up with you pretty soon anyway thanks to Ruth at the flower shop."

"Ah yes. I'd forgotten about her."

"And once we'd got to you and found that you matched the descriptions we'd already received ... well ... it was only a matter of time."

Corbett gave a deep sigh of resignation. "I suppose so."

Rayner intervened again. "Look, Mr Corbett. So far as improving the standards of English is concerned, I'm on your side. It would be marvellous if we could somehow turn back the clock and eradicate some of the ghastliness that has been allowed to creep in. It would be lovely to have decent English spoken on the BBC again. They can't all be like John Snagge, but it would be nice if some of them were. It's not your aims that I'm against, it's your methods."

"So what do you suggest? The position of Director General of the BBC's already spoken for."

"Well ... you could try writing to the press," Rayner suggested sympathetically.

"I told you, I've already tried that. Not a single letter's ever been published. Anyway, I suppose I'll soon be in prison. How many letters are you allowed to write from there? Particularly to the press?"

"I don't think you need be inside for very long. Perhaps not at all if they give you a suspended sentence."

"Keep trying, Mr Corbett," Zoë added in support. "Don't give up."

"What's the point?" asked Corbett in a defeated voice.

"As a matter of fact," said Rayner, "with luck there might be some press coverage of your case. Of your trial. If would make a good story. Man imprisoned, or whatever, for trying to save the English language. If you handled it right you might get just the sort of exposure you need. Articles, perhaps interviews in the press, on the television even."

"Hmm," said Corbett.

"And there are organisations like the Plain English Society and the Queen's English Society. You could try joining those."

"After what we saw on the television a few minutes ago?"

"I'm going to come back to that in a minute," said Rayner. "Or what about writing a book on the subject? You said you'd been reading Lynne Truss's one. That's caused quite a bit of interest. Why not try it?"

Corbett gave a sad smile. "If I end up inside, perhaps it would help pass the time."

"John Bunyan wrote *Pilgrim's Progress* in prison," Zoë contributed.

"So he did." Corbett nodded slowly. "So he did."

Then Rayner had a brainwave. "I'll tell you what," he said. "There's something else that you might find interesting. You could kill several birds with one stone. Help people who are illiterate; promote higher standards of English; and, come to think of it, you'd be doing me a favour to boot."

"How?" enquired Corbett.

Rayner explained the Step by Step Reading Plan. "My wife's part of a team that's promoting the project. Countrywide if all goes well."

"Hmm. I see the point," said Corbett. "And by involving me, assuming I'm going to serve time, you'd be setting a thief to catch a thief."

Rayner shook his head. "I hadn't thought of it in that way. It just seemed to me that it would perhaps give you a mission in life. Not far removed from the mission that you've already adopted. Someone with a love of English, helping those who don't have your advantages. Grass roots stuff."

"Maybe."

"It wouldn't necessarily be easy. My wife and her associates tend to come up against a lot of stonewalling amongst the prison authorities. They have to be won over. It's a challenge and it takes time and patience. I'd put you down as someone who likes a challenge."

"I'll think about it."

"Good," Rayner smiled. "No hurry, but if you'd like to get involved I can arrange for my wife to explain the nuts and bolts to you."

The policeman re-entered the room carrying a sheaf of papers. "Thank you," said Rayner, taking them, and he proceeded to read the contents quickly. The others waited in silence. Then Rayner looked up. "This is the statement that we've drafted." He handed the papers to Corbett. "Here you are. Have a look. If you'd like to make any changes or add anything, go ahead. Take your time."

Corbett took the papers and read through them. When he came to the end he said, "Looks Okay to me." Then he added, "You said you were going to come back to the Queen's message."

"Oh yes," said Rayner, hoping that he would be able to choose his words carefully. He thought for a moment and then started to explain. He just hoped that this final denouement would not hurt Corbett even more than the earlier one. "I'm afraid that ... well, let's say that what I'm going to tell you is good news and bad news."

"What do you mean by that?" asked Corbett. "Are you going to ask me whether I want the bad news or the good news first?"

"I'll start again. I'm going to tell you something which will probably make you very angry but which, when you think about it, could make you very happy. I just hope that the happiness will outweigh the anger, if not at once, then in time."

"Curiouser and curiouser," said Corbett. "Go on then."

"What you saw on the television just now was not the Queen's Christmas message."

"Wasn't the Queen's message? Of course it was."

"No. It was a fake. I'm sorry ..."

"A fake? What do you mean " a fake?" Corbett asked in puzzlement.

"It was a tape, put together by a team of police experts. I won't go into the details of how it was done, but the long and short of it is that what you saw was not what you thought. And, most importantly, the Queen's words were not her own, even though they appeared to be. She has not just broadcast a speech to the public saying 'like' instead of 'as if'. Apart from the people in this room and the people who put the tape together nobody else has seen it. Or will ever see it. She's probably just finished giving her real message about now."

As Rayner spoke, Corbett's puzzled look was replaced by one of gradual enlightenment. Then his jaw tensed as he realised the enormity of what he had just been told.

"My God!" he said slowly. "You bastard. You deliberately, callously, put me through all that ... that pain ... that agony ..." He could not go on. He shook his head in disbelief.

"I'm sorry. It was done with the best of intentions. But I agree it was cruel."

"Cruel! Christ!" Corbett spat out the words. "Why? Why? Why?"

"We wanted to see your reactions ..."

"Reactions!"

"And to get your confession."

"Ah! My confession." Corbett spoke the words softly. "Ah yes. My confession."

"I regret very much having put you through that ordeal." Rayner put as much sincerity into his voice as he could.

"You fooled me. You were just playing with me." Corbett was accusing now.

"If you had come clean sooner we would not have used the tape. I can understand your feelings now, but if you can manage to look beyond them I hope that at least you'll be pleased to know that the Queen did not actually say the things that upset you. I'm sure that she never has and never will. The Queen's English is safe with the Queen."

"Yes. I suppose that's true," said Corbett, and added, "Thank God for that." Then he looked at the papers in his hand. "And if, after all that, I refuse to sign this?"

"We have it all on camera and tape," said Rayner.

"But in a court of law ..." Corbett began, but Rayner cut him off.

"And I think you'll find that Carstairs is waiting to go home."

Corbett thought for a few seconds, as Rayner and Zoë watched him anxiously. Then he said, "Right," and signed the statement. "Initial at the bottom of each page?" he asked.

"Please," said Rayner.

Corbett complied and then looked up at Rayner. "I don't like what you did to me, Chief Superintendent. But ... you're a bloody good policeman. You too Sergeant." He held out the papers to Rayner, who took them.

"Thank you, Sir." Zoë was not sure whether Rayner was thanking Corbett for the compliment or for the papers, but she was pleased to hear the 'Sir'.

"What now?" asked Corbett.

"A few formalities and we can all bugger off home," said Rayner cheerfully. "There's still a bit of Christmas left." Then his voice became serious. "But you do understand, don't you, that I'm putting myself out on a limb for you? No more nastinesses through letter boxes or whatever. Not even any rats, I'm afraid."

"I understand," Corbett replied.

"And one more thing, Sir," said Zoë, adding her own 'Sir' as a contribution to the truce. "We know what you've been through today. Are you ... Okay now? Will you be Okay at home? On your own?"

"I'm not sure that I would have been if that ... if that Queen's message had been genuine." Corbett shuddered. "But, as things stand ... yes, I'll be all right."

"Nothing silly then?"

"Nothing silly."

"Right," said Rayner, getting to his feet. "There'll be a few formalities to go through and you'll need to pick up your belongings. Constable, can you do the necessary?"

"This way, please," the constable said. Corbett followed him to the door, then stopped and turned towards Rayner and Zoë.

"Is that it then?" he asked.

Rayner nodded. "I suppose it is," he said. "We'll meet again in court, If not before. Merry Christmas Mr Corbett." He hesitated and then held out his hand.

Corbett stood for a moment before taking a step forward and, to Zoë's delight, taking the proffered hand and shaking it. "Merry Christmas, Chief Superintendent." Then he turned to Zoë, holding out his hand in turn. "Merry Christmas, Sergeant."

Zoë felt the strength and confidence of Corbett's grip. "Merry Christmas, Sir," she said. "And good luck."

Five minutes later Corbett had cleared out his cell and retrieved the rest of his belongings from the security desk. The duty officer assured him that a patrol car was on its way to take him back to Rudgwick and before Corbett could enquire about Carstairs there was a commotion outside and suddenly the dog was bounding in, with a red ribbon decorating his collar, tail wagging furiously and giving a combination of snorts and whimpers at the joy of being reunited.

Corbett hugged Carstairs and looked up, smiling. "Something tells me that he's had a rather better Christmas day than I have," he said to the duty officer. "Come on, Carstairs. Let's go home."

CHAPTER FOURTEEN

Later that evening Rayner excused himself from the family ritual of opening the Christmas presents. Earlier he had taken leave of Roberts and Zoë and thanked them for a job well done. They had earned what remained of their Christmas break. There was only one thing left to do to bring this stage of the case to a close. He went into the study and picked up the telephone to call the Commissioner.

The Commissioner was irritated to be called away from the cosy pre-dinner drinks with his wife, daughter, son-in-law and son-in-law's parents. The son-in-law's father was a television producer. One of the series for which he was responsible was the hugely popular, "The Law and You", whose presenter was rumoured to be thinking of moving to another channel. With retirement just round the corner an invitation to be the new presenter of the series would be more than welcome, thought the Commissioner. A nice little earner to accompany the knighthood which, if he played his cards right and if there was any justice in the world, would be coming his way when he finally hung up his uniform.

"Yes?" said the Commissioner into the telephone, not bothering to disguise his irritation.

"Rayner here, Sir. Sorry to disturb you."

Briefly Rayner updated the Commissioner and said that he was glad to be able to tell him that the ASIF case had been successfully concluded. Subject to the trial, of course, but given that the suspect had made a full confession the outcome of the trial was not in doubt.

"Right," the Commissioner said. "I'll tell the Home Secretary." Before ringing off he remembered to add, "Oh ... and well done."

"Anything important, darling?" his wife asked, when he rejoined the drinks party.

"No," replied the Commissioner. "Not particularly."

* * *

Zoë sat in her armchair in front of the television, watching Claude Raines rounding up the usual suspects for the umpteenth time. Beside her, her mother had been asleep for the past twenty minutes but Zoë knew better than to turn off the video before *Casablanca* had finished. It did not matter very much anyway. She had not really been watching it. Her mind had been elsewhere. In a few minutes she would help her mother up to bed before going back to the kitchen to do the washing-up. But for the moment she was trying to come to terms with the feeling of guilt that she had experienced when she realised that she had been wondering how her mother would react to a dead rat or even a Mark IV thunderflash being shoved through the letter box.

* * *

Corbett sat in his drawing room, pondering. On arriving back home he had thanked the police driver for the lift and again agreed to abide by the pre-arraignment bail conditions set by Rayner. He had turned on the central heating, lit the drawing room fire, poured himself a large whisky, fed Carstairs, despite guessing that the dog had already eaten more than enough for one day, and called his sister to say that he was feeling a bit better now and would be in touch again over the Christmas holiday. He had taken a left over portion of shepherd's pie out of the freezer and put it in the oven where it was now defrosting at a low temperature.

While he waited for his Christmas dinner to be ready he sat with Carstairs at his feet. He had not bothered to switch on any of the television sets. To do so would have been too easy and might have tempted him to fall back into a routine that he knew he would have to abandon. Instead he had put on a CD. Initially he had chosen Mozart's Requiem, but as he listened to it he found that, despite the beauty of the music, the subject matter had brought depressing thoughts. He knew the direction in which they might lead. He knew that Annie would not approve. Then he remembered Sergeant Henderson's earlier remarks about his not doing anything silly and thought that she would not approve either. So he had taken off the Mozart and replaced him with Fats Waller.

He had a wide choice of subjects on which to ponder. Once he had forced the depression out of his mind he thought about what Rayner had suggested. The man was ruthless, of course, and could reasonably be described as a shit of the first order after what he had done with that video. If he worked for the *Guardian* newspaper he would certainly deserve a dead rat through his letter box. But, it had to be said, he was only doing his job and he had succeeded and there was nothing to be gained by dwelling on the pain of the afternoon's events. On the other hand, if you looked to the future, as Annie and perhaps even Sergeant Henderson would want, then what Rayner had said made quite a lot of sense. Corbett was not quite sure about the Plain English Society or the Queen's English Society. Worthy organisations though they might be, they had little enough success to show when it came to upholding the standards of the English language. But the possibility of media coverage of his forthcoming trial was certainly worth thinking about. This could present the opportunity of furthering his cause which had so far been denied him. Had his past efforts to communicate with the media about the falling standards of English not been ignored, he would not have had to resort to the campaign of direct action which had landed him in this mess. If he seriously asked himself whether countless hours of watching what was often a load of rubbish on the box, or reading the painful prose of a lot of tabloid hacks, had been enjoyable, the answer would have to be "No". He supposed he had got a bit of a buzz out of delivering dog turds and thunderflashes through people's letter boxes but was that really him? Was that the true Alan Corbett? More like the British National Front! Yes, he would certainly want to explore the trial coverage avenue. It could lead to great things.

Then there was the Step by Step Reading thing. Not to be able to read, and therefore probably unable to write either – that must be a terrible thing. Awful, particularly as half the illiterate prisoners were probably unwilling to own up to their illiteracy; which in turn would probably make them even more aggressive in their attempts to cover up their deficiency and would in all probability lead them back to crime. They certainly needed help. That would be something worthwhile to get involved in. He wondered whether the project might allow him to teach a bit of grammar, too. Just imagine. All those ex-cons speaking proper English! Saying 'as if' instead of 'like'!

Finally there was the book. Another interesting suggestion from Rayner. A book about the English language, treading in the footsteps of Lynne Truss and John Humphrys, if not John Bunyan. It might even be a natural follow-up to any media publicity coming out of the trial. Was he up to it? He had never written a book before; the thought had never occurred to him. There would be no problem with the subject matter. It would just be a question of working out the structure. It would take time, of course, but having abandoned his TV-vigil and newspaper-reading routine he would have plenty of that. Yes. He would do it, or have a damned good crack at it. If Fats Waller was going to sit right down and write himself a letter, Alan Corbett was going to write himself a book! He went to the desk, got out an unused notebook and returned to his chair. He tapped the end of the biro against his teeth. What should he call it? Nothing too pretentious or highbrow. Nothing too boring either. He could not start the book without a title. A title, chosen by him, would help to make the project his project, the book his book. He spent several minutes in deep thought and then the title came to him. It had been staring him in the face all the time. Three words. Then he remembered Rayner explaining to him how they had been barking up the wrong tree. Yes. He rather liked that. Two words would be more fun. On the cover of the notebook he wrote the title – LIKE ASIF.